I0761664

The Saffron Tide

The Saffron Tide

Kingshuk Nag

Published in Rainlight by
Rupa Publications India Pvt. Ltd 2014
7/16, Ansari Road, Daryaganj
New Delhi 110002

Sales centres:
Allahabad Bengaluru Chennai
Hyderabad Jaipur Kathmandu
Kolkata Mumbai

ISBN: 978-81-291-3127-0

First impression 2014

10 9 8 7 6 5 4 3 2 1

In the memory of my friend, Alok Mukherjee,
with whom I spent hours discussing everything under the sun but who,
alas, departed early.

Contents

Introduction

The Battle for Hindu Votes

In December 1967 at Jana Sangh's plenary session at Calicut (now Kozhikode), the newly elected president of the party, Deendayal Upadhyaya, thundered: 'The enlightened mind of the country regards untouchability in social life as a sin. But, curiously, in political life, the practice of untouchability is something that some of the enlightened people feel proud about.' He added: 'Sometimes the sheer political arithmetic would prompt others to overlook, for the time being, Jana Sangh's untouchability and do business with it.' He gave the example of the Samyukta Vidhayak Dal (SVD) governments that were formed in many states earlier that year after general elections. In some states, the Communist Party of India (CPI) had allied itself with the Jana Sangh to form the government.

But why were parties mostly reluctant to partner with the Jana Sangh—a phenomenon that has continued for decades? The answer can be found in the Jana Sangh's (and later the Bharatiya Janata Party's or the BJP's) concept of 'cultural nationalism' and Hindutva, which defined its political ideology. This concept was spelt out for the first time in the BJP's election manifesto ahead of the 1998 elections: 'The BJP is committed to the concept of one nation, one people and one culture... The unique cultural and social diversity of India is woven into a larger civilizational fabric by thousands of years of common living for common shared values and beliefs and customs. Our nationalist vision is not merely bound by geographical or political identity of "Bharat" but it is referred by our timeless heritage. This cultural heritage that is central to all religions, regions and languages in a civilizational identity constitutes the cultural nationalism of India and which is the core of Hindutva.'

Many found this theory of the BJP abhorrent because it seemed to convey that India was monocultural. There was no scope for diversity, the diversity that promoted unity. What added to the discomfort of many was the aggressive sloganeering by Sangh Parivar outfits in the mid-1980s: '*Garv se kaho ki hum Hindu hain*. (Say with pride that we are Hindus.)' This war cry had been coined by M.S. Golwalkar, the long-standing sarsanghchalak of the Rashtriya Swayamsavk Sangh (RSS), BJP's parent body. Critics compared BJP's vision to that of Jawaharlal Nehru, the prime minister of India for seventeen years after Independence. Nehru had endeavoured to model the Indian Republic on the basis of western democracies with secularism as the cornerstone of his policies. Many said that this was a better model to run a country comprising people of many religions and sub-nationalities.

But is it possible to run a country where 85 per cent of the people are Hindus without catering to their interests? Is it possible to win elections in India without polling the Hindu vote? Was Nehru's Indian Republic really secular or was the Hinduness of the country couched in secular terms? Did the BJP become a victim of criticism because of promoting its cause too blatantly? Was this the same cause that the Congress had been promoting, albeit in a softer fashion?

Sample this: India's first major communal conflagration post-Independence took place in Jabalpur, Madhya Pradesh. Though there are different versions of how the riots of February 1961 started, Prime Minister Jawaharlal Nehru was very disturbed by the turn of events. What troubled him more was that members of his party did nothing to stop the riots even though the reigning government in the state was that of the Congress. On his first visit to Bhopal after the riots, Nehru addressed Congressmen and asked them why they had hidden in their homes like women in burkhas when the riots broke out.

Undoubtedly, Nehru sought to govern India as a secular republic. But, in reality, this secularism was only skin-deep; on paper, the country was administered as a secular republic, but barring a few men like Nehru, others were quite 'pro-Hindu' in their thinking. These men—many of whom adorned the top echelons of administration in Delhi and other states—were not communal. At least, they did not feel that they were communal. For them, Hinduism was the Indian way of life and reflected the ethos of the country. So being Hindu was the natural thing. For them, this also did not mean that they were disrespectful of other religions or their adherents. These leaders found nothing wrong with being secular and Hindu at the same time.

The Congress party reflected Hindu thinking even before Independence. In fact, the British thought that the Congress was full of seditious Brahmins. Jinnah's Muslim League gained traction only because it was able to hammer in the point that the Congress reflected the interests of the Hindus alone, though this was not true. But what the party practiced was full of Hindu symbolism—'Vande Mataram' was the anthem of the freedom fighters—drawn from Bankim Chandra Chattopadhyay's *Anandamath*, the song is sung in the novel by Hindus rebelling against their Muslim kings. Mahatma Gandhi talked of Ram Rajya and his favourite hymn was the Gujarati bhajan, 'Vaishnav Jana toh Tene Kahiye'.

The Congress party—both before and after Independence—had

leaders who reflected their Hindu thinking. A good example is that of Mehr Chand Khanna who, as Nehru's rehabilitation minister, was in charge of settling refugees from West Pakistan. Hailing from Peshawar, Mehr Chand entered politics at an early age and founded the Hindu Sabha. Later, he joined the Hindu Sikh nationalist party and became the finance minister of the Peshawar state government. After Partition he was arrested and put in jail in his home state. Ultimately he came to India and joined the Nehru government after getting elected to the Lok Sabha from the New Delhi seat. Mehr Chand served the Nehru cabinet later as the housing as well as the law minister.

He was not the only one with Hindu credentials in the Nehru cabinet. Ministers like Kanaiyalal Munshi were even more Hindu in their approach. Munshi, the founder of Bharatiya Vidya Bhavan set up in 1938 to promote Indian culture, was a member of the Constituent Assembly and later the food and agriculture minister in the Nehru cabinet. He was a well-known Gujarati writer of historical fiction. After the Gujarat riots of 2002, analysts held the popularity of his novels (that had themes like the continual assaults on the Somnath temple by Mahmud of Ghazni) as one of the contributing factors for the Hinduization of the state.

Morarji Desai requires no introduction. He was the prime minister of India and was known as an eminent Gandhian. Before joining the Independence movement, Morarji was an officer of the Bombay Provincial Civil Service and served as the deputy collector of Godhra—the same Godhra that was etched in the collective psyche of the nation after the train burning of 2002—in 1927. It was during this period that communal riots broke out in the town and Morarji was blamed for siding with the Hindus. Desai has himself recounted this incident in his autobiography, *The Story of My Life*, that was published in 1974. He wrote: 'I had received a notice from the Commissioner saying that the Collector of Panchmahals (which covered Godhra) had asked for an inquiry about my part in the riots. The burden of the issue framed by the Commissioner was that I was a communalist and that I had supported the Hindus against the Muslims.' Morarji says that he presented his case to the Commissioner in a personal hearing and through written submissions. 'In April 1930 I received the government's decision. I was held guilty of acting in a partisan way on account of personal bias...no action was taken against me for my good record of twelve years but I was degraded by four places in the list of seniority,' he adds. Subsequently he was transferred to Ahmedabad in a junior position. It is then that he resigned from service and joined the freedom struggle in 1930. Morarji believed that injustice had been done to him and that he was certainly not communal.

There were many other senior Congressmen in the early 1950s with the reputation of being soft Hindus. This included Purushottam Das Tandon, the Congress president in 1950. India's first home minister and deputy prime minister, Vallabhbhai Patel, also had views that were strongly Hindu. There are many other telling examples, far too numerous to be recounted here.

The point of relating all this is to highlight that the original Hindu party of India—the party that reflected the Hindu interests—was the Congress party and not the Jana Sangh or the BJP. The Congress party—professing to be secular—remained in power so long as the Hindu vote was with them. When the Hindus started perceiving that the Congress did not serve their interests, they started deserting it and began searching for an alternative. This was a continuous process and took place in different states in different ways and at different times. In that way, and for a long time, the fortunes of the Jana Sangh (and later the BJP) were dependent on the vagaries of the performance of the Congress. Till date, the BJP relies on the lack of performance of the Congress party for its election showing, even though this dependence has reduced in the last couple of decades. This is true even of the 2014 elections, although in the latest case, the BJP led by Narendra Modi built on the massive disenchantment of the electorate with the Congress to offer a proactive programme of change, hope and decisive leadership.

All through the 1950s and till 1967, the Congress party had a virtual monopoly over the Hindu votes across the country. Thus, the party remained in power unchallenged. There was a lull of four years after 1967 but the party's fortunes revived under Indira Gandhi in 1971. Her historical achievement in dismembering Pakistan and creating Bangladesh had the Indian nation in rapture. Indira Gandhi was hailed as Goddess Durga and the Hindu vote once again gravitated to the Congress. The Jana Sangh stood no chance in this scenario. Then, four years later, Indira Gandhi imposed the Emergency to beat her disqualification from electoral politics for six years—the penalty imposed on her by the Allahabad High Court for misusing official machinery during the elections. All Opposition leaders were imprisoned; they were released only nineteen months later at the end of the Emergency. It was then that they came together to form the Janata Party in 1977. Thus ended act one of the Jana Sangh that was to be reborn three years later in 1980 in a different avatar.

▪

The Jana Sangh was founded by Syama Prasad Mookerjee in 1951 as a reaction to the problems of thousands of Bengali Hindu refugees forced to flee to West Bengal from East Pakistan in the wake of Partition. He wanted the Jana Sangh to be a national democratic alternative to the Congress. Obviously Syama Prasad believed that the Congress was not reflecting the Hindu cause adequately and not effectively securing Hindu interests. A former Congressman from Bengal who came from a distinguished family of educationists, Mookerjee had strayed into the Hindu Mahasabha in the 1940s.

The Hindu Mahasabha lost steam because it propagated a very conservative Hindu viewpoint. As such, it could not capture the imagination of Hindus who were part of a nation on the move. Progress meant not only growth and development but also social reforms. After quitting the party in the wake of the assassination of Mahatma Gandhi, Mookerjee joined the Nehru cabinet only to resign and establish the Jana Sangh.

Mookerjee died in 1953 not too long after the party was founded, thus altering the fortunes of the Jana Sangh. He was a career politician and had been in electoral politics since 1930. This had made him practical and taught him to negotiate the twists and turns of politics. After his death, the party came under the control of the RSS, a socio-cultural organization which had no experience in electoral politics. The RSS enlisted a young pracharak, Deendayal Upadhyaya, to run the party with the assistance of a few other chosen pracharaks. Though dedicated, hard-working and endowed with great organizational abilities, Upadhyaya was limited by his background, experience and the network of the RSS, which in those days was limited to parts of Madhya Pradesh and Uttar Pradesh. The party was also influenced by the Arya Samaj with many of RSS's members and supporters having worked with that organization. As a result, the party developed a North-Indian ethos, that is, it promoted concepts that could only be popular in these parts. Hence, promotion of Hindi as India's national language was one such idea that the Jana Sangh espoused.

A result of this was that the Jana Sangh could not become popular in South India where Hindi was anathema. In fact, Madras state (now Tamil Nadu) was gripped by anti-Hindi agitations. Incidentally, the status quo—the dominance of the Congress—was first challenged in Madras by the Dravidian parties. Very soon the Congress was put out of business and the Dravidian party Dravida Munnetra Kazhagam (DMK), representing the intermediate castes, established its hegemony. This was the first dent on the Hindu vote. In Madras state, in the initial years after Independence, the Hindu vote could be taken to roughly denote the electoral preference of the entire Hindu community including Brahmins, intermediate castes and the Dalits.

The Jana Sangh could also make no headway in West Bengal from where the party's founder had hailed. Here, the Congress's hegemony was challenged by the Left parties who represented industrial workers and peasants. Marxism was on the rise; under its influence votes got divided across professions rather than on the basis of caste and community.

The Jana Sangh did not realize that to win against the Congress party it would have to cultivate a different voter base and establish support amongst groups who wanted to challenge the Congress base. The Congress was essentially controlled by the higher castes—led by the Brahmins—across the country, though the Dalits, who formed the lowest level of the social pyramid, also supported the Congress. They had not evolved enough in the first two decades after Independence to chart their own path. But the intermediate castes in North India were getting restive. Originally a part of the Congress, they were looking for political outfits who would reflect their interests and aspirations. During the 1960s, socialist parties like the Praja Socialist Party and Samyukta Socialist Party, and even the Communist Party of India had a support base of these intermediate castes. In Madras state, the Dravidian movement (roughly representing the same social classes as the intermediate castes in the north) had succeeded because of two reasons. First, the movement had begun in the mid-1920s and, second, the Brahmins comprised a miniscule proportion of the total population (unlike in the north).

The Jana Sangh's support base was still restricted to the Brahmins and the Banias in North India. It failed to articulate the concerns of these rising intermediary castes (who were Hindus) and this acted as a deterrent to its growth. For instance, the party was involved in a movement opposing cow slaughter which was seen as an upper caste movement. Although this had the potential of mobilizing even the lower castes in North India, in reality the movement ran out of steam.

Though Jana Sangh leaders were locked up in jail and the RSS was banned during the Emergency, this came as a boon for the saffron party. The merger of the Jana Sangh into the Janata Party allowed the leaders of the former to mix with leaders of parties that constituted the latter. This close interaction opened new vistas for the leaders of the erstwhile Jana Sangh and broadened their thinking considerably. Deendayal Upadhyaya had by now died tragically after being thrown out of a moving train and the leadership of the party had passed on to Atal Bihari Vajpayee. Though an RSS man with exposure to the Arya Samaj, Vajpayee had been coaxed by Upadhyaya to join electoral politics. This was after he realized that Vajpayee was a great orator. On Upadhyaya's insistence, Vajpayee contested elections to the Lok Sabha from three seats in 1957 and got elected from one. He was a little over thirty then and his tenure in the Lok Sabha, and later Rajya Sabha, exposed him to the art of legislative politics. This stood him in good stead when the leadership of the party fell into his lap a decade later when Upadhyaya suddenly died.

Vajpayee had understood quite early in his legislative life that flexibility and liberalism were a must for a successful political life. However, his elevation to the head of the party was not a smooth affair. He was challenged by Balraj Madhok, the first secretary of the Jana Sangh, who had drafted the charter of the Jana Sangh and had got Syama Prasad interested in Kashmir's affairs. But, for all his strengths, Madhok was very mercurial and espoused extreme views about minorities. With the help of a young lieutenant called Lal Krishna Advani and the blessings of the top echelon of the

RSS, Vajpayee was able to wrest control of the party in the early 1970s. Over the next few decades till 2004, this duo ran the party together—in part cooperation and part competition.

The Janata government collapsed and the Janata Party broke up because of the members of the erstwhile Jana Sangh. The latter insisted that they would remain members of not only the Janata Party but also of the RSS. For them, RSS was their alma mater, the organization where they had been schooled in the cause of the nation, and there was no question of excising the umbilical cord. But other members of the Janata Party were suspicious of the designs of the RSS. They thought that the RSS with their dedicated cadres would take over the party and the outfit would become Jana Sangh by another name.

All these doubts about the RSS could be traced to the assassination of Mahatma Gandhi. Before the killing of the father of the nation, it is believed that Sardar Patel thought highly of the RSS, which, at the time of Independence, was twenty-two years old. The organization played an important role in organizing relief for refugees streaming into India after Partition and Patel was impressed by their dedication and work. In fact, Sardar Patel had nudged the sarsanghchalak of the RSS, M.S. Golwalkar, to go to Srinagar to persuade the then Maharaja of Kashmir to accede to India. When the Mahatma was assassinated in 1948 by 'Hindu fanatics', however, the home minister presumably thought that he should not be perceived as someone who had close ties to the RSS. The RSS was banned and Golwalkar was jailed. In reality, the assassination was planned and executed by right wingers in the Hindu Mahasabha. But the fact that the assassin Nathuram Godse had a RSS background complicated matters. In public view, the RSS became the organization that was responsible for the heinous murder. Though Golwalkar was released from jail and the RSS absolved from the crime, public opinion persisted. The personal views of Golwalkar were very strong and unpalatable. It is doubtful whether he really thought they were implementable but the fact that Golwalkar controlled the RSS for a long time (from 1939 to 1973) made the organization suspect in various quarters.

When the Janata Party was being formed, doubts were expressed by some parties about allowing the Jana Sangh to become part of the outfit. But Jayaprakash Narayan, under whose leadership the battle for democracy was being fought, gave the green signal. Leaders of the Jana Sangh had released all the documents relating to the assassination of the Mahatma and he was convinced that the RSS had had no role in it.

The erstwhile Jana Sangh reinvented itself in June 1980 after breaking off from the Janata Party. The new name they adopted was Bharatiya Janata Party (BJP) and Gandhian socialism became their new credo. Vajpayee was convinced that this was what would sell in India: the Jana Sangh was too aggressive and non-inclusive. Unfortunately, this formula did not work—not for any fault of the leaders running the BJP, but because of extraordinary circumstances. Indira Gandhi, who had consolidated her Hindu credentials by constantly visiting temples, was assassinated on the last day of October 1984, just ahead of the elections. Riding the massive sympathy wave, the Congress won 414 seats in the Lok Sabha—a performance not seen even in the heydays of Nehru and Indira Gandhi. The BJP won just two seats—even less than the seats they had won the first time they had contested elections as the Jana Sangh in 1951. All Hindu votes had gone to the Congress! There was some reshuffling in the BJP ranks and Vajpayee, the boss of the party, was sidelined, his position taken over by his old associate, Lal Krishna Advani.

In 1980 when the BJP chose the credo of Gandhian socialism, the RSS was upset. Its boss, Balasaheb Deoras, was worried: he felt that the party was abandoning its Hindu base. He proposed using the Vishwa Hindu Parishad (VHP)—a twenty-year-old outfit that was distantly a part of the Sangh Parivar—to represent the Hindu cause. The immediate provocation was the conversion of a village of Dalits to Islam in Meenakshipuram in Tamil Nadu in March 1981. Under the guidance of the RSS, VHP began its Hindu mobilization programme in Uttar Pradesh (UP), the most populous state in India. When the 1984 elections were fought, it is believed that the RSS men canvassed for votes for the Congress.

Very soon, Advani jumped on to the VHP bandwagon and hitched the BJP's fortunes to the former. This was when the party decided to use the issue of Ram Janmabhoomi to mobilize Hindu society. In Ayodhya, a small town in UP's Faizabad district, stood a mosque that had been the subject of a dispute for over 125 years. Local Hindus believed that the mosque had been built by the invading armies of Babur in 1528 by razing an ancient temple that stood there—a temple that was believed to have been erected at the very place where Lord Ram had been born. In 1949, just two years after Independence, the local Hindus had asserted themselves and managed to smuggle in an idol of Ram into the mosque. A court intervention resulted in a stay order and the mosque was shut, but the idol remained in the mosque where, at appointed times, the priest would offer pujas. Entry to the Hindu devout was, however, banned. The dispute was local and so did not arouse national passions.

Under Advani, the BJP took up the Ram Janmabhoomi issue in earnest, helped to a large extent by the VHP which was constantly mobilizing Hindus through various religious yatras across UP. All this was happening in the late 1980s when television, too, played a huge role in Hindu revivalism. The popularity of the *Ramayana* and *Mahabharata,* two epics being serialized during the period was tremendous and it is not an exaggeration to say that on Sunday mornings when they were aired, the roads would be empty. The result of this was a significant rise in Hindu consciousness in urban and semi-urban areas. The BJP capitalized on this by putting up some actors of *Ramayana* and *Mahabharata* as candidates for the Lok Sabha polls in 1989. They won.

▪

Rajiv Gandhi was elected prime minister on the basis of the major mandate he got, but the former Indian Airlines pilot had little political acumen. Surrounded by his advisors—most of them not chosen judiciously—Rajiv's government stumbled from one controversy to another. The Bofors issue—which revolved around pay-offs in the purchase of guns from a Swedish company—soon became a major scandal. Rajiv's finance minister and later defence minister V.P. Singh who had raised his voice against the deal soon formed his own party—the Janata Dal—which became a major Opposition party to the Congress. In the ensuing elections in 1989, the Janata Dal and BJP joined hands and won more seats than the Congress. The Janata Dal formed the government with V.P. Singh as the prime minister and the BJP decided to support it from outside.

But V.P. Singh wanted to go down in history for doing something that would leave a lasting impact. He brought out the Mandal Commission report that had been gathering dust for over a decade and proposed to introduce reservations of other backward castes (OBCs) in institutions of higher education and government jobs. The BJP was alarmed: the party was trying to consolidate Hindu votes but V.P. Singh's move had the potential to divide Hindu votes into OBCs and higher castes. Advani immediately embarked on a motorized rath yatra from Somnath on the western coast of Gujarat to Ayodhya to galvanize Hindus on the Ram Janmabhoomi issue. He felt that this was the only way he would be able to counteract the impact of the Mandal Commission's recommended reservations. It was a long yatra that passed through many states, stirring Hindu sentiments on the way; there were also law and order issues in many places in the wake of the yatra as there were frequent Hindu-Muslim clashes. When the yatra was passing through Bihar, the new chief minister of the state, Lalu Prasad Yadav of Janata Dal, halted the procession and arrested Advani. The BJP immediately withdrew their support from the V.P. Singh government, which fell as a result. A few months and the stop-gap government of Chandrasekhar later, polls were held. Halfway through them, Rajiv Gandhi was assassinated. The Congress, hence, enjoyed yet another sympathy wave in the second phase of polling. As a result, the party came back to power in mid-1991 with P.V. Narasimha Rao at the helm.

In UP, a BJP government was formed and, taking advantage of this, the party and the VHP intensified the Ram Janmabhoomi movement which aimed at building a Ram temple at his birthplace, thereby reclaiming the Hindu heritage that they said had been destroyed by continuous invasions by the Muslims in the medieval ages. This would redress the grievance of the aggrieved Hindus, it was argued. On 6 December 1992, the Babri Masjid was razed to the ground by Hindu activists who had gathered in droves at the spot under the leadership of Advani, other BJP leaders and VHP activists. The congregation was to lay the foundation stone for the temple at a site that was a little away from the mosque. It is unclear what Narasimha Rao was doing when this happened and why he was unable to save the mosque, but the consensus is that he was looking the other way. Rao had the reputation of being a soft Hindu.

Though what followed was a series of communal riots across the country, the Ram Janmabhoomi movement was a watershed for the BJP. The party that had been struggling in the Jana Sangh days and that was decimated in the wake of the assassination of Indira Gandhi had now arrived. The felling of the Babri Masjid was the culmination of the Ram Janmabhoomi movement and created a captive Hindu vote for the BJP. Earlier, the political scenario in the country was marked by the Congress on one side and other smaller

Opposition parties on the other. From here on, it was the Congress on one side and the BJP on the other. A motley group of other parties combined with either the Congress or the BJP.

The BJP may have emerged as a major force in the country in many states but it lost power in UP in the next state assembly elections. In fact, the party's clout weakened in UP thereafter, primarily because of the rise of the Dalits under the Bahujan Samaj Party (BSP) and the consolidation of the intermediate castes—which stood to benefit from the Mandal reservations—in the Samajwadi Party.

Several goof-ups by the Narasimha Rao government brought the BJP to power in New Delhi for the first time ever in 1996. The government lasted thirteen days because of the reluctance of other parties to support those purportedly responsible for the demolition of the Babri Masjid and the subsequent communal violence. Two unstable governments later, the BJP came back to power, this time for thirteen months. Another election later, the BJP stayed in power for five years. In the aftermath of the Babri Masjid, the BJP also decided to change its leader. Vajpayee, who had been sidelined for a long time, was brought back to the helm and Advani was now relegated to the number two position. It was Vajpayee who became the prime minister, leading a coalition government called the National Democratic Alliance (NDA) that comprised a clutch of parties including the Akali Dal, Shiv Sena, DMK, Biju Janata Dal (BJD), Janata Dal (United) and the Telugu Desam Party (TDP). The BJP had realized that Vajpayee would be acceptable as prime minister to constituents of the NDA and not Advani, who had zealously led the Ram Janmabhoomi movement.

The Sangh Parivar and the VHP, which had tasted blood after the demolition of the Babri Masjid, wanted to dictate the agenda of the government. But Vajpayee outsmarted them; he built a wall around him by choosing advisors who had little to do with the

Sangh Parivar and depended on them to run the government. Brajesh Mishra, a retired foreign service officer; Jaswant Singh, a BJP member with no Sangh Parivar background; former bureaucrat Yashwant Sinha; and socialist George Fernandes comprised his core group, though the first two were more important. Advani was the home minister but Vajpayee steadfastly refused to make him the deputy prime minister. At the same time, Vajpayee pushed the nationalistic agenda of the BJP by detonating a nuclear device that demonstrated the strength of the country while on the other hand pushing for peace with Pakistan. To a vast number of countrymen it seemed that Vajpayee was following on the footsteps of the liberal Nehru. At the same time, Vajpayee did not relent on the economic agenda and pursued the liberalization process that had been started in the time of Narasimha Rao. This helped him cultivate an alternate support base that was more interested in economic growth and believed that this was both desirable and achievable.

Vajpayee had a virtually pristine track record until the Gujarat riots of 2002. The riots caused a furore both nationally and internationally, and Vajpayee found it difficult to defend his party's government in the state due to its inability to control the riots effectively and with promptness. At the same time, there were strong allegations that elements of the VHP had fanned the violence. The state's chief minister, Narendra Modi's stance remained firm, making life even more difficult for Vajpayee, who was further stymied by Advani and his group of hardliners in the party. Vajpayee soon beat a hasty retreat. Advani became deputy prime minister and Modi continued in his role as chief minister of Gujarat. A few months later, in December 2002, the Modi-led BJP romped home to victory in the state elections.

But in the general elections in 2004, much against people's expectations, the BJP lost the polls, albeit narrowly. The party had gone into the elections on the back of its good economic performance but the events in Gujarat hung round its neck like a millstone. There was a consolidation of minority votes against the BJP (and in favour of the Congress) and this brought the Congress to power. Vajpayee was aghast and said in interviews that it would have been better if he had axed Modi in 2002.

From then on, the BJP fell into disarray. Vajpayee decided to withdraw from politics and his place was taken by Advani. But Advani was past seventy-five at that time and the BJP needed second-rung leaders to take over the mantle of the party. Most of the next level leaders in the party were headquarters-based politicians. They had great elocution skills and even the aptitude to draw up brilliant strategies, but none were leaders with a significant support base. Only one of the leaders, Pramod Mahajan, had the ability to network and raise resources for the party; many at that time thought that the party would eventually be led by him a few years down the line. But he was tragically shot dead by his own brother after some dispute. So Advani continued to lead the party with second-level leaders like Sushma Swaraj, Arun Jaitley, and Venkaiah Naidu. With Vajpayee out of the picture, the RSS intensified its grip over the party and appointed a little-known leader, Rajnath Singh, as president. The BJP went to polls in 2009 under the leadership of Advani, but the party lost—badly. If in 2004 the difference in the seats tally between the Congress and BJP was marginal, this time the grand old party had improved its performance vastly and the saffron party had fallen. It was clear that there was a stronger consolidation of minority votes against the BJP as the sceptre of Gujarat 2002 continued to haunt them.

After its defeat in 2009, another round of introspection was initiated within the party about how best to run it. This was even as the RSS tightened its control over the BJP and replaced Rajnath Singh with a president who was lesser known than him. Advani continued to be in the party but many discerned that after two successive losses his innings was over. There was an acute leadership crisis because it was not clear who could take the party to victory in the next elections. Winning the second successive election in Gujarat in 2007, Narendra Modi became a contender for leading the party. Though he could not get rid of the communal taint, he was able to warm up to industries through progressive policies to attract investments. In Madhya Pradesh, Chief Minister Shivraj Singh Chauhan and, in Chhattisgarh, Chief Minister Raman Singh were also doing well. Sushma Swaraj continued to push her case forward as one of the senior-most female members of the party. In 2013, months after Modi won his third election in Gujarat, the RSS decided to have him anointed as the prime ministerial candidate of the BJP. The elevation passed through two stages in quick succession. First, Modi was appointed as chief of the campaign committee of the BJP for the election and then, a few months later, as the prime ministerial candidate. The appointment, however, did not go smoothly as Advani, who still fancied his chances as the party's prime ministerial candidate, threw a massive tantrum—to little effect.

Meanwhile, the Congress in its second term became blasé and took things for granted. The feeling had grown in the party ranks that as long as Modi was at the helm of the BJP's campaign, the saffron party had no chance. Minority votes could always be secured by holding up the threat of Modi's pro-Hindu stance. As these minority votes accounted for 15 per cent of the total registered voters, the Congress party began to tailor some of its policies to benefit them. The Sachar Committee was set up to think of ways to benefit minorities by way of reservations and favourable bank loans. The Andhra Pradesh government—formed by the Congress—introduced reservations for Muslims in jobs (this was subsequently struck down by the courts which said that there could not be religion-based reservations).

While the BJP had for decades been labelling the Congress as a 'pseudo secular party' interested in appeasing the minorities, most Hindu voters did not perceive the Congress party as one that pandered to the minorities. However, after 2009, the feeling began to permeate amongst some section of Hindus that the Congress party was playing to the interests of the minorities alone. Incidentally, the minorities did not themselves feel that the Congress party was doing anything substantial for them. They were of the opinion that they were only being used as a vote bank by the Congress—something the party had been accused of by the BJP as well.

The fact that the head of the Congress party, Sonia Gandhi, is Italian by birth has allowed the feeling to deepen. Other factors like the continuous influx of Bangladeshis into India, that has converted many border districts of West Bengal into Muslim majority areas, have been seen as Congress's increasing partiality towards minorities. Many political analysts think that the rainbow coalition of all Hindus and minorities that the Congress had created sixty years ago has now been dismembered. As a result, the party is now largely dependent on the minorities to get elected. In these circumstances, the party has taken recourse to schemes like the National Rural Employment Guarantee Act (NREGA) to substitute its support base. But these schemes have caused severe distress to the economy. It has assured incomes and wages for the poor but has not ensured them regular jobs. A lot of money has also been siphoned off. Moreover, this has led to a shortage of labour in small scale industries, the household sector and in the unorganized sector. At the same time, those who have gained from these programmes do not necessarily vote for the Congress. In other words, these schemes have not created a support base that is as committed as the voter base it had earlier. In the past couple of years, the major gainer of the Congress's identity crisis has been the BJP.

Ultimately, however, the story of Indian politics is the saga of who captures the Hindu vote and how. The Congress controlled this vote for a long time but now has given way to the BJP. Thus, the story of the Jana Sangh and the BJP is essentially the tale of how they built their strong, faithful Hindu vote base.

chapter 1

A Party Is Founded

In the end, it was the plight of Bengali Hindu in East Pakistan that forced Syama Prasad Mookerjee to act. Although the eve of Partition was shattered by communal violence, large-scale migration had not taken place in Bengal. This was unlike the situation in Punjab, where Hindus and Sikhs had fled en masse to India and Muslims had migrated to Pakistan. However, in East Pakistan Bengali Hindus were undecided whether to migrate to India lock, stock and barrel or try their luck by remaining where they were. Things only became worse for them as violence against them increased and they were marginalized, making living a life of dignity impossible. Everyday, incidents of killings, plundering, rapes, abductions and conversions of Hindus were being reported and, disturbed by these stories, Mookerjee wanted Prime Minister Nehru to take strong action to protect them. Though economic relations between the two countries had been severed in December 1949, Syama Prasad, who had joined the Nehru cabinet on 15 August 1947, felt that not enough had been done to protect Hindus in East Pakistan. And he was not alone—some socialist leaders like Ram Manohar Lohia and Jayaprakash Narayan were equally alarmed by the turn of events and wanted the military action taken in Kashmir and Hyderabad to be replicated in order to protect the Bengali Hindus.

Under pressure, Pandit Nehru invited the then prime minister of Pakistan, Liaquat Ali Khan, to discuss the problems minorities were facing in both countries and concluded the Delhi Pact on 8 April 1950 after six days of talks. This was an agreement for the protection of minorities in the two countries but Syama Prasad was not satisfied: he believed that it was not strong enough to take care of the interests of the Hindus in the neighbouring country. He, in fact, did not even consider it necessary to engage the Pakistani government in talks on this matter. To mark his protest, he resigned from the union government in which he was serving as the minister for industry and supplies along with another Bengali minister of the Nehru cabinet, K.C. Neogy. Both of them actually resigned on 1 April but the cabinet tried hard to keep them on board; one week later, though, as the Delhi Pact was signed, their resignations were accepted. Mookerjee was also miffed that Nehru had discussed the matter privately with select ministers before inviting Liaquat Ali but had not consulted him.

In an elaborate statement made eleven days later in the Lok Sabha, Mookerjee said that Nehru's policies were disastrous and could lead to a situation that would be worse than the Partition of India. He pointed out that 'life for minorities...[had] become nasty, brutish and short' in East Pakistan and how 'in the course of two or three weeks events of tragic character had broken out almost simultaneously resulting not only in wanton loss of lives and properties but resulting also in forcible conversions of a large number of helpless people and shocking outrages on women. As a result since January at least ten lakh people had come to West Bengal.'

Simultaneously, Syama Prasad started mulling over how to establish a political party that would be a democratic and nationalist alternative to the Congress party and broadly represent the interests of Hindus.

Syama Prasad's apprehensions about the agreement were proven true by subsequent events: in the months following the pact, more than a million Hindu refugees migrated to West Bengal. For the record, this Indo-Pakistan Delhi Pact allowed refugees to return to their erstwhile homeland 'unmolested' to dispose of their properties, and abducted women and looted property were to be returned to them. Moreover, forced conversions were unrecognized and minority rights were confirmed. Minority welfare commissions were established in both the countries to implement the agreement. But everything remained on paper alone.

Despite being a rising star in the Hindu Mahasabha, a political organization that represented Hindu interests, Mookerjee quit the party in the wake of Mahatma Gandhi's assasination, which he condemned in no uncertain terms. An extreme wing of the Hindu Mahasabha was held responsible for the killing of the Father of the Nation and those tried included their leader, V.D. Savarkar, who had, decades ago, served a term at the notorious Cellular Jail in the Andamans for participating in the struggle for India's freedom. Savarkar was later acquitted on technical grounds.

After he quit, Syama Prasad was roped in by Nehru and given a cabinet berth because the prime minister was acutely conscious of the allegation that the Congress did not represent all sections of society. In fact, the growth of the Muslim League in pre-Partition India was also attributed to the inability of the Congress to address the concerns of the Muslims adequately. Nehru wanted a national government for Independent India that could face up to these allegations and hence many others from different ideological persuasions were inducted into the cabinet.

Along with Mookerjee, Dalit leader Dr B.R. Ambedkar was inducted as law minister and Sardar Baldev Singh as defence minister, Shanmukham Chetty as finance minister and John Mathai as railways and transport minister. Incidentally Mookerjee had begun his political career in 1929 as a member of the Bengal legislative council representing the Congress party but he resigned later when the party decided to boycott the legislature in 1930. He later got re-elected to the legislative council as an Independent candidate. A barrister by profession who later became the youngest vice chancellor of Calcutta University at thirty-three years of age, Mookerjee became the finance minister of Bengal when a Progressive coalition led by Fazlul Haq was in power. He started out as the leader of Opposition but with Bengal getting increasingly communalized, he resigned from his position in the ministry and joined the Hindu Mahasabha and subsequently became its president in 1944.

Initially opposed to the partition of Bengal, his view changed later because Mookerjee felt that Hindus would not be safe in a Bengal with a Muslim majority (the province had 56 per cent Muslims and 42 per cent Hindus in the 1940s). Mookerjee vehemently opposed a move for an independent Bengal that was floated by Congressman Sarat Chandra Bose (the elder brother of Netaji Subhas Chandra Bose) and H.S. Suhrawardy, the highly polarizing Muslim League leader in the state. Mookerjee was deeply affected by the riots of October 1946 in the Noakhali district of East Bengal where an estimated 5,000 Hindus were lynched by Muslim mobs for over a week, many women were raped, and hundreds of people were forcibly converted to Islam. The Great Calcutta Killings of August 1946 where Hindu-Muslim riots saw more than 4,000 people lose their lives in just three days convinced Syama Prasad of the futility of members of the two communities staying together in an undivided Bengal. The killings began on 16 August 1946 which was declared as Direct Action Day (for the creation of Pakistan) by the Muslim League. The chief minister of Bengal—who was none other than Suhrawardy—ensured that there was no police force on the streets.

This gave a free reign to the rioters resulting in mass killings.

After resigning from the Nehru cabinet, Syama Prasad identified the Arya Samaj and the RSS as the two organizations that might be interested in establishing this nationalist alternative and got his associate, Balraj Madhok, to write to them. Although the Arya Samaj responded, the RSS remained silent. This was in spite of the fact that Mookerjee had been given a rousing public reception in New Delhi after his resignation and many of the organizers of the reception—like Hansraj Gupta and Vasant Rao Oke—owed allegiance to the RSS. But an official silence from the organization was not unexpected.

In the wake of the assassination of Mahatma Gandhi, the RSS had been banned and their leader, M.S. Golwalkar, had been jailed. Though there was no evidence to link the RSS to the heinous crime, Home Minister Sardar Patel felt that the organization was indulging in 'dangerous activities'. Less than a year ago in the wake of Partition, Patel had praised the RSS for defending vulnerable sections of Hindus and Sikhs. In July 1949, the ban was lifted and Golwalkar, popularly known as Guruji, was released from jail. But the home minister extracted an indirect declaration from the RSS that it would function as a solely cultural organization, adopt a more democratic structure and give itself a constitution. Under these circumstances, the RSS was circumspect about giving Syama Prasad any formal help for establishing a political party. In fact, there seems to have been two views within the RSS with one group wanting the organization to take the lead in setting up a party. But Guruji was not at all in favour of doing so. There was another twist to the tale: there was talk that the Congress party would open their doors to RSS members. This would allow them to be a part of mainstream politics.

Syama Prasad was in a hurry. The Constitution of India had been adopted and it was expected that the elections for the first Lok Sabha and the state assemblies would be held in 1951, and he wanted to launch the party before the elections. He returned to Calcutta (his hometown) from New Delhi—where he had been camping earlier—and after meeting his supporters announced the formation of the Indian People's Party. The news received wide publicity in the media and immediately stirred the leadership of the RSS.

The RSS leaders who had sorely felt the lack of support from any political party when it was banned in 1949 now decided to wholeheartedly support Mookerjee's initiative and conveyed this to him. However, the RSS said that it would prefer a Hindi name for the party and suggested two names: Bharatiya Lok Sangh and Bharatiya Jana Sangh. They also suggested that the party have a kesari (saffron) flag. Mookerjee chose the name Bharatiya Jana Sangh over Bharatiya Lok Sangh. Jana Sangh conveyed the impression that it was a people's collective, whereas Lok Sangh merely seemed to indicate a crowd of people.

On 21 October 1951, the Bharatiya Jana Sangh was officially formed with Syama Prasad Mookerjee elected as its first national president. Balraj Madhok was elected as the first national general secretary of the party. The RSS deputed three men to help Mookerjee set up the party organization. One of them, Deendayal Upadhyayaya, was to become president of the Jana Sangh later. The others were Sundar Singh Bhandari and Bhai Mahavir who was the son of Bhai Parmanand, a staunch Arya Samaj member who was president of Hindu Mahasabha in the early 1930s. At the opening meeting Mookerjee said that the party's stand on public policy would be guided by Bharatiya sanskriti and maryada. 'While we therefore aim at establishing a Dharma Rajya or a rule of law, we only abide by the highest of Bharatiya sanskriti, that binds all people together in ties of real amity and fraternity.' The 'deepak'—the earthen lamp which brightens the humble hamlets and cottages where the real India lives—was symbolically chosen as the logo of the new party.

It broadly represented here the party's interests lay. It was thus that a national democratic alternative that broadly represented Hindu interests came to be established.

▪

The Jana Sangh was, however, not the first attempt at setting up a political front to represent Hindu interests. The first such initiative was taken when the Hindu Mahasabha was founded in 1914 at Amritsar. The party was headquartered in Haridwar, clearly establishing what interests it represented, and the first leaders were Madan Mohan Malaviya (who later went on to establish the Banaras Hindu University) and the Arya Samaj leader Lala Lajpat Rai. The Mahasabha campaigned for education and economic development of Hindus and reconversions of Muslims to Hindus. The party was, however, conservative in its approach, including politics: thus, it preferred to keep away from the non-cooperation and non-violent civil disobedience policies of Mahatma Gandhi. This is not to say that it was loyal to the British raj, but it believed in using constitutional methods to fight them. The party was against untouchability but otherwise believed in orthodox Hindu laws and customs. Not surprisingly, it was dominated by upper caste Brahmins and this limited its appeal.

In the late 1920s, the organization came under the influence of Savarkar who opposed the secularism of the Congress and felt that the latter was unnecessarily wooing Muslims. The approach of the Hindu Mahasabha became more strident in the 1930s and 1940s as the Muslim League became strong and demanded a separate homeland for Muslims. Savarkar agreed with Mohammed Ali Jinnah's view that Hindus and Muslims belonged to separate nations. In 1946 after communal violence claimed thousands of lives in various parts of undivided Punjab and Bengal, Savarkar asserted that Gandhi's adherence to non-violence had left Hindus vulnerable to armed attack by Muslims. The assassination of Mahatma Gandhi struck a severe blow to the party. Though the Hindu Mahasabha did not disintegrate, it was clear that the party could never again serve the interests of the Hindus effectively and become a democratic alternative representing them. In 1925, a Hindu Mahasabha member, Dr Keshav Baliram Hedgewar, left the party to raise a Hindu volunteer force. Launched on the day of Vijaya Dashami, the RSS was to abstain from active politics and work at resuscitating the nation's civilizational ethos, which was a cultural task. But the mission did not foreclose its impact on politics. 'All of us must train ourselves physically, intellectually and in every way so as to be capable of achieving our cherished goal,' Hedgewar said in his inaugural message at his home in Nagpur. A shakha, literally meaning a formation, formed the basic unit of the RSS. Nitya shakhas (daily meetings of the formations) commenced with a salutation to the bhagwa dhwaj (saffron flag) and concluded with a prayer. The cadets were trained in wielding the lathi and the danda and there were also lessons in physical exercise. All of these sessions ended with discourses on national affairs. The RSS also initiated weekly route marches by its members synchronized to a band playing 'Jhanda Hindu Rashtra Ka'. From its base in Nagpur, the RSS spread to Benaras, Punjab and the Central Provinces, followed by Bombay Presidency.

Though not aligned with the Congress, the RSS actively supported some of the work done by the former. For instance, when the Congress passed the resolution for Purna Swaraj on 26 January 1930, RSS members were ordered to celebrate the day as Independence Day. Similarly when the Congress launched its Quit India movement in 1942, some RSS members in their individual capacities participated.

However, the RSS came under the adverse gaze of the government from almost the very beginning. In 1932, the government in

Mahakoshal banned government employees from joining the RSS. The administration of Bombay Presidency did the same in 1938. In 1940, the British government banned the RSS uniform as well as the route marches that the shakhas would hold periodically. That the RSS was becoming a significant force is also evident from the fact that Syama Prasad Mookerjee met Hedgewar as early as 1940 to discuss the plight of Bengali Hindus in Bengal which was fast becoming communal and where Muslims were in a majority.

On 3 June 1947 when the Congress agreed to the Partition, the RSS was stunned but was not in a position to do anything. The organization, however, swung into action and set up 3,000 relief camps in the wake of the Partition. Additionally, the then RSS leader, M.S. Golwalkar, flew to Srinagar to plead with Maharaja Hari Singh of Kashmir to merge with North India. It is said that Golwalkar had travelled to Kashmir after being gently nudged to do so by Sardar Patel.

▪

Within two months of the Bharatiya Jana Sangh's formation, the first general elections were announced. There was considerable excitement in the country as this was Independent India's first experience with democracy. There were many sceptics who predicted that elections would not work in a caste-ridden, multi-religious and backward society like India where the number of illiterates ran into millions. They argued that universal franchise could only work where there was universal literacy. Some described the elections as a leap in the dark, yet others labelled it as an act of faith. The elections were held over a four month period—from 25 October 1951 to 21 February 1952. Candidates and party chiefs campaigned vigorously; Pandit Nehru's campaign, for instance, covered 40,000 kilometres and if Balraj Madhok is to be believed, he targeted Syama Prasad Mookerjee and the Bharatiya Jana Sangh at many rallies.

The Jana Sangh won three Lok Sabha seats in the elections. Two were from West Bengal: Syama Prasad won the Calcutta (East) seat while Durga Charan Banerjee was elected from Midnapore-Jhargram. The third seat came from Rajasthan: Jana Sangh's candidate Uma Shankar Trivedi emerged successful in the Chittor seat. Trivedi had studied law with Syama Prasad in England and his victory was attributed to his local popularity. The Jana Sangh had contested 94 seats and in 49 seats the party's candidates lost their deposits. Nation-wide, the party won 3 per cent of the votes. It was not an impressive performance but then the party had just been formed. Not all Hindus who would have been part of the Jana Sangh's campaign had voted for it. Though the Hindu Mahasabha was now in a declining phase, the party actually won four seats more than those won by the Jana Sangh. One of the successful candidates was N.C. Chatterjee whose son, Somnath Chatterjee, made his mark in the Lok Sabha many decades later as a speaker as a representative the CPM. There was another Hindu party in the fray in the elections: the Akhil Bharatiya Ram Rajya Parishad (RRP) which won three Lok Sabha seats. Founded in 1948 by Swami Karpatri (or Har Narayan Ojha) of Pratapgarh, Uttar Pradesh, the outfit was a dharmic party that did not believe in the concept of the nation state. Karpatri was a monk of the Hindu dashnami monastic tradition and the party wanted a uniform civil code in India that was based on the manava dharma shastra with ahimsa as its creed. Karpatri was a leader of the movement against the Hindu code bill and made pointed references to B.R. Ambedkar, the law minister and a Harijan, and said that he had no business to meddle in matters that were the preserve of Brahmins. More than a decade and two Lok Sabha elections later, the party merged with the Bharatiya Jana Sangh.

Once the Lok Sabha was constituted, one of the first things that Mookerjee did was to gather like-minded (broadly speaking) parties like Jana Sangh, Hindu Mahasabha and the RRP into a block. He wanted the block to be recognized as a composite group, but the then speaker of the Lok Sabha did not agree. Mookerjee frequently clashed with Nehru on the floor of Parliament. On 2 June 1951, there was a verbal duel between the two stalwarts. Nehru called Mookerjee communal, and Syama Prasad retorted saying that Pandit Nehru was an 'arch communalist responsible for the partition of the country.' He went on to say that there was no communalism in the country except the policy of Muslim appeasement which had been started by Pandit Nehru in order to win the elections. He added that Nehru had repeatedly sacrificed Indian nationalism at the altar of Muslim communalism and even after the Partition, had surrendered to the whims and howls of the Pakistani government. Mookerjee also said that Pandit Nehru was 'raising these issues to side track real issues like hunger, poverty, exploitation, maladministration, corruption and abject surrender to Pakistan.' Duels between the two had taken place even at cabinet meetings. It seems that when the Nehru-Liaquat pact was being negotiated, Mookerjee had questioned Nehru in a cabinet meeting: 'When Muslims in Kashmir were attacked you sent the Indian armed forces and spent crore of rupees. What do you care for Bengali Hindus? What do you care for criminal assaults on our women?' Nehru had reacted angrily even as some cabinet ministers, uncomfortable with the exchange, exited from the meeting. This apparently included Sardar Patel.

After the troubled accession of Kashmir into India that was accompanied by an Indo-Pak war and occupation of a part of the state, Nehru entered into an agreement with Sheikh Abdullah, who was the most popular leader in Kashmir. This pact, also called the Delhi agreement, was signed in July 1952. It stated that the hereditary rule of the Dogra kings who reigned till then was to be abolished in Kashmir. A new constitutional head of state called Sadr-i-riyasat was to be elected by the assembly which in turn would be elected by the people. Further citizenship was to be denied to non-subjects of the state. The state would also have a separate flag and constitution. Syama Prasad was livid; he, on the other hand, had been talking about integrating Kashmir into India. On 26 June 1952, he asked in Lok Sabha: 'How is Kashmir going to be integrated into India? Is Kashmir going to be a republic within a republic? [...] If you want to play with the winds and say we are helpless and let Sheikh Abdullah do whatever he likes then Kashmir would be lost. I say this with great deliberation that Kashmir will be lost.'

In a speech delivered on 7 August 1952, he asked why Sheikh Abdullah was asking for special treatment. 'Wasn't he [a] member of the Constituent assembly of India which had finalized terms for the princely states? If these were good enough for others why were they not for him?' He repeated the same points in a letter to Jawaharlal Nehru dated 8 February 1953. Nehru, however was of the opinion that Kashmir had become a part of India with great difficulty and Syama Prasad was needlessly forcing the issue. Syama Prasad's views in the matter were partly influenced by his aide, Balraj Madhok, who had earlier been a part of the Praja Parishad in Jammu, many of whose Hindu populace was not quite convinced by Sheikh Abdullah's leadership. They perceived that only the full accession of Kashmir into India would give them comfort. Syama Prasad had a prolonged correspondence with both Nehru and Abdullah on the subject. At one point he conceded that: 'We would readily agree to treat the Valley [Kashmir Valley] with Sheikh Abdullah as its head in any special manner and for such time as he would like but Jammu and Ladakh must be fully integrated with India.'

However, Sheikh Abdullah would not agree. He wrote on 4 February 1953: 'You are not perhaps unaware of the attempts that are being made by Pakistan to force a decision by disrupting the unity of the state. Once the ranks of the people of the state are divided any solution can be foisted on them.' By this Abdullah obviously meant that any solution could be forced by international agencies. Abdullah also pointed out to Mookerjee that 'you were also part of the government when arrangements for Article 370 were made,' referring to the time that Syama Prasad was part of the union cabinet. But Mookerjee had served in the capacity of industry and supply minister and could hardly have been in a position to influence policies relating to Kashmir.

Syama Prasad was unmoved by Abdullah's argument and he lent his support to the Jammu Praja Parishad agitation that there could not be two flags, two prime ministers and two constitutions in the same country. It was due to the Jana Sangh president's efforts that the issue was brought to the nation's attention. For Mookerjee it was not a question of parity; there could not divided loyalty, he asserted.

Matters, however, came to a head on the issue of permits. By arrangement outsiders from the rest of India could enter Kashmir only with a special permit. The permit system had been introduced by the Sheikh in an understanding with the defence ministry—Nehru and Abdullah were aligned on the issue. But Syama Prasad decided to challenge it. With the cooperation of the Hindu Mahasabha and the RRP, the Jana Sangh launched a massive satyagraha against the permit system. Mookerjee travelled to Kashmir in what would be his last journey and tried to enter without a permit. He was arrested on 11 May 1953 and housed in a dilapidated building as a detainee. As a result, his health deteriorated as proper medical attention was not made available to him. He suffered from dry pleurisy and coronary troubles and in spite of being allergic to penicillin was administered the drug. When his health became precarious he was shifted to a hospital in Srinagar in a car instead of an ambulance. But it was too late: Syama Prasad expired late in the evening on 23 June 1953. This was a day before a habeas corpus petition was to heard at the High Court. Mookerjee's party men believed that he had been slow poisoned to death in a conspiracy because he was becoming a thorn in the flesh of the powers that ran the country. His own mother, Jogmaya Devi, demanded an inquiry into the circumstances that led to the death of her son. But Pandit Nehru, to whom the mother had made her demand, rejected the plea. Whatever be the case, the sudden demise of Mookerjee—he had died thirteen days short of turning fifty-two—was a blow to the fledgling party—one that would change its course completely and alter the way it would be run in the future. A few months later, Kashmir politics also changed with Sheikh Abdullah being arrested and sacked for anti-national activities. In some sense it was a vindication of what Mookerjee had been fighting for.

chapter 2

RSS Takes Control

With the sudden death of Syama Prasad there was a leadership vacuum in the Bharatiya Jana Sangh. Pandit Mauli Chandra Sharma, the vice president of the party, was forced to take over the reins of the fledgling party.

Sharma had actively promoted the cause of the RSS and when the organization had been banned in the wake of Mahatma Gandhi's assassination he had zealously tried to defend it in the face of criticism from all quarters. He had started the Jana Adhikar Samiti, which many considered to be an organization set up to help members of the RSS under the cover of protecting the civil liberties of people. Sharma worked in liaison with certain functionaries of the Government of India for this purpose. This included Rajendra Prasad, then president of the Constituent Assembly and later president of India, and Deputy Prime Minister Sardar Patel.

During this period, Sharma was also arrested under Section 3 of the Public Safety Act at the time for an alleged inflammatory speech. But he was later released because on inquiry it was found that the speech had been wrongly reported by the police official who was present at the spot. After being imprisoned, Sharma angrily wrote to

Rajendra Prasad questioning the basis of his arrest: '...this is blatant untruth and groundless. Who is to decide whether my speech had prejudicial colour—the police or the court of justice?' In turn, Prasad referred the matter to Patel who was also the home minister. Patel wrote back to Rajendra Prasad saying, 'With regard to a complaint against him [Mauli Chand] in regard to a speech which he is alleged to have made at a meeting of the Jana Adhikar Samiti, our enquiries have brought out that the speech was fabrication by a person who was drunk at that time. The police acting on information had put Sharma under arrest.' Incidentally Rajendra Prasad also wrote to Sardar Patel that: 'Congress people generally think that [the] Jan Adhikar Samiti is an organization which has been started only to help the RSS people under the pretext of protecting civil liberties.' But in the same letter, Prasad says that 'the Samiti gets unreserved support from Congressmen and that senior Congressmen [such] as P.D. Tandon had addressed their meeting' and even he had been invited to do so.'

Mauli Chandra also played an active role in getting the ban lifted on the RSS and urged the then home minister of Madhya Pradesh, D.P. Mishra, to be an intermediary for this purpose. The Government of India wanted a guarantee that the RSS would not indulge in political activities as a pre-condition for lifting the ban on the organization. But the RSS's supreme leader Guru Golwalkar, though in jail, would not agree to this. In the end, Mishra came up with a roundabout plan: Guruji would write a letter to Sharma that the RSS would not participate in political activities. Thus, such a letter was written and Sharma showed it to the powers that be. On the basis of it, the ban on the RSS was lifted. In any case the ban had not been very effective and this is again was made clear in a correspondence between Rajendra Prasad and Sardar Patel. Prasad wrote on 13 October 1948: 'There is a general movement to revive the RSS about which people from different places have spoken to me. I hear that in Delhi itself occasionally rallies, drills and physical exercises, which they used to have in a large body, have been started.' This made lifting the ban easier.

When the Jana Sangh was formed, Sharma, with his acumen in matters of public affairs, became the vice president. Sharma was, however, not officially a RSS man: on the contrary, he owed allegiance to the Congress even though he was an inactive member of the party. His father, Deen Dayal Sharma, one of the founding members of the Hindu Mahasabha, was also very close to Madan Mohan Malaviya. After becoming vice president of the Jana Sangh, Sharma also contested the first general election as the Jana Sangh's candidate from the Outer Delhi seat. In the first general election two candidates could be elected from some constituencies: Outer Delhi was one of them. But Sharma lost and so did the other Jana Sangh candidate, Pat Ram Singh. Both the winners were Congress candidates. Sharma secured 74,077 votes or 16 per cent of the votes cast.

It seems that after his defeat Sharma lost interest in electoral politics and became relatively inactive in the Jana Sangh. But when Syama Prasad died, Sharma found himself heading the organization. The RSS—which after its initial hesitation was now fully charged with the idea of a political party—probably thought that with a weak Sharma at the helm it would control the organization and its day-to-day affairs. On paper, however, the RSS kept an arm's length as they had done before. In this way it was able to circumvent the ban imposed on it.

But Sharma had other ideas. Now that he had stepped into the shoes of the towering leader that was Syama Prasad, he began running the party as he deemed fit. Soon enough, trouble began to brew between Sharma and the RSS. The RSS tried to rein him in but failed. The turning point was when Mauli Chandra refused to accept a draft list of office bearers drawn by the RSS for appointment. Sharma said that as per the constitution of the Jana Sangh the president had the sole authority to appoint office bearers.

Frustrated, the RSS bosses of Nagpur now used the young and energetic Deen Dayal Upadhyaya, who was serving as the Jana Sangh's organizational secretary, to force Sharma out of the party. On 3 November 1954, Sharma resigned from the president's post but not before making public his resignation letter that was reproduced in national newspapers. He said: 'Acute differences of opinion on the question of interference by RSS in the affairs of the Jana Sangh have been growing over a year. Many RSS workers have entered the party since its inception. They are welcomed as RSS leaders had publicly declared it as a purely cultural body having nothing to do with politics and its members were perfectly free to join any political party. In practice, however, it did not prove to be so.' Sharma's resignation letter went on to say: 'The late Dr Mookerjee was often seriously perturbed by the demand of the RSS leaders for a decisive role in matters like [the] appointment of office bearers, nomination of candidates for elections and matters of policy. We, however, hoped that the rank and file of the RSS would be drawn into the arena of democratic public life through their association with the Jana Sangh.' Sharma stated that a vigorous and calculated drive had been launched to turn the Jana Sangh into a competent handle of the RSS and that orders were issued from their headquarters through emissaries and the Jana Sangh was expected to carry them out. Sharma also claimed that many workers and groups all over the country resented this and the Delhi State's Jana Sangh as a body refused to comply with the orders.

The RSS, however, felt that Sharma was interpreting the Jana Sangh's ideology as per his political convenience. The RSS bosses also suspected that Sharma also nursed ambitions of disengaging the party from its parent organization and that he ran the party with the help of a coterie. The committee of office bearers of the Delhi Jana Sangh was dissolved and reconstituted with hard-core

RSS pracharaks. With the ouster of Mauli Chandra Sharma and his groupies—including Guru Dutt (the president of Delhi Jana Sangh) and Kanwar Lal Gupta who was to return to the party many years later and represent the Delhi Sadar seat in Lok Sabha—Jana Sangh truly fell into the hands of the RSS. Sharma himself joined the Congress party. In sense it was the end of the legacy of Syama Prasad Mookerjee.

The new man at the helm of affairs was Prem Nath Dogra, a leader from Jammu who had earlier founded the Praja Parishad in 1947 to fight for the cause of Hindus who lived in the region. A former official of the Maharaja of Kashmir who started off as a naib tehsildar and rose to be a deputy commissioner, many thought that Dogra had set up the Praja Parishad at the behest of the deposed maharaja, Hari Singh. This speculation was fuelled by the fact that Dogra had in the past been a leader of the Hindu Sabha, an organization that had supported the Maharaja of Kashmir's aspiration for independence and refusal to accede to India. Whatever be the case, Dogra was popularly known as sher-e-duggar. However, his approach was narrow; his interests were confined to Jammu and Kashmir and therefore from an all India perspective, he was a poor choice. But the Bharatiya Jana Sangh had no other towering personality so the mantle fell on Dogra automatically. Subsequent events proved his narrow focus: Dogra was elected as a member of the J&K assembly in 1957, 1962 and 1967. He could never rise above the politics of the northern hill state.

Dogra served as the president of the Jana Sangh only in 1955. The next year, 1956, which was a pre-election year, saw the induction of a new president who was even more remotely connected to national politics than Dogra—Debaprasad Ghosh, a professor of mathematics at Calcutta's Ripon College. A refugee from the Barisal district of undivided Bengal, Ghosh, popularly called Acharya by his admirers, was inducted to shore up the position of the party in

Bengal where the Jana Sangh was floundering after the demise of Syama Prasad Mookerjee. Ghosh had earlier been with the Hindu Mahasabha and joined the Jana Sangh on its inception in 1951. The Acharya was however a titular president—all the powers of his position had passed on to the RSS who operated through Deen Dayal Upadhyaya. The RSS found Ghosh to be very congenial and he continued as president from 1956-60 at a stretch and again become president in 1962 and 1964. His presence, however, did nothing to rev up the party in Bengal. In 1957, it all but disappeared in the state and has never gained fraction, until the recent elections in 2014. Interestingly the presidency of the party was offered to the Hindu Mahasabha MP N.C. Chatterjee from Bengal right after the death of Syama Prasad. But Chatterjee, under the influence of Veer Savarkar, refused to accept the position.

The Bharatiya Jana Sangh won four seats in the 1957 polls—one more than in the first elections. The party got 5 per cent of the votes and Atal Bihari Vajpayee, who would become the prime minister of India forty years later, was elected to Lok Sabha for the first time. Vajpayee contested from three seats in Uttar Pradesh, winning the Balrampur seat but losing Lucknow and Mathura. Since he was a good orator his bosses were keen that Atal Bihari enter Parliament and eloquently put forward the Jana Sangh's viewpoints. The party had been handicapped ever since Syama Prasad's death: they had found it difficult to find an equally talented orator.

The Jana Sangh won another seat in UP: Sheodeen was declared the winner of the seat from Hardoi. The party also won two seats in the Bombay province. Both of them were in the Maharashtra area (in those days, Bombay state also included present-day Gujarat)—Uttamrao Patil secured 55 per cent votes in Dhulia to be declared elected while Premjibhai Assar won a whopping 70 per cent votes in Ratnagiri to sail through to the Lok Sabha.

The party had contested 130 seats in all and its candidates lost their deposit in 57 seats. However, the party got a good percentage of votes in Delhi (19 per cent), Punjab (16 per cent), Madhya Pradesh (13 per cent) and Rajasthan (11 per cent). In West Bengal it got merely 1 per cent of the votes. In all, the party had contested elections in eleven states.

In terms of vote percentage, the Jana Sangh had improved its performance since the first general election. This was not surprising: the Hindu Mahasabha and the Ram Rajya Parishad were on the decline and the hardcore Hindu vote was shifting to the Jana Sangh. The party bosses were, however, pleased with the performance. The Central Working Committee (CWC) of the party, at a meeting to review the election performance, noted that Jana Sangh had secured over seventy-two lakh votes in the elections compared to the thirty-two lakh votes in the first general polls and this was a 'definite advance'. The CWC also blamed 'casteism and communalism especially Muslim communalism' that had been whipped up by the 'party in power and some other Opposition parties'. The committee also lamented the lack of resources and organizational base for its poor performance in some states.

The late 1950s were still early years after Independence and the public's love affair with the Congress party was intense. The party, under the leadership of Mahatma Gandhi, had won freedom for India and although Gandhi was now dead, his able lieutenant Jawaharlal Nehru was unfolding his dream for India. The country had become a Republic in 1950 and a democracy with universal suffrage. The five-year plans had been unveiled and promised growth and prosperity. Industrial development was to be sped up by increasing public investments in strategic sectors like steel, capital goods and manufacturing. By doing this, India was trying to follow the same model adopted by the USSR. Zamindari had been abolished and land was being redistributed, laying the basis for an equal society. The Congress party had declared that a socialistic pattern of society would be set up and began laying the basis for heavy industry which not only would provide domestic capability to produce complex products like steel and machinery but also provide massive employment in the public sector. 'There was a new hope. There were new dreams. While inaugurating the Bhakra Nangal dam, Nehru had termed it as a temple of modern India. Everybody lived this dream and believed that India would become a developed country and poverty would be banished. What is more they believed that these would fructify under the leadership of Pandit Nehru,' says Ashok Chaudhuri, a retired engineer recollecting the memories of those days. 'In these circumstances the electors were not ready to give a chance to parties who promised an alternate vision of India,' he adds.

Little wonder then that the polls were swept by the Congress which won 371 of the 490 seats in the Lok Sabha after the polls 1957. The party secured 47 per cent of all the votes cast. Other than the Jana Sangh, the other main contenders for power were the Communist Party of India (CPI) and the Praja Socialist Party (PSP). The CPI won 27 seats and 8 per cent of the votes cast while the PSP won 19 seats and garnered 10 per cent of the votes. Thus it was clear that left-wing parties had a better following in the country than a right-wing party like the Jana Sangh. 'Even the Congress leaned to the left and those voters who were even more radical than what the party represented voted for CPI or PSP. There was little support for the right ideology that the Jana Sangh represented. The mood of the country was clearly socialistic, left of the centre,' says C.K. Basu, an educationist.

The major support for the Jana Sangh came from the trading community and a small proportion of Hindu refugees from West Pakistan who had taken refuge in Delhi. Many of them were connected to the RSS from their pre-Independence days in Punjab. The RSS had made rapid inroads into the undivided Punjab in direct proportion to the growth of the Muslim League. The Sikh refugees from West Pakistan gravitated towards the Akali Dal. Yet, there were exceptions to this. 'I was a refugee from Lahore and had lost all. But we did not blame the Congress for the Partition. Rather the Muslim League led by Jinnah was the villain of the piece. So as we rebuilt our life with generous dollops of support from the government, our support for the Congress party did not wane,' says Chaman Chopra, who was only twenty-years-old in 1947. The Government of India's works and rehabilitation minister, Mehr Chand Khanna, who was himself a displaced person from Peshawar was responsible for providing relief to refugees.

The party, however, made some strategic mistakes that cost it some support. Under the influence of Arya Samaj, whose members had joined the party in large numbers in Punjab, it pursued the cause of Hindi (as opposed to Punjabi) aggressively. It is conceivable that if the party had taken up the cause of Punjabi, perhaps the Jana Sangh could have garnered Sikh votes as well. But the party was suspicious of the Akali Dal and averred that they probably wanted to set up a Sikh state which at a later stage could seek independence from India as the Muslim League had.

The Jana Sangh's manifesto for elections and resolutions reflected the aspiration of its party support base: for instance, in the 1950s, the party was constantly talking about how sales tax was regressive and proving to be a hurdle for both the traders and common people. The party wanted the abolition of sales tax on goods that were necessary and demanded a uniform sales tax rate across the nation for all other goods. The Jana Sangh also wanted the central sales tax to be abolished. The party asked for inculcation of the swadeshi spirit and what it called 'Indianization' of foreign industries (it was the first decade after Independence and the industrial landscape was replete with British companies and the party named mining, tea, coffee and rubber plantations in this context). The Jana Sangh also demanded the nationalization of the defence industry but wanted private enterprises to flourish in all other sectors but subject to state regulation. It specifically named banking, insurance and road transport as sectors where the party did not want state ownership. In order to achieve economic democracy the party wanted that the government unveil plans that would lead to the creation of more employment and not take recourse to moves that would lead to the creation of labour saving devices. The party in 1958 also wanted minimum salaries to be fixed at Rs 100 per month and maximum salaries at Rs 2000 per month. Salaries of ministers should be pegged at Rs 500 per month, the Jana Sangh said.

In 1960 there was a change at the helm of the party with Pitambar Das being made the head of the Bharatiya Jana Sangh He was a veteran Congressman from UP who had joined the RSS in the mid-1940s and had risen quickly within the organization. In 1961, Avasarala Rama Rao, an MLC from Andhra Pradesh was elected as president. This was a deliberate move to establish a party base in the Andhra area. But the move did not succeed. Three Jana Sangh candidates won elections to the legislative assembly in the state but that was five years later in 1967. Rama Rao himself contested and lost the polls for a Lok Sabha seat in 1962.

India's tryst with Jawaharlal Nehru continued till the Chinese invasion of India in October 1962. After that the popularity of Nehru took a hit and even he was heartbroken by Chinese treachery. However the 1962 elections were earlier in the year. If there was any anti- incumbency against the ruling party it was not reflected in the voting patterns. The Congress secured 44.72 per cent of the votes and won 361 seats.

The Jana Sangh's vote tally improved marginally to 6.44 per cent. However the Indian electoral system is such that the number of seats won by a party does not necessarily reflect the percentage of votes polled. The Jana Sangh won fourteen seats, but party stalwart

Atal Bihari Vajpayee lost narrowly (Vajpayee was inducted into the Rajya Sabha shortly after that and he became the chief of the the Jana Sangh's parliamentary party). Seven of the seats came from UP, three each came from Madhya Pradesh (MP) and Punjab and one seat was won from Rajasthan. All the three seats won in Punjab were from the region that is now Haryana. Besides, the party won a massive 32 per cent of votes polled in the five Lok Sabha seats from Delhi. Although the Jana Sangh won no seat here, it was clear that the party was a major contender in the capital of India.

One of the losing candidates in Delhi was Balraj Madhok. A year earlier in 1961, Madhok had entered the Lok Sabha in a by-election from a Delhi seat. In UP, MP and Punjab, the party won between 15-18 per cent of the votes. Earlier on when elections for the newly formed Delhi Municipal Corporation were held in 1959, the Jana Sangh had won 25 seats in a house of 80—only two short of the Congress's tally of 27. The party had clearly arrived in Delhi. In 1951, Jana Sangh had won five seats in the Delhi assembly and secured 21 per cent of the votes. The Delhi assembly was suspended thereafter, only to be revived many decades later.

Hence, at the end of the first decade, the Jana Sangh still remained a marginal force, save in a few places like Delhi. Though much of it was due to the popularity of the Congress and Nehru there was another reason that played a role. After the RSS took control of the party it lost a practical edge and ideological considerations became paramount. The RSS was keen on a political outfit which fought elections with its vision of India. The thinking was that this would be a slow process but would nevertheless succeed. To the bosses of the RSS, the spread of ideology and organization was more important than election results. It is for this reason that RSS swayamsevaks and sarsanghchalaks were deputed to the Jana Sangh to augment its organizational base. An example of the manifestation of this organizational purity is the fact that the RSS did not allow the

Hindu Mahasabha to merge with the Jana Sangh. A proposal to this effect had come up as early as 1951 when Syama Prasad Mookerjee was at the helm. Mookerjee's thinking was that the Hindu vote in the country should be consolidated and not divided—as would be the case if Jana Sangh and Hindu Mahasabha competed in the electoral arena. On his death it was Mauli Chandra Sharma who took the proposal forward. But the RSS objected because it perceived that the Hindu Mahasabha had opened the doors to disgruntled princes and zamindars (who had lost land and estates after Independent India came into being) and communalists. The issue of merging the Hindu Mahasabha with the Jana Sangh continued till 1957 and was actively pursued by the president of the former, N.C. Chatterjee. It is important to note here that the RSS was not averse to individual members of the Hindu Mahasabha—in fact, there were several transfers from the former organization to the latter.

Another example of maintaining organizational purity was the refusal of the organization to collaborate with the local zamindars in Rajasthan who were very influential and who did not want to be part of the Congress party as they had taken away their land. But the RSS's stand was that it did not want to make the Jana Sangh a feudal outfit. In fact, the RSS did not wish to align itself with any social groups. Interestingly in the first election in 1952, the Bharatiya Jana Sangh had won eight assembly seats in Rajasthan, and six of the candidates were landowners/zamindars. When the party began supporting the abolition of zamindari, these MLAs resigned and even efforts by Syama Prasad Mookerjee to explain the new emerging realities to them proved to be a failure. One of the MLAs who remained was none other than Bhairon Singh Shekhawat, who rose to be the vice president of India.

Throughout the decade of the 1950s and even in the early years of the 1960s, the Jana Sangh felt that the Nehru raj was very dictatorial in its approach and followed totalitarian policies. It passed resolutions to the effect and also alleged that the distance between the Congress party and the government was getting narrower by the day. 'It is making increasing use of official patronage and machinery to raise funds and suppress the opposition,' the party said while passing a resolution at its all India session at Bangalore in 1958. The party also lamented how in the union territory of Delhi (where the Jana Sangh was strong), the government had made no efforts to co-opt representatives of the party in various official committees and had packed them with Congressmen.

The story of the Jana Sangh in the decade of the 1950s will not be complete without the party's preoccupation with a matter which would, in retrospect, look like a fad—the banning of cow slaughter. The RSS had much to do with pushing the party to engage in this agenda. At its all India session of 1952 at Delhi—barely a year after the party was formed—the Jana Sangh declared that it would give full support to the RSS's demand for a ban on the slaughter of cows. It passed a resolution that said: 'From pre-historic times there has been a ban on cow slaughter and [the] cow has been the accepted [as a] symbol of Indian culture. In spite of five years of Independence, the present government has taken no steps to ban cow slaughter. The RSS has collected record signatures in favour of such a ban and has organized public opinion. Jana Sangh is grieved to see Prime Minister Nehru insisting that he would not permit a central law for [a] ban on cow slaughter though he has given up his objection to states passing laws.' The resolution added that 'this is a regrettable symbol of his [Nehru's] fascist tendencies. It is but proper to fulfil this national demand on a national level by a central law instead of 20-25 different laws.' The Jana Sangh also requested the president 'to compel the government to respect the people's feelings for the sake of national honour'. The president of India at that time, Rajendra Prasad, was known to be more sympathetic to Hindu causes than Nehru. The resolution concluded by declaring that if nothing happened, the 'Jana

Sangh will be compelled to take forward the agitation against cow slaughter and assures RSS's full cooperation.' Two years later, when there was no forward movement, the Jana Sangh complained about the government's 'obstinate behaviour' and again declared that 'the repeated and arrogant rejection at the hand of the government of the truly national demand has left the people with no alternative but to take the last resort of satyagraha.'

The Jana Sangh continued to work zealously on this issue. By 1958, as a result of co-sponsored agitations along with Hindu organizations, cow slaughter was banned in UP, Punjab, Bihar, MP and Mysore. Even the states of Orissa, Andhra Pradesh and Bombay began to seriously consider the possibility of doing so. But the party was in for a shock because, in June 1958, the Supreme Court ruled that it was lawful to allow slaughter of old and disabled cows and bulls. The central working committee of the party passed a resolution that 'with the court order, the values and objectives which prompted the states to ban cow slaughter had been rendered ineffective in practice'. In June 1961, the party at its Lucknow all India session demanded that the Constitution be amended to completely ban the 'slaughter of cow and its progeny'. The Constitution only mentioned cow protection as Article 48 of the directive principles of state policy.

It may not be out of place to mention that the cow protection movement had begun in India in modern times courtesy of the Arya Samaj founder, Dayananda Saraswati. Though the Arya Samaj represented a reformed version of Hinduism that did not believe in the caste system, rituals, idol worship, child marriage and widow celibacy, Dayananda pushed for cow protection. Many think that this was with the idea of mobilizing Hindus. Dayananda and his followers toured large parts of the country setting up gourakhshini sabhas (cow protection committees). The movement was at its peak in 1893—by which time Dayananda was dead—when communal riots broke out in Azamgarh district of the United Provinces on this matter and spread across with sporadic incidents reported from as far as Bombay and Rangoon (now in Burma). The Muslims were not at all pleased with the cow protection movement and saw it as Hindus mobilizing against them.

However, this was when winds of modernity and development were blowing in the country, which is why the party was not able to make much headway. In 1966, the Jana Sangh, along with Hindu organizations, made a last-ditch attempt to achieve their goal—an all India Cow Protection Committee began an agitation that involved satyagrahas, dharnas, hunger strikes and courting arrests. On 7 November 1966, the day of Gopashtami, a massive demonstration was held outside Parliament House. Violence ensued as the agitators (that included a large number of sadhus) tried to storm into the building. The government resorted to police firing and eight people were killed, two of whom were sadhus.

Though the Jana Sangh later denied any hand in the violence, the permission to hold the rally had been sought by the party's secretary for Delhi, Kedarnath Sahni. Even after this massive show of strength, the then Prime Minister Indira Gandhi refused to ban cow slaughter. Instead, she asked Home Minister Gulzarilal Nanda to resign for failing to maintain law and order. Nanda was a rival of Indira Gandhi's and also a votary of cow protection. The Jana Sangh, meanwhile, did not pursue the matter beyond the next few days: it realized that the issue was not moving the public strongly enough. Moreover, all sorts of elements—Naga sanyasis, et al.—over whom the party had no control were starting to participate in the agitations and the Jana Sangh knew that, in the event of further violence, the government could take punitive action against it.

chapter 3

The Decade of Deen Dayal

At around 3.45 a.m. on 11 February 1968, a railway points man at Mughalsarai Junction in Uttar Pradesh spotted the dead body of a man near the tracks. The police was informed and they came at the crack of dawn with a doctor in tow to certify that the man was indeed dead. This done, the unidentified body was brought to the nearby station where a small crowd had gathered. Suddenly, someone recognized the body. 'This is the president of the Jana Sangh, Deen Dayal Upadhyaya!' the man shouted, causing a commotion on the platform. Subsequent investigations by the police and the CBI revealed that Upadhyaya had indeed been pushed out of the first class compartment of the Delhi-Howrah Express shortly after the train had taken off from Mughalsarai. The CBI suggested that two urchins had pushed him out after Upadhyaya had found them stealing his luggage, but this version did not find many takers. Most believed that it was cold-blooded murder. In fact, the case against the urchins did not stand in the court of law and the Jana Sangh insisted that Upadhyaya, who had had no personal enemies, had been done away with because he was the architect behind the rise of the party.

Upadhyaya died barely forty-one days after he had taken over the presidency of the party at its annual session at Calicut in December 1967. However, the Jana Sangh of that time bore his imprint notwithstanding his short tenure. Deen Dayal had been the organization's secretary and then general secretary ever since its inception and had steered the party for the better part of its existence. Before Upadhyaya took over the reins of the party towards the end of 1967, the Jana Sangh had been scouting for known political figures to assume leadership. Even then the party could not find really big names to lead, hamstrung as it was by the paucity of members and its restricted following.

After the sudden death of Syama Prasad Mookerjee, the mantle of strengthening the organization and charting its course had fallen on the able shoulders of Upadhyaya. A simple man who had spent most of his life travelling from place to place to lay an organizational base for the Jana Sangh, Upadhyaya had joined the RSS after completing his masters' degree. He had the complete trust of the RSS boss, M.S. Golwalkar, and on the latter's direction took charge of the party after Mauli Chandra Sharma stopped listening to the directives issued from Nagpur. He was a favourite of even Syama Prasad Mookerjee, who used to say that if he had 'two more' like Upadhyaya, he could transform the fortunes of the Jana Sangh.

In 1963 following the debacle at the hands of the Chinese, Jana Sangh appointed well-known linguist and Indologist Raghu Vira as the new president. A PhD from London and a DLitt from Holland, Raghu Vira had attracted the attention of Jawaharlal Nehru, who had him elected to the first Constituent Assembly in 1948. In the assembly he played a significant role in getting cow slaughter prohibition included in the directive principles of state policy. Subsequently, he served two terms as an MP in the Rajya Sabha. But Raghu Vira was decidedly anti-communist and anti-China and pleaded for an alliance of Buddhist Southeast Asian countries to combat them. More importantly, he was against Nehru's China policy and resigned from the Congress because of this. Subsequent events proved him correct and the Jana Sangh invited him to become the party's president. Raghu Vira accepted but his tenure was short—he died in a road accident near Kanpur as he was proceeding to canvass candidates for by-elections. Faced with the sudden demise of its leader, the party went back to the good old Debaprasad Ghosh who continued as president for the remaining part of 1963 and 1964.

In 1965, however, the party decided to experiment. It decided to elect a president from within its ranks, someone who had risen through the pecking order gradually over time. Deen Dayal Upadhyaya was the most appropriate choice but he was not game for the job at the time. He preferred to continue his work while staying away from the limelight, rather than lead the organization. The second choice was Bachhraj Vyas who had been in the party since its inception and who had also been an MLC from Vidarbha. But there was dissent within the party regarding Vyas's elevation to party president and two important leaders boycotted the annual session at Vijayawada in protest—the chief of the party in Parliament, Atal Bihari Vajpayee, and Balraj Madhok, one of its founding members.

In order to assuage their hurt feelings, Madhok was elected president the following year even as the prospects of the Opposition party were looking up due to the economic crisis plaguing the country. The victory of India in the war with Pakistan in August 1965 had buoyed the national mood but the unprecedented food shortages that followed, which led the Indian government to extend a begging bowl to the world, was doing nothing to rev up the fortunes of the ruling Congress party. To make matters worse for them, Prime Minister Lal Bahadur Shastri had suddenly died in January 1966.

The Jana Sangh sought a new food policy through which the sale and purchase of food grains would be the prerogative of the central government alone. The state governments were to be responsible for increasing food production. The party also wanted all restrictions in the movement of food grains across the nation to be removed.

The year 1967 was a watershed election year for India. The Jana Sangh went to polls under the presidency of Madhok and though the Congress won a majority in the Lok Sabha, it was a small majority. In a house of 520, the halfway mark was 260 and the Congress could only get 283 seats. Clearly, the election results revealed the anti-incumbency of the Congress party despite it having been in power for two decades. The Bharatiya Jana Sangh won 35 seats and 9 per cent of the votes. The Congress's share in votes was 40 per cent. In some states, Congress performed dismally while the Jana Sangh showed impressive results. In Delhi, for instance, the Jana Sangh won six out of the seven Lok Sabha seats, Madhok being one of the victors. In Madhya Pradesh, the party won 78 and, in UP, 98 assembly seats. In Rajasthan, too, the Jana Sangh did well and got 22 assembly seats.

Due to the fractured mandate, coalition governments were formed in most states including West Bengal, Bihar, Punjab, Uttar Pradesh and Haryana. Opposition parties, forgetting their ideological differences, came together. In some states, the Congress, finding itself in a minority position, allied itself with independents and breakaway groups to form governments. The most interesting coalition was seen in UP, where the Congress party with 199 seats in a house of 425 could not get a clear majority; its top leader, Kamlapati Tripathi, lost the election as well. The Congress, however, staked a claim to power and formed a government under C.B. Gupta. This incensed another chief ministerial aspirant, Charan Singh, who refused to join the ministry. Within a fortnight, the government collapsed as Charan Singh split the party and formed his own party, the Jana Congress (later renamed Bharatiya Kranti Dal). Charan Singh was sworn in as chief minister as he cobbled up a coalition called the Samyukta Vidhayak Dal (SVD) that included parties as disparate as the Jana Sangh, Swatantra Party, Praja Socialist Party, Samyukta Socialist Party, communists and independents. A common minimum programme was drawn up to guide the functioning of the ministry and, for the first time in the history of Independent India, it was the party chief who decided which members would be part of the ministry and not the chief minister. There was great euphoria—after all, this was one of the first times that a non-Congress government was coming to power.

But, soon enough, the cracks began to show: constituents became increasingly suspicious of the Jana Sangh. Soon, outfits like the CPI, SSP, PSP and the Swatantra party, critical of the Jana Sangh's activities, were charging the latter with utilizing government machinery to spread its influence and ideology. As internal differences grew, Charan Singh, on 16 August 1967, sent his resignation to the secretary of the SVD saying that the 'unreasonable attitude of the constituents of the coalition government' was making it difficult to run the government. He was persuaded to stay on, but this reprieve was temporary and, soon, the internal dissensions were out in the open. CPI backed out of the coalition and the Jana Sangh said that it would stay neutral if a non-confidence motion was brought. Charan Singh resigned and President's rule was clamped down on the state. Fresh elections were held in 1969 and the fractured Opposition enabled the Congress to come back to power.

Similar experiences were repeated in other states even as trading of MLAs began in a big way. Party discipline broke down as MLAs were lured by money and positions. The term '*aya Ram, gaya Ram*' which reflects legislators frequently changing parties to be on the side of the winning coalition was coined in 1967 after defections became an everyday phenomenon. However, two parties were able to keep their flock together and maintain internal discipline: the Bharatiya Jana Sangh and the Communist parties.

Reflecting on the state of affairs in the country after the elections, the Jana Sangh passed a resolution during its CWC meeting on 14 March 1967: 'Because of the defeat of the Congress and the inability of anyone to form a government it is impossible in many states to form a government unless all Opposition parties come together. This situation is not conducive to [the] development of democracy. It can encourage elements that do not believe in democracy. Hence the central working committee favours inclusion of Jana Sangh in the governments. These members will remain in the ministry so long as they can effectively serve the people on [the] basis of the principles and programmes of the Jana Sangh.' The party also said that 'anti-Congressism' could not become the credo of the party. This party line was forged by Deen Dayal Upadhyaya who was the most dominant voice in those days. At the same time, the party was very disturbed by the tendency of many outfits to treat the Jana Sangh as a political outcast. Since the communist parties were the most vocal about their mistrust of the the Jana Sangh, Upadhyaya mentioned them specifically while pointing out that although the Jana Sangh did not agree with the strategies, tactics and political cultures of the communists, this did not justify them treating the Jana Sangh as political untouchables.

Deen Dayal Upadhyaya, however, always strove hard to maintain high standards in politics. He was responsible for pioneering a code of conduct for legislators of the party and in June-July 1959 conducted a workshop for Jana Sangh legislators for this purpose. The next year at the annual session of the party at Nagpur, Deen Dayal moved a resolution stating that 'the base of the Jana Sangh being principled, we urgently require training camps and workshops. Without these we will not be able to assess the different approaches of political parties.' Deen Dayal went on to say: 'Walking out of the house and a tendency to create chaos through shouting or sloganeering which are aimed at capturing newspaper spaces are not considered right by the Jana Sangh. We have advised our members to keep away from such conduct, they should not protest in this unbecoming manner.'

The late 1950s and early 1960s were early days for the Indian Republic and Deen Dayal Upadhyaya was trying to ensure that his party conducted itself in a democratic fashion. Since the party had been attacked by many for its sectarian approach, Upadhyaya wanted to make sure that the public conduct of party representatives was above reproach. 'What you thought of the party depended on which side of the political divide you were. Undoubtedly the public behaviour of their members was good but many like us saw the Jana Sangh as a reactionary party. This was because some of their members, especially at the ground level, were quite vociferous while talking about minorities,' recollects Bimal Bose, who started going to college in Delhi in the late 1960s. 'On me, the party made a great impact. I was impressed by the public oratory of their leaders who seemed very earnest. Jana Sangh members were always volunteering for neighbourhood public causes,' says Sunita Budhiraja, who grew up in west Delhi in the same period.

These were also the times when the Jana Sangh was vying to catch the attention of the people along with those of competing philosophies like the Congress, the communist parties, socialists and the newly formed Swatantra Party. Deen Dayal was critical of all of them. Of these, the Swatantra Party was closest to the Jana Sangh in terms of its economic ideology of free market enterprise. But unlike the Jana Sangh, which drew its cadres from the lower middle class and the middle class rungs of society, the Swatantra party comprised ex-rulers who had been deposed after Independence, landlords whose land had been redistributed, capitalists who were affected by the Congress government's socialistic policies, and defectors from the Congress. Though the Swatantra Party was a highly effective party since its inception in 1959, Deen Dayal told his party men to keep away because 'the centre of interest of the party was the individual and not principles or even the party.' Interestingly, the Swatantra Party had been started by C. Rajagopalachari who was associated with the freedom struggle but opposed Nehru's socialism. In the 1962 elections, the party polled almost 7 per cent of the votes and won 18 seats. In the 1967 elections, it secured 9 per cent of the votes and emerged victorious in 44 seats. This made it the principal Opposition party. The Swatantra Party had a strong base in Bihar, Rajasthan, Gujarat and Orissa.

Deen Dayal's anger, however, was reserved for the Communist Party: 'We must go deep into society in order to shake them from their roots. People who understand the language of community, regionalism and their own selfish interests must be taught the real meaning of nation and dharma.' In fact, Deen Dayal was trying to build the Jana Sangh on a philosophy that provided an alternative to both capitalism (on the basis of which the Swatantra Party was running) and communism. Deen Dayal called his philosophy that of integral humanism which provided a basis for statecraft consistent with what he called 'the laws of creation and the universal needs of the human race'. Deen Dayal believed that integral humanism led to harmony in society and that this could be achieved by satisfying the needs of the body (food, shelter), the needs of the mind (ingraining traditions), intelligence (reforms in society) and the soul (achieving the common aspirations of the people that shape their unique culture). This philosophy was expounded by him in a series of four lectures given in Bombay in 1964 where he suggested that western political philosophies are preoccupied with materialism and overlook the social well-being of individuals. Therefore, they lead to greed and exploitation, resulting in social anarchy. 'As a concept it was good and based on principles of old Hindu philosophy. But in practice it could never work and never did. The Jana Sangh and its successor, the Bharatiya Janata Party, never based its policies on this,' says a BJP leader who did not wish to be identified.

Though the Jana Sangh did well in the northern states in 1967, it failed to make any impact in the south. This was not surprising. The philosophy and the idiom used by the party was very North India oriented. The man who built the organization—Deen Dayal Upadhyaya—having grown up in Mathura, Kota, Agra and Kanpur was steeped in North Indian traditions and as such had no real understanding of what moved people in South India. South Indian culture and politics were totally divergent from that of North India, and Upadhyaya and his colleagues were oblivious of this. Even the RSS that was the ideological guide of the party could not help in this regard: they, too, had been cast in the mould of North Indian Hindu culture. But the Jana Sangh did try to make forays in the south and even held its annual conferences there: Bangalore in 1958, Vijayawada in 1965 and Calicut in 1967. This had little effect, however. The Jana Sangh made the cardinal mistake of pushing for Hindi as the official language and this had the effect of reinforcing the party's image as a Hindi-belt outfit.

When India became a Republic on 26 January 1950, it was decided to keep English as the official language for fifteen years and then take a call on the future course of action. As 26 January 1965 approached, there was a clamour for and against Hindi. The Jana Sangh was campaigning for Hindi as the undisputed language of communication throughout the country and a categorical removal of English. There were widespread disturbances and agitations in Madras (which was yet to be renamed Tamil Nadu) against such a ruling. At the forefront of the agitations were the Dravida Munnetra Kazhagam (DMK) and C. Rajagopalachari, the first governor general of Independent India. The Jana Sangh misread the situation badly: not only did it continue to fight for the cause of Hindi zealously, it dubbed the anti-Hindi agitations as being instigated by missionaries and Islamists. This was a blunder because Hindi and Hindu was not the same thing. After the dust had settled down and the Government of India chose to continue with English, the party passed a resolution at its Calicut session at the end of 1967 that said: 'The Jana Sangh does not favour any move that would deprive non-Hindi speaking people. Jana Sangh demands that exams of UPSC should be held in regional languages and there should not be any compulsion for learning a particular language for recruitment. Those who wish to use English during the period of transition should be allowed to do so.' But it was too late. In the manifesto for the 1967 elections, the Jana Sangh said that Sanskrit should be declared the country's national language but that it should be used on special occasions. The party also suggested that in provinces, the provincial languages should be used and that the central government should use Hindi or provincial languages to communicate with the people. There was no mention of English.

In its manifesto released before the 1962 elections, the party had called for the setting up of a high powered commission on languages whose recommendations would be binding on all. It had also said that it favoured the formulation of a five-year plan for the development of Hindi and other Indian languages. It was of the opinion that though regional languages and other Bharatiya languages could be the medium of secondary and higher education, Hindi had to be compulsory.

In the late 1960s, the party had to countenance internal demands to take up a strong ideological line, propagated by none other than Balraj Madhok who, besides being one of the founding members of the party, was also its president. Always known as a hothead, he advocated the 'Indianization' of Muslims which basically meant that non-Hindus would have to adopt the Hindu way of life. In 1968, he emphasized in the Lok Sabha that the temple of nativity of Ram in Ayodhya, the temple of nativity of Krishna at Mathura and of Shiva in Kashi Viswanath in Varanasi are as holy and important to Hindus as Kaaba in Mecca is to Muslims and Bethleham is to Christians. 'Can anybody deny that Muslims have destroyed thousands of temples and churches? We Hindus want these temples returned to us. In return we will give land for building the concerned mosques,' he said.

Madhok, who was also a prolific writer, expounded that 'nationalism is not a question of political loyalties only. It demands a feeling of attachment and a sense of pride for the country's heritage and culture as well.' He added: 'India should be a homogeneous nation state. There has to be total assimilation of Muslims into Hindu culture.' Justifying why the Hindu way of life should be adopted in India, he pointed at the Malaysian law that prohibited marriage between a Muslim and a non-Muslim unless the non-Muslim has converted to Islam. He pointed out that during a visit to Kuala Lumpur, he had raised the matter with the Deputy Prime Minister Tun Abdur Razaq, who had apparently quipped: 'Why should anybody grumble? Our being secular only means that we respect all forms of worship, but this does not mean that Malay Muslims who constitute the dominant stream in Malaysian national life should not have special privileges.'

Many in the party subscribed to the philosophy of Madhok but did not want to rake up this issue publicly because it unnecessarily brought the party into focus at a time when the dominant philosophy in the country did not match its own. However, from time to time, the party passed resolutions on matters concerning minority affairs that showed its more hardline character.

At a time when the Congress party was showing signs of decline it was becoming imperative for the Jana Sangh to collaborate with other parties to jointly oppose the ruling party. In fact, this was what the SVD coalition government was about. In this situation, Madhok was proving to be a liability to the party though he occupied a position of eminence within its ranks. Although an RSS man, he was not really loved by the bosses in Nagpur. They thought that he was not disciplined enough and that he had not even completed the Officers' Training Scheme that was essential for graduation to higher levels of the party. He had come into the limelight because he had intimate knowledge of Kashmir's affairs—he belonged to Jammu and had worked as a pracharak in the state in the 1940s before setting up the Praja Parishad. Matters relating to Kashmir were top priority for the party in the 1950s and, more importantly, Balraj Madhok had been close to Syama Prasad Mookerjee.

In fact, it was to check the influence of Balraj Madhok in the affairs of the party that Deen Dayal, after remaining in the shadows for so many years, consented to be president. He was egged on by Guru Golwalkar. While Golwalkar would have preferred Deen Dayal to concentrate exclusively on organizational affairs, he felt that the continuance of Madhok could lead to problems for the party. But as bad luck would have it, the premature death of Deen Dayal created a crisis of sorts for the Jana Sangh just when the party seemed to be gaining in popularity among the masses.

▪

The story of the Jana Sangh in the 1960s cannot be complete without a reference to the formation of the Vishwa Hindu Parishad (VHP). The VHP was formed on 29 August 1964 on Janmasthami day with the express purpose 'to consolidate Hindu society and serve and protect Hindu dharma'. Though officially founded by a Sanskrit scholar, Keshavram Kashiram (Keka) Shastri, with Swami Chinmayananda as its first president, in reality the organization was catalyzed by the RSS. M.S. Golwalkar, the supreme leader of the RSS, was of the opinion that 'all faiths of Indian origin need to unite'. By this, he meant the Buddhists, Jains, Sikhs and Hindus. The purpose of this clarion call was to 'save Hinduism from Christians, Islam and Communists'. Thus, the VHP was a Sangh Parivar member, very much like the Jana Sangh. However, it was officially stated that the VHP had been established by the 'saint shakti of Bharat'. Hence, the Jana Sangh was engaged in electoral politics while the VHP concentrated on mobilizing the Hindus masses with the stated objective of protecting their interests and the unstated objective of creating a vote base for the former. The Jana Sangh could not directly take up the causes that were taken up by the VHP due to the fear that it would minimize the appeal of the party and limit its reach. However, the late 1960s were still early days and whatever the VHP did had little impact on the electoral prospects of the Jana Sangh at the time. Two-and-a-half decades later, though, the VHP played a major role in changing the fortunes of the Jana Sangh, which had by then metamorphosized into the Bharatiya Janata Party.

chapter 4

The Turbulent Seventies

Atal Bihari Vajpayee was anointed president of the Jana Sangh after the sudden death of Deen Dayal Upadhyaya. A liberal within the party who was known to tread a more tolerant and secular line, Vajpayee had already made a mark as a Parliamentarian and won the admiration of none other than Jawaharlal Nehru for his oratory. In the party, however, he faced some criticism from members who felt that he was not fully committed to the cause of the party. Leading this pack was Balraj Madhok who, at the time of his stewardship of the party, had even complained to Guru Golwalkar about Vajpayee's lifestyle which he thought was amoral. In the words of Madhok as revealed in his memoir, *Zindagi Ka Safar*, Golwalkar, the supremo of the party, had responded by saying that he knew the weaknesses of everyone but since he ran an organization he had to take everybody's interests into account. Madhok writes, 'When I was the president of the party Jagdish Prasad Mathur in charge of the central office who was staying with a senior leader at 30 Rajendra Prasad Road complained to me that the leader had turned the house into a den of immoral activities. I had discovered that the senior leadership of RSS was bent upon making this leader the president of the Jana Sangh. I went to Golwalkar and told him what Mathur had said. After hearing me Golwalkar was quiet for sometime. Then he said: "I know about the weaknesses of people. But I have to run an organization, I have to take everybody together. So like Shiva I have to drink poison everyday."' It is an established fact that the bungalow at 30 Rajendra Prasad Road was allotted to Vajpayee. He had a long standing relationship with a former classmate of his with whom he lived till she passed away in May 2014 and Madhok's complaint was probably an allusion to this.

Vajpayee also had the confidence of Deen Dayal Upadhyaya who, with his pleasant manners and moderate ways, was able to balance both Madhok and Vajpayee. After the 1967 elections when the Jana Sangh realized that the Congress had been defeated in many states but no single party had won enough seats to come to power, there was a furious debate within its ranks. A large number of Jana Sangh leaders led by Madhok were strongly against allying with other parties to come to power, but Vajpayee tried to convince them that this was a time to take tactical advantage. He said that the Jana Sangh should ally with other parties like the socialists to keep the Congress out of power, especially as there was no chance of the Jana Sangh being able to come to power on its own. Deen Dayal Upadhyaya took Vajpayee's advice and formed an alliance with non-Congress parties that included the Praja Socialist Party, Samuykta Socialist Party and the Bharatiya Kranti Dal. This was the second time that the party was allying with other non-like-minded parties. Earlier in 1964, the Jana Sangh had formed a coalition for four Lok Sabha seats in the by-elections. Deen Dayal Upadhyaya had contested a seat from Jaunpur but lost in his only electoral contest.

Jana Sangh's advantage did not last long, but this had little to do with the happenings within the party. Indira Gandhi displayed her prowess when she gained total control of the Congress party at the end of 1969 in a series of political manoeuvres. After the sudden death of Lal Bahadur Shastri in January 1966, Indira had been pushed into the prime ministerial position by the old guard in the party led by K. Kamaraj, Atulya Ghosh, S.K. Patil and S. Nijalingappa who calculated that she would be nothing but an instrument in their hands. They wanted to foil the rigid and strong minded Morarji Desai who was a strong contender for the post. In the 1967 general elections when the Congress returned to strength with a lesser majority, many of the elected MPs owed loyalty to Desai. So both the syndicate (as the old guard was called) and Indira Gandhi were forced to accept Morarji Desai as deputy prime minister and finance minister. But Indira was distinctly apprehensive of Morarji and of the syndicate who were trying to control her turf. Meanwhile, a group of young Turks were fast emerging in the party and they sought radical reforms in the country. Under pressure from them and with a view to marginalize the old guard, Indira got the Congress Working Committee (CWC) to adopt a radical ten-point programme including social control of banks, nationalization of general insurance, state trading in imports and exports, ceilings on urban properties and income, curb on business monopolies, etcetera. The syndicate did not oppose the resolution, planning to foil it if the government tried to implement the programme.

But Indira Gandhi would not rest before wresting total control of the Congress party. Though a proposal to divest the princes of their titles and privy purses failed in its first attempt, Mrs Gandhi nationalized major banks in the country in July 1969 after getting the All India Congress Committee (AICC) to pass a resolution demanding such a move. Morarji Desai, the finance minister at the time, had his portfolio taken away ahead of the nationalization, which led to his resignation. By November, the differences between the syndicate—smarting under the offensive by Indira Gandhi—and Mrs Gandhi grew. On 12 November 1969, the Congress president, S. Nijalingappa, expelled Indira Gandhi from the party 'for fostering a cult of personality.' What precipitated matters was the election for the president of India necessitated by the untimely death of Zakir Hussain. The syndicate put up Neelam Sanjeeva Reddy as the official Congress candidate but Indira Gandhi prompted labour leader and Congressman V.V. Giri to file his nomination as an independent candidate. She then declared that Congressmen should vote as per their 'conscience'. Ultimately, Giri won even as Indira Gandhi set up the Congress (R). A majority of Congress MPs went with her and the Election Commission of India recognized her party as the real Congress party. Mrs Gandhi had established herself as the supreme leader and the slide of the Congress since 1967 had been reversed. But Indira was still leading a minority government and managed to remain in power with the help of parties like the DMK.

The Vajpayee-led Jana Sangh had to deal with this newly-formed threat. Though billed as a national democratic alternative, the party in all these years had been concentrating on issues of Bharatiyata, which roughly meant pushing for Hindu interests. The party had sparse knowledge on economic ideology and, worse still, hardly any intellectuals of stature in its ranks. The rank and file came from the RSS school of thought and their grooming in shakhas did little to acquaint them with concepts like means of production and theories of consumption and distribution. However, at a broader level, the Congress's left-of-centre economic agenda did not appeal to the party. If anything, the party leaned right-of-centre. But there was no choice because the popular mood in the country was in favour of a left-leaning programme.

Yet, as an Opposition party, the Jana Sangh could not applaud the government. At its working committee meeting in Delhi on 30 August 1969, the party said that it 'rejects both capitalism and statism' (implying state monopoly). It added: 'Evils flowing out from private monopoly can be checked through state regulation but concentration of political and economic authority in the hands of

[the] state results in totalitarianism incompatible with democracy.' The Jana Sangh also went on to declare (correctly, of course) that the 'decision to take over commercial banks was guided by political considerations and not based on any objective assessment of the economic situation and its requirements.' The party also wanted more power for the Reserve Bank of India. In a bid to rein in Indira Gandhi, the party declared that the 'RBI should be an autonomous monetary authority equal in status and power to the legislative, executive and judiciary'.

That the public at large were appreciative of the moves by Indira Gandhi was clear when the next general elections were held—elections that were advanced by one year by Indira who felt that she did not have any room to manoeuvre with a minority government. The Congress bagged 352 seats—up from 283 in the previous elections—while the Jana Sangh's tally fell. The party won just 22 seats of the 157 it contested, down from the 35 it had won in the 1967 elections. The party's vote proportion also fell to 7 per cent. In Delhi, which was a stronghold of the Jana Sangh, the party failed to win a single seat. Eleven of the Jana Sangh's seats came from Madhya Pradesh where Atal Bihari Vajpayee was himself elected from Gwalior. Vijaya Raje Scindia, who would later become the party's vice president, won from Bhind. Newspaper magnate Ram Nath Goenka won on a Jana Sangh ticket from Vidisha while Madhav Rao Scindia, who later joined the Congress and became an important leader, won from Guna.

After the 1971 elections, armed with a two-thirds majority, Indira Gandhi was unstoppable. With the Indo-Pak war of 1971, she managed to divide Pakistan after a bitter clash and separate its eastern wing which is now known as the independent nation of Bangladesh. Her popularity was its peak. The Jana Sangh could not criticize her: after all she had given a bloody nose to Pakistan, the country it had been campaigning against for so long. With her prowess, Indira Gandhi was now also poaching on the core constituency of the Jana Sangh. Little wonder that after India's victory in the 1971 war, even Atal Bihari Vajpayee was forced to liken Indira Gandhi to Goddess Durga in the Lok Sabha. 'With [this] victory Indira Gandhi was able to give India her pride back. It was a great assertion of the self-confidence of the nation,' points out Brij Mohan Pande, a retired archaeologist from New Delhi recollecting the public mood. In fact, the win over Pakistan was a culmination of events. India had started drifting after the 1965 war which had put pressure on public resources. This, coupled with bad crops, led to famine-like conditions in 1965. Food grains were imported from the US who gave aid but demanded that the economy be liberalized. Then fresh in office, Indira Gandhi responded by sharply depreciating the Indian rupee. This caused disenchantment within the country and the public saw the devaluation of the rupee as loss of national prestige. But the devaluation did not satisfy the western lobby pushing for liberalization. The US now wanted Indira Gandhi to support the war that they had been waging against Vietnam and held back aid. Mrs Gandhi was incensed but could do nothing. She ordered that the government take steps to shore up foreign exchange. She also decided that whenever the country needed to import food grains, it would buy it commercially from the market and not extend a begging bowl. Fortunately for her, the green revolution increased crop yield dramatically and changed the situation.

Armed with new confidence in the wake of the liberation of Bangladesh, Indira Gandhi went full throttle at nationalizing the coal and petroleum industry and accentuated the drive towards the public sector, expanding it greatly. New licensing regimes were kicked in and other restrictions were put in place for industry. This was around the time that her slogan of 'Garibi Hatao' was coined.

Meanwhile, the Jana Sangh continued to be on the back foot. This is reflected by the resolutions it passed during 1969-71. In its

1971 election manifesto, the Jana Sangh also talked about a war on poverty and providing full employment to the people, saying that the five-year plans had not resulted in solving any problems. Finding that the initiative had been snatched by Indira Gandhi, the party resorted to rhetoric in the 1971 manifesto. 'Never before has it been that a prime minister in a democracy entered into such open collusion with anti-national and anti-democratic forces. Never has the clique in power treated judiciary and Parliament with such contempt,' the manifesto said.

Atal Bihari Vajpayee was facing a double whammy. Not only was his party smarting under the offensive of Indira Gandhi, but he was also facing attack from Balraj Madhok internally. The latter seemed to have developed a personal animosity against him and put forth his opposition on every conceivable matter. Vajpayee pushed the party to adopt policies that would be in tune with what Indira Gandhi was pushing for. This would also make the party reflect the aspirations of the people. But Balraj Madhok was opposed to any move that would give the impression that the party was veering to the left. He, in fact, wanted the Jana Sangh to ally itself more with the Swatantra Party that promoted free enterprise but was largely seen by the public as an outfit that espoused the cause of big businesses and dispossessed landholders and princes. In fact, Madhok also advocated that the Jana Sangh be merged with Swatantra Party.

In these difficult days, a new party member was to occupy centre stage and later became an able associate of Vajpayee—Lal Krishna Advani, a convent-educated Karachi boy who had been exposed to the RSS even before Partition. After 1947, Advani migrated to India and was deputed by the RSS to Alwar, Rajasthan. In the late 1950s, he caught the attention of Deen Dayal Upadhyaya who drafted him for party work in Delhi and asked him to look after the affairs of the Delhi Municipal Corporation. In 1967, Advani got into the Delhi Metropolitan Council and, in 1970, he was given a berth in the Rajya Sabha. Advani's rise in the party was due not only to his organizational experience but also his good oratory and drafting skills in English.

But Madhok looked at him with suspicion. Many years later, in an interview to Pankaj Vohra of the *Hindustan Times*, Madhok recalled that although Advani had been nominated by the party as a candidate for the elections of the Metropolitan Council, two days before the nominations, he wanted to opt out. Advani's argument: his seat had a significant rural electorate over whom the party had little influence. Advani's wishes were granted and someone else was put up instead. Even then the party swept the polls. Madhok, the president of the party then, was approached by Deen Dayal Upadhyaya who suggested that Advani be nominated as metropolitan councillor and be made the chief executive councillor. There were five nominated posts of councillors. Madhok said he resisted partially, agreeing to nominate him as an executive councillor but not to making him the chief executive councillor. Instead, Advani was made the chairman of the council, a post like that of the speaker.

However, Advani has a different take on this incident that he recounts in his autobiography, *My Country My Life*. Advani writes: 'I had not contested the council elections since I was entrusted the responsibility of organizing my party's city unit for polls. Under the Delhi Municipal Act, the union home ministry could nominate five members for the council. Atalji persuaded Home Minister Y.B. Chavan to nominate me to the council.'

In those days, along with Advani, Vajpayee's closest colleagues in the party were Nanaji Deshmukh and Jagannath Rao Joshi. Deshmukh, despite hailing from Maharashtra, had considerable experience in building the organization in Uttar Pradesh where he had worked as a RSS pracharak in Gorakhpur and was the party in-charge of Jana Sangh of the state. Joshi, a Kannadiga, had won a Lok Sabha seat from Madhya Pradesh. All of them felt that Madhok had grown too big for his boots and the process of sidelining the leader began. Madhok, however, had the support of Deen Dayal Upadhyaya (even though Madhok would later criticize Upadhyaya's theory of integral humanism by suggesting that it was nothing but an adaption of the radical humanism philosophy by M.N. Roy). This allowed Madhok elbow room in the party but with the demise of Deen Dayal, the former's opinions did not carry much weight within the party. In March 1973, he was expelled from the party on the flimsy charge of leaking some party documents to the media. It seems that the party took a formal nod from RSS boss Guru Golwalkar before taking the extreme step. At that point, Golwalkar was unwell and a few months later passed away from cancer. Incidentally, Vajpayee had pushed Advani into the president's slot by then. Since Vajpayee had completed his five years, he wanted to pass on the baton to somebody else in his camp. The responsibility fell on Advani after both Vijaya Raje Scindia and Bhai Mahavir refused to take up the position.

With Advani by his side, Vajpayee had started working on how the Jana Sangh could be a winning party. He realized that the party would have to expand its support base and for this the Jana Sangh would have to take up causes of the poor and underprivileged and not just of those who lived in big cities. Vajpayee advised state units of the party to take up farmers' causes and agitate for them. He also asked them to take up programmes that would appeal to the scheduled castes and the other backward classes. However, this initiative does not seem to have been a great success though the party nominees had won a few seats from reserved constituencies, the winners being members of the scheduled caste.

On Vajpayee's request, Advani also started looking at the electoral system and suggesting reforms that would benefit a smaller party like Jana Sangh against larger parties like the Congress. This included ways to stem defections from parties and stop the inordinate use of money power in elections. Advani was also concerned about the first-past-the-post system of elections or the winner-takes-all system of polls in India. By this, a party could win elections even without attaining a majority of votes. Advani at that time preferred the system of proportional voting by which parties win seats in proportion to the votes that they win (it is, however, doubtful that, with his party now having grown enourmously, Advani would still subscribe to this system).

In 1972, elections for state assemblies were to be held. This was the first time ever that state elections were to be held separately from the general elections which had been advanced by a year. The Jana Sangh decided to offer itself as 'the only alternative' to the people. Its manifesto said: 'The ruling Congress wants a vote for itself in the name of victory and stability. The fact is that it can claim neither. What we have just won is a glorious war made possible by our gallant forces.' It went on to claim that 'the Congress has made defections into a major industry. [The] PM has been toppling provincial governments with an abandon more appropriate to puppet play... The constitution has been dehydrated and the country pushed into the direction of a one-man dictatorship. Efforts are being made to subvert the independence of the judiciary and the press.'

The 1972 elections may not have thrown up great results for the Jana Sangh but an opportunity came their way when Indira Gandhi, armed with extraordinary powers, really started going berserk. The government went out of its way to promote her son Sanjay's auto venture, Maruti, in contravention of all norms. This blatant nepotism caused a lot of public anger because the press was reporting the matter with vigour. Meanwhile, prices also started rising and, in 1973, after the oil crisis, there was record inflation. At the same time, evidence of corruption started surfacing from everywhere and this touched not only cabinet ministers (like railway minister Lalit Narayan Mishra) but also Congress chief ministers (like Chimanbhai

Patel of Gujarat). People were getting visibly angry and rising in protest. In 1974, there was a huge strike by railway men and the Nav Nirman Andolan (re-invention movement) was organized in Gujarat by students that led to the ouster of the chief minister. The old Congress socialist Jayaprakash Narayan, though past seventy years of age, led a major students' movement in Bihar. In a little over three years from the day she dismembered Pakistan, Indira Gandhi had reached a nadir, with her popularity dipping every day. Opposition parties including the Jana Sangh began to informally coalesce into a composite group around Jayaprakash Narayan who was fast emerging as a symbol of resistance to the anti-people rule of Mrs Gandhi. Jayaprakash Narayan gave a call for 'sampoorna kranti', galvanizing the masses in North India. It is interesting to note that, once upon a time, JP—as the leader was popularly called—was a trenchant critic of the RSS. This was especially after the assassination of Mahatma Gandhi. JP thought that the RSS had some hand in the assassination. Why JP agreed to include the Jana Sangh in the informal coalition of parties is a mystery, though he may have decided to be practical. Advani in his autobiography says that JP asked him, 'I hear persistent questions about RSS's alleged role in Gandhiji's assassination. I want to study the matter in detail and would like you to furnish me all the information'. A few days after all the information with documentary evidence was sent to him, JP called Advani and said: 'I have studied the matter fully and am now convinced that RSS has had no hand in the assassination of Mahatma Gandhi.'

Things came to a head on 12 June 1975 when the Allahabad High Court, ruling on an election petition filed earlier, unseated Indira Gandhi from her Rae Bareli Lok Sabha seat for taking recourse to practices not permitted in the elections in 1971, including the misuse of the official machinery. She was barred from contesting elections for six years. Even as pressure mounted on her to quit,

Indira Gandhi struck back and imposed internal emergency on 26 June 1975 saying that anti-social forces were out to subvert the country. Simultaneously, she packed off the leaders of the Opposition parties to jail, including all Jana Sangh leaders like Vajpayee, Advani, Sunder Singh Bhandari and Vijaya Raje Scindia, as well as hundreds of others. A large number of other activists were also jailed as a reign of terror was unleashed. The RSS was also banned. All civil liberties were suspended and the Supreme Court ruled that the fundamental right to life was also suspended.

On 12 June, the day that Indira Gandhi was unseated, there was another significant happening that was scarcely noticed nationally. In the elections held in Gujarat after the Congress government fell—as a result of the Nav Nirman Andolan—the Jana Morcha got the highest number of seats. The Jana Morcha was a coalition that had been cobbled out of several Opposition parties, chief among which was the Jana Sangh. This was the first time that the party was in power in Gujarat. The successor of the Jana Sangh, the BJP, was to strike very deep roots in the state in the next two decades.

The Emergency made Indira Gandhi overconfident and even as her son, Sanjay Gandhi, ran riot, she remained cut off from what was happening on the ground. The press was censored and thus, with no reality check, Indira Gandhi believed all that her loyal band of party men told her; not surprisingly, the lackeys said that the country was greatly appreciative of the Emergency and the discipline it had inculcated. Trains ran on time, industrial production was up and, for the first time, family planning was being pursued with vigour. The twenty-point programme had enthralled the masses, the loyal brigade asserted. Influenced by this false sense of well-being, Indira Gandhi thought that she would sweep the polls when they were held; reports from the Intelligence Bureau also suggested so. The term of the Lok Sabha that was to end in March 1976 had, in any case, been extended by a year. In order to get a fresh mandate,

Indira Gandhi announced that elections were going to be held on 18 January 1977.

Even in the midst of the Emergency—expecting that elections would have to be organized sooner or later—Opposition parties had been confabulating. A majority of the top leaders were jailed but lesser representatives of the Jana Sangh, Congress (O), Bharatiya Lok Dal and the Socialist Party along with 'eminent individuals' met in Mumbai on 20 and 21 January 1976. Jayaprakash Narayan, who had been released from jail as his kidneys had failed, also attended. The purpose of the meeting was to construct a national alternative to the Congress.

In May 1976, the working committee of the Jana Sangh met to take the agenda forward. It was a low-key affair because thirty members of the national executive of the party, including the president, were in jail. The working committee felt that all Opposition parties should come together to form a national alternative, but since their senior members were not present they failed to officially pass a resolution. The members present said that it would be great if joint committees of representatives of the parties could be set up at the central, state, district and taluka levels as a prelude to the formation of a single party.

Even in those difficult times there was a certain apprehension against joining hands with the Jana Sangh to form a coalition party. Many socialists felt that the link between the Jana Sangh and the RSS made the party communal. To address these concerns, on 26 September 1976, the working committee of the Jana Sangh met and appealed to all parties to 'unconditionally merge their separate entities in a single party that would be the rallying ground for all defenders of democracy, irrespective of their personal non-political affiliations.' The Jana Sangh also asked the political parties to 'avoid scrupulously the alienation of any democratic forces whose constituents have contributed to the struggle during the Emergency' and 'conduct itself in a manner suited to commanding confidence of all the various patriotic and anti-establishment forces'.

Hence, when elections were announced, it was only within a matter of a few days that the non-communist political parties merged their identities and coalesced into a single unit called the Janata Party. The architect behind the party was Jayaprakash Narayan although Morarji Desai was appointed as its chairman. Ramakrishna Hegde was the general secretary while the spokesman was Lal Krishna Advani. The Janata Party, in its manifesto titled *Bread and Liberty*, declared that the forthcoming elections were a 'choice between freedom and slavery, democracy and dictatorship, between abdicating the power of the people and asserting it and between the Gandhian path and the way that has led many nations down the precipice of dictatorship, instability, military adventure and national ruin.'

There was so much public anger against the Emergency regime in North India that it did not take much effort for the Janata Party to storm into power with 295 seats. South of the Vindhyas, where the rigours of the Emergency had not been felt so intensely, the Congress performed well and this enabled it to win 154 seats. In Uttar Pradesh, the Congress met with a thrashing and did not secure a single seat. Both Indira Gandhi and Sanjay Gandhi lost.

Ninety-three Janata Party MPs were of Jana Sangh origin. This made them the largest group in the party: Congress (O) origin MPs totaled forty-four, Charan Singh's Bharatiya Lok Dal origin MPs accounted for seventy-one members. The socialists contributed twenty-eight MPs whilst Jagjivan Ram, who had quit the Congress before elections, contributed twenty-eight MPs who were elected from his Congress for Democracy group.

Morarji Desai was anointed as prime minister even as Atal Bihari Vajpayee was appointed as the external affairs minister. L.K. Advani became the information and broadcasting minister. Brij Lal Verma, the third minister from the Jana Sangh, was appointed as the communications minister. The Janata Party government came into being on 24 March 1977. State governments formed by the Janata Party also came into office in cow-belt states such as Haryana, Uttar Pradesh and Bihar.

But the common cause made against the Emergency did not last too long. Mutual suspicions started coming to fore once again and within a year fissures in the Janata Party started showing. The socialists in the Janata Party felt that the Jana Sangh elements—propelled by the RSS—were trying to further their ideological cause through the government. They received support from the Bharatiya Lok Dal (BLD) whose leader, Charan Singh, although the home minister, nursed ambitions of occupying the prime ministerial slot. To make matters worse, the Jana Sangh faction in Janata Party did nothing to allay the apprehensions.

On 2 December 1978, O.P. Tyagi, a member originally owing allegiance to the Jana Sangh, introduced the freedom of religion Bill in Lok Sabha. This Bill sought to make religious conversions by the use of fraud, force and inducements a criminal offence and immediately raised the hackles of Christians who thought that their involvement in running missionary schools and hospitals could be construed as inducements. Among those disturbed by the Bill was no less than Mother Teresa, who wrote to the prime minister. A few months later, there were massive protests by the Christians in Delhi and the Bill was never passed by the Lok Sabha.

But the damage had been done. In May 1979, Janata Party general secretary, Madhu Limaye, who had earlier owed allegiance to the Socialist Party, convened a conference to discuss if there was a possibility of having a non-authoritarian, non-communal third front. The meeting was attended by many anti-RSS members of the Janata Party like George Fernandes, who criticized the Jana Sangh elements in the party and pointed to Tyagi's Bill as an illustration of how they were trying to hijack the official agenda. Many Congressmen (the Congress had split by now) and Communists also attended the meeting. Attendees across party lines agreed to commit themselves to cooperate in the Lok Sabha on issues of national unity, democratic freedoms, communal harmony and social justice.

A month earlier in April 1979, Raj Narain, the man whose election petition had resulted in the high court order unseating Indira Gandhi, had demanded that the Janata Party officially break all ties with the RSS. Jana Sangh elements gathered support from the hundred MPs of the Janata Party and demanded the expulsion of Raj Narain, who was the incumbent health minister from the Janata Party. Raj Narain had also contested against Indira Gandhi in the 1977 Lok Sabha polls and defeated her. The MPs further demanded the expulsion of UP Chief Minister Banarasi Das who led a Janata Party government but without a single minister from the erstwhile Jana Sangh. Banarasi Das had replaced Ram Naresh Yadav who had to quit after losing his majority in the legislature party after he had sacked all ministers who had Jana Sangh origins. Similarly, in Haryana, Devi Lal had to quit after sacking misters of Jana Sangh origin from his government. In Bihar, Chief Minister Karpoori Thakur lost his confidence vote, a move that was engineered by legislators with Jana Sangh origins.

A series of communal riots in North India in late 1978 and early 1979 also did much to cause fissures within the Janata Party and their socialist members looked at the RSS with even greater suspicion. This was the primary cause of tension within the Janata Party in Haryana, UP and Bihar. The end game began after Raj Narain left the Janata Party and formed a breakaway group: the Janata Party (Secular). By 11 July 1979, forty-nine MPs from Janata Party had joined Raj Narain's outfit. This reduced the Janata Party to a minority in the Lok Sabha and when the Congress party leader Y.B. Chavan brought a vote of confidence in the lower house, Morarji Desai resigned (on 15 July) before the vote actually could be taken.

What happened in the next few days was even more bizarre. Y.B. Chavan, who was invited to form the government, declined the offer and then Charan Singh, who barely a few months ago as home minister had attempted to imprison Indira Gandhi, staked claim to the government. This he did with the support of Indira Gandhi's Congress which now had seventy-one MPs! Charan Singh became prime minister on 28 July but soon thereafter Indira Gandhi's party withdrew support. This made Charan Singh's continuance untenable. He resigned, and the then President Neelam Sanjiva Reddy, without asking anybody else to form the government, dissolved the Lok Sabha and announced fresh elections. Hence, Charan Singh continued as prime minister for six months. The Janata Party experiment had failed and the man who was responsible for cobbling together the party, Jayaprakash Narayan, had also died in the interim.

chapter 5

Jana Sangh and the Minorities

Born in the wake of the Partition, the Bharatiya Jana Sangh was, from the very beginning, suspicious of developments that it averred could lead to fissiparous tendencies and affect the unity of the country. As a result, it passed resolutions and took positions that would look odd from a liberal perspective. Since the body politic was governed by the concepts of Nehruvian secularism, these views did not find favour with large sections of the electorate. This was a major reason that stymied the growth of the party.

A glimpse of the party's attitude towards minorities at that time can be gleaned from the foreword the then Jana Sangh President Atal Bihari Vajpayee wrote to the compilation of party documents in 1973. Vajpayee, who was otherwise considered a moderate, writes (talking of developments in the country in the first two decades): 'Congress hopes that [the] creation of Pakistan would put an end to the agonizing chapter of communal violence and animosity had been falsified. The Hindu-Muslim conflict had only enlarged into an Indo-Pakistan confrontation. There was widespread discontent in public mind regarding the government's Pakistan policy which in effect was only an extension of the Congress's Muslim appeasement policy.'

Not just the Muslims, the Jana Sangh was equally suspicious of the Akalis. Within a few years of India becoming a Republic, the Akalis began demanding a Punjabi suba (province). This was against the backdrop of the demand for creating linguistic states that was coming up in many parts of the country. The Jana Sangh started becoming apprehensive; it felt that behind the demand for creating a Punjabi suba was the plan to create a Sikh state. The party was echoing the views of many Punjabi Hindus who had begun declaring Hindi as their mother tongue to prevent a Punjabi-speaking state. On 28 August 1955, the All India General Council (AIGC) meeting at Calcutta passed a resolution that stated that the party expressed 'grave concern' created by 'communal elements such as Akali Dal carving out separate territories...with little regard to symbols of national honour and unity.' The party also said that the 'Akali Dal cloaked its intention of establishing a communal and theocratic state by putting forward the demand for a Punjabi-speaking state.' The Jana Sangh also claimed that this demand was only supported by a section of the Sikhs. Whether this was correct or not, the States Reorganization Committee (SRC) set up by the central government also did not recommend a Punjab consisting only of Punjabi-speaking areas. Punjab in those days also included present-day Haryana.

The demand for a separate Punjabi suba, however, caught momentum once again in the mid-1960s after the Indo-Pak conflict in which Sikh soldiers played a sterling role. This incensed the Jana Sangh and the party's central working committee passed a resolution at Kanpur on 15 January 1966 saying: 'The CWC regrets that immediately after the ceasefire, [the] Government of India has rushed to reopen the issue of [a] Punjabi suba. The move of the government is unwarranted, inadvisable, inopportune and fraught with grave consequences. It is essential to maintain [the] unity of Punjab in order to meet [the] aggressive designs of neighbouring hostile countries.'

By March, the government had decided to reorganize Punjab. The Jana Sangh could not sit still. At its all India session held on 1 May 1966 at Jalandhar, it passed a resolution: '[The] Government of India's move to reorganize Punjab in March goes counter to expert opinion and wishes of the people. Jana Sangh considers this decision unfortunate.' It added that the central government had to acknowledge that there was a force in Punjab other than that of the Akalis and this was manifested through popular sentiment. The Jana Sangh said that this force 'cannot be disregarded'. In the end, the party said that Jana Sangh 'regards Sikhs as part and parcel of the Hindu society'.

Says political scientist Jyotirmaya Sharma: 'This was the problem with the Jana Sangh: they looked at everything from the perspective of Hindu and non-Hindu [groupings] and found it difficult [to conceive] that non-Hindus could exist as separate entities in India.'

If this was their attitude towards Sikhs, little wonder then that the party was suspicious at anything relating to Muslims. On 31 December 1952, the party passed a resolution at its all India session that was prompted by a demand for recognizing Urdu as an official language in some northern states. The resolution said: 'Agitation in Delhi, Bihar and UP for recognizing Urdu as an official language, in the view of Jana Sangh, is being encouraged by anti-national and separatist tendencies. Urdu, a trumped-up language by distorting Hindi with foreign words and foreign thoughts, was one of the many methods adopted by foreign rulers to weaken the unity of the nation. After Independence, it is the duty of the rising nation not to encourage a distorted form of Hindi exploited by anti-national elements.'

In 1965, the Jana Sangh's venom was reserved for Aligarh Muslim University (AMU). The party passed a resolution at its central working committee meeting on 10 July 1965 at Jabalpur: 'AMU was founded mostly with the set purpose to develop and consolidate separatist trends among Indian Muslims to keep them out of the national movement. The ideology of Pakistan was born and developed from this university.' It went on: 'After Partition, most of their students and teachers migrated to Pakistan. It was generally believed and expected that this poisonous plant will be allowed to die its own death and nothing would be done to enable it to take roots in the Indian soil again. But quite the opposite happened. The national government of free India began to rebuild [it] as a central university. But while doing so there were no steps taken to end its separatist and communal character and make it a national institution. As a result, communalism is manifesting itself and communal riots and communal incidents are taking place year after year.' The provocation that the Jana Sangh was reacting to was the move by the vice chancellor of the university, Ali Yavar Jung, to reduce the reservation of Muslims from 76 per cent to 50 per cent that was met with stiff resistance from within the institution. The Jana Sangh said that the statute of AMU should be completely changed to end the communal character of the university: 'All teachers and officials of the university must be thoroughly scanned to clear the university of all anti-national characters.'

It may be noted here that, a few years earlier in October 1961, the AMU had been affected by riots. The violence that occured before the 1962 general elections happened after the AMU student elections where not a single Hindu student made it to the union. After Muslims held victory processions, a counter procession was organized by Hindu groups. This led to a clash between students. A rumour that one Hindu student had been killed in the campus sparked off full-scale violence where fourteen lives were lost, mostly those of Muslims. This provided the background to the Jana Sangh resolution on the university.

Earlier, the CWC of the party had adopted a resolution on 22 April 1961 that said: 'The way in which the question of debarring communal parties for participating in elections has been raised by the ruling party in the context of Jabalpur and the indecent haste with which the administration has sought to be equipped with necessary new and vast powers is a matter of deep concern for all lovers of democracy'.

Jabalpur saw Hindu-Muslim riots in February 1961, in what was billed as the first major conflagration between the two communities post Independence. The riot was linked to the emergence of a small class of successful Muslim entrepreneurs that created a new economic rivalry between the Hindus and the Muslims. Two hundred people were killed and Muslim houses were targeted after the daughter of a prominent Hindu businessman involved in the bidi trade eloped with a Muslim. According to another version, a Hindu girl was raped by some Muslim students providing the spark for the communal riots.

The Jana Sangh's CWC resolution also said: 'It is an unpleasant fact that nothing has been done to destroy the two nation theory which directly led to the partition of India and which today lies at the root of Muslim communalism in the country. The unholy Congress alliance with the Muslim League (in Kerala) has lent respectability to communalism and inspired and encouraged the Muslims living in other parts of the country to organize themselves on [a] communal basis. The situation has been aggravated by efforts of Pakistan to become the self-styled protectors of Indian Muslims.'

A few years later, the Jana Sangh became more strident. This was evident from its resolution at the all India session of the party on 28 December 1969 which said: 'The spate of communal riots and rapid erosion of the rule of law is a cause of concern. The communal riots—for example, those at Ahmedabad, Jagatdal and Varanasi—have set up a pattern. They are invariably started by that section of Indian Muslims which...[has] stuck to the ideology that led to the Partition of the country in 1947 with the direct or indirect help and abetment of the CPI, CPM and a section of the Congress which have developed vested interests in perpetuating communalism and separatism among the Muslims and keeping them away from the mainstream of Indian life.' It went on to say that Pakistan was striving for another Partition of India and this was clear from the recent writings of Mr Bhutto and Maulana Bhashani (a leader from East Pakistan). Bhutto was a leading baiter of India in Pakistan in those days and a votary of covert Pakistani operations in Kashmir. The dependence of the Indira Gandhi government on the Muslim League for support had given new import to the communal problem, the resolution said. Incidentally, the Justice Jaganmohan Reddy Commission that had been set up to inquire into the causes of the aforesaid Ahmedabad riots had concluded that Hindu nationalist organizations were responsible for causing it.

A year earlier at its Guwahati session on 14 June 1968, the Jana Sangh had expounded on 'foreign-inspired riots' and said that, '...forces in the country are actively conspiring to create disorder and anarchy by fomenting communalism. The possibility cannot be ruled out that these rioters have been receiving arms and money from some foreign powers.' Slogans of 'Pakistan zindabad' and 'parading of foreign flags' lent strength to suspicions, the party said. The Jana Sangh went on to note that: 'Parties which tom-tom the loudest about secularism are foremost in patronizing communalism. The extraordinary rise in strength and influence of Jamaat-e-Islami is an index that the Muslim masses are increasingly coming under the grip of fanatic mullahs and maulavis who hold that the security and progress of Muslims can be ensured only under a state ruled by Muslims in accordance with the shariat.'

In 1969, the Jana Sangh was agitated with the move of the Kerala government to carve out a Muslim majority Malappuram from the existing Calicut district. At its Delhi CWC meeting on 16 February 1969, the party resolved 'to intensify the agitation against the proposal to create Malappuram district which it feels is thoroughly communal and a grave threat to the nation's integrity and security.' The resolution added: '[The] Muslim League in Kerala made this demand from its inception. The demand for Mopalastan is as old as Pakistan. There is recorded evidence that Jinnah, when approached by League leaders from Kerala, advised them to strive for carving out a Mopalastan within the Indian Union, which when the proper time comes we can link with Pakistan.' This obsession with the Muslims of Kerala continued. In the manifesto for the 1971 elections, the party harped: 'Ever since the Congress split [in November 1969], Indira Gandhi has headed a minority government to maintain herself in power. She has leaned more and more on communists and communalists. As a price for their support she has turned a blind eye to the anarchic conditions created by the former and promoted the ominous revival of the Muslim League in the country's political life. In the Kerala mid-term polls the ruling Congress entered into an open alliance with the Muslim League. In a bid to cloak this unbiased opportunism the PM has publicly certified the Kerala Muslim League as "not communal".'

In the mid-1950s, the Bharatiya Jana Sangh was also much disturbed by the activities of foreign missionaries in Madhya Pradesh and launched an agitation called 'the anti-foreign missionary week'. The agitation forced the state government to appoint a high level committee headed by the retired chief justice B.S. Niyogi. The committee's recommendations—like legal prohibition of religious conversions that are not completely voluntary and other strict measures—found favour with the Jana Sangh. The central working committee of the party considered the report on 21 July 1956 and said that it 'supported the recommendations as it is intended to put an end to undesirable activities of foreign Christian missionaries'. The CWC also added that the 'Indian Christian community should gather under an united independent Indian Christian church without being dependent on foreign support and should thus constitute a devoted, loyal and valued section of the citizens of India'.

The Jana Sangh was also worried about the state of affairs in Assam and its neighbouring states and the missionaries working there. 'All foreign Christian missionaries operating in the Assam hills, NEFA (which is now Arunachal Pradesh) should be immediately expelled,' the Jana Sangh's CWC said after a meeting in Guwahati on 14 June 1968. At the same meeting, the party declared: 'The foreign Christian missionaries, in their bid to have a Christian majority state in the hill areas of Assam, have been playing the game of Communist China and Pakistan. They have been systematically converting and denationalizing the hill tribals by reversing the process of their cultural assimilation with the people of the plains through their common allegiance to Hinduism.'

On 30 December 1956, the all India session of the party passed a resolution titled 'Eradication of Communalism through Indianization'. A reading of the resolution gives a deep insight into the thinking of the party. It stated: '[The] Jana Sangh holds that the territorial unity alone cannot be the basis for nationalism. For being a nation, people require the underlying bonds of culture. Indian nationalism is ancient; despite political divisions, the people of India have remained one through the bonds of one national culture. When foreign rulers of this country began destroying this unity for their selfish ends and thrust culture foreign to the genius of Indian life, and when foreign values began to be respected, our nationalism was endangered. The success of the two nation theory and the consequent vivisection of the Motherland are their results. Even then, again, a supposedly separate Muslim culture is being promoted and protected resulting in the continuance of the two nation theory mentality.'

In the 1950s—more specifically after the death of its first president Syama Prasad Mookerjee—the Jana Sangh had raised the slogan of 'Akhand Bharat'. In a resolution passed by its All India General Council on 15 August 1953, the sixth anniversary of Independent India, the party said: 'India while she attained her freedom was also divided into two independent states...which cuts at the roots of the spirit of one nationhood. The Partition of the country was done without the consent of the people and a large majority of nationalist forces have since repudiated it.' It added: 'The Bharatiya Jana Sangh stands for one nation, one country and one culture. We reaffirm our faith in united India and pledge ourselves to renewed efforts for the fulfillment of Akhand Bharat.'

Again in its 1957 election manifesto, the Jana Sangh declared: '[The] Partition of India was a great blunder and it has benefitted neither the Hindus nor the Muslims. The number of people who are beginning to realize that the annulment of Partition is essential for the well-being of the country...[is increasing] in Bharat and Pakistan.' It went on to say: 'Most of Indo-Pakistan problems can be permanently solved only by establishment of Akhand Bharat in which Hindus and Muslims and people of other faiths can live as loyal citizens of one great nation.'

After 1957, the party realized that it was futile to continue harping on Akhand Bharat. Instead it came to the internal understanding that fissiparous tendencies could possibly be contained by strengthening the centre. This meant that the states should be weakened. This is what the Jana Sangh effectively declared in its manifesto for the 1962 elections. The manifesto said: 'The Constitution calls the Centre...[a] Union of provinces or states. This separate and somewhat sovereign status of constituents is a hindrance to national unity. Bharatiya Jana Sangh will amend the Constitution and declare India as a unitary state with [a] provision for decentralization of power to the lowest level with [the] creation of district councils or janapada.' It is obvious that with the weakening of the states and strengthening of the centre, the voice of the minorities would be dimmed.

However, during the 1960s, when Deen Dayal Upadhyaya was at the fore of party matters, the Jana Sangh proposed the concept of an Indo-Pak confederation. Upadhyaya, who was friends with and influenced a lot by socialist leader Ram Manohar Lohia, propounded this concept along with the latter. While publicizing this concept, Upadhyaya said that he was well aware that there were expectations that Pakistan would be forcibly merged into India if the Jana Sangh came into power. But Upadhyaya stressed that the party did not propose to do such a thing; instead, it would call for an Indo-Pak confederation which would guide bilateral relations. The proposal for the confederation repudiated the concept of Akhand Bharat and was expounded after the Indo-China war of 1962 which highlighted the need for maintaining good relations with neighbours.

chapter 6

The Metamorphosis

Indira Gandhi romped back to power in the 1980 elections. The Janata Party was decimated: it could only manage to win 31 seats in the Lok Sabha. The voters were extremely upset with the internal fights within the party that had been played out in the public. 'The Congress asked for votes for a government that works and the disgusted public voted for Indira Gandhi with a vengeance,' says Rajeev Saxena, then a post-graduate student at the Delhi School of Economics. In this total tally of 31 seats, former Jana Sangh members held 16. But even after getting decimated in the elections, the infighting in the Janata Party showed no signs of abating. The issue of dual membership of former Jana Sangh men again came to fore and the assembly elections slated for the middle of the year (the state governments had been dismissed by the new Congress government) necessitated that the matter be resolved once and for all.

Meanwhile, the ex-Jana Sangh men perceived that they were being targeted, not because of their association with the RSS, but because they had come from a cadre-based party which meant that they had greater reach on the ground. Others who were part of the Janata Party were afraid that the party would ultimately be dominated by these members and this prompted the virulent anti-RSS and anti-dual membership campaign. Acutely conscious of these apprehensions, the Jana Sangh men had been satisfied with only three ministerial berths (Vajpayee, Advani and Brij Lal Varma) in the Janata government, even though their numbers justified a much higher representation. This was to allay the fears of the non-Jana Sangh section of the Janata Party. But this was to no avail because the non-Jana Sangh members would be satisfied with nothing less than the resignation of Jana Sangh men from the RSS. The Jana Sangh worthies led by Vajpayee announced that they would do nothing of this kind and a showdown soon became imminent.

▪

On 4 April 1980, the executive committee of the Janata Party resolved to throw out members who had come from the Jana Sangh. The latter had, however, anticipated this. They held a two day national convention on 5 and 6 April at New Delhi's Feroz Shah Kotla ground. Over 3,000 members attended the conference and it is here that the formation of the Bharatiya Janata Party (BJP) was announced. Atal Bihari Vajpayee was made the president of the new party while L.K. Advani became the general secretary along with Suraj Bhan and Sikandar Bakht. The latter was a Muslim belonging to the walled city of Delhi. He had originally been in the Congress (O) and was the minister for works and rehabilitation in the Morarji Desai government. He had a Hindu wife and his marriage in the early 1950s had sparked off trouble with Hindu groups protesting against it. But the BJP was determined not to be known as a Hindu party and therefore had opened its doors to not only Muslims but also those who had no RSS background. Thus, eminent lawyer Ram Jethmalani joined them as did the former judge of the Supreme Court K.S. Hegde, who had been passed over by the Indira Gandhi regime for the post of chief justice of India. Lawyer Shanti Bhushan, who had been the Janata government's law minister, also became a member of the new party.

Before the BJP was born, there were furious debates among members on what to name the new party; going back to the old Jana Sangh name was also discussed. But the consensus reached by Vajpayee was that a new party with a new philosophy would serve to bring the erstwhile Jana Sangh to the political centre stage. Going back to the Jana Sangh would once again make the party vulnerable to criticism that it was a Hindu communal outfit and limit its attractiveness to the masses. According to official documents of the BJP, members who attended the first session of the party were asked whether they wanted to go back to the name Jana Sangh but less than 'half a dozen' of the 3,000-odd attendees voted for it, and so the name Bharatiya Janata Party stuck.

After the meeting, consensus emerged on Gandhian socialism being the credo of the new party; in other words, it would fashion itself like the Janata Party. In this, Vajpayee and Advani were influenced not only by what they had seen of Jayaprakash Narayan but also by their excellent working relationship with Morarji Desai. The then prime minister was a die-hard Congressman in the Gandhian mould but the Vajpayee-Advani duo found him to be on the same page as them on many ideological matters.

For instance, Morarji Desai was instrumental in getting an amendment to the Constitution passed in Lok Sabha in May 1979 that put cow protection on the concurrent list. This was earlier in the state list and putting it on the concurrent list meant that the Government of India could also legislate in the matter. Desai said that after the amendment he would ban cow slaughter across the nation. The amendment was passed in the face of stiff opposition from the Congress, Muslim League, Communist parties and even the socialist faction of the Janata Party. But the move had warmed the hearts of the ex-Jana Sangh members of the Janata Party. In another instance, Morarji also supported the Private Members Bill introduced by O.P. Tyagi on Freedom of Religion that actually sought to prohibit illegal conversions. Though the Bill did not say so explicitly, it was targeted at stopping conversions of Hindus to Christianity. However, later Morarji withdrew his support of the Bill when he was faced with tremendous opposition but it showed where his sympathies lay. In 1975—before the Emergency—it was at Morarji Desai's instance that the Congress (O) and Jana Sangh tied up for elections for the Gujarat assembly. The Congress (O) chief in Gujarat, Hitendra Desai, protested and left the party, but Morarji did not relent.

Incidentally, the adoption of Gandhian socialism did not find favour within influential quarters of the party led by Vijaya Raje Scindia. Many were skeptical about using the term socialism because it denoted affinity to the communists who were avoided like a plague by the RSS. Others thought that adopting Gandhian socialism would make the BJP appear like a copycat: taking up what was essentially a Congress programme. Others suggested that the adoption of Ram Rajya would convey the same meaning as Gandhian socialism. It is believed that even Balasaheb Deoras—who was now the top boss of the RSS—did not like the idea of adopting Gandhian socialism but agreed, stating that organizations like the Vishwa Hindu Parishad would have to be used for Hindu mobilization in the new situation.

Some RSS men were also critical of the BJP for going out of the way to appear non-Hindu by including Muslim members. Nevertheless, for the state elections in 1980, the newly formed BJP adopted the Janata Party manifesto of the 1977 general elections. 'The stress from the beginning was not on harking back to our Jana Sangh past but on making a new beginning,' Advani wrote in his autobiography. In line with this, the BJP's inaugural convention had pictures of not only Syama Prasad Mookerjee and Deen Dayal Upadhyaya but also those of Jayaprakash Narayan. The lotus was the new symbol adopted by the party but its new flag was like that of the Janata Party: one-third green and two-thirds saffron with the lotus in the latter part. Positive secularism, according to the BJP, meant '*sarva dharma sambhava* (all dharmas are equal)' and this was in sharp contrast to the Congress party's secularism that was biased in favour of minorities for the purposes of creating a vote bank. To gain acceptability, the BJP also got a Bill introduced in the Lok Sabha in mid-1980 through Ram Jethmalani and Sikandar Bakht to legalize religious conversion. This was to dispel the impression of intolerance created in the wake of the O.P. Tyagi Bill of 1978 and emphasize the secular background of the new party. In the last week of December 1980, the first plenary session of the party was held in Bombay and attended by thousands. Newspaper reports estimated that over 40,000 attended the meet that was held in Bandra at a ground christened Samata Nagar for this purpose alone. The name was chosen to reflect the goals of the party: equality for all sections of society. Advani in his autobiography claims that twenty-five lakh members had been already enrolled in the party since its formation a few months ago as compared to the sixteen lakh members that the Jana Sangh had at its peak.

The newly formed BJP tried to get to the centre stage from the day it was founded but came up against a strange role reversal—Indira Gandhi became religious with a vengeance after coming to power in 1980 and began visiting temples with fervour. In public imagination, the impression created was that of a Hindu lady seeking the benefaction of the Gods. The policies in her tenure were also interpreted as being pro-Hindu. In the 1983 assembly elections held in Jammu and Kashmir, the Congress took a strong position against the Farooq Abdullah government and polled the Hindu votes in the Jammu region. This was at the cost of the BJP which, since its Jana

Sangh days, had been strong in the Jammu region.

The early 1980s were also marked by skirmishes in Assam and Punjab. In Assam, trouble was sparked by the continuous infiltration of immigrants from Bangladesh who, over a period of time, were assuming Indian citizenship, with voters' identification and ration cards being given to them, much to the chagrin of the locals. In Punjab, the demand for an independent Khalistan for Sikhs fostered trouble and led to violence in several parts of the state. For starters, the response of the Indira Gandhi-led government was not very effective and did little to contain the situation in Punjab. This provided the BJP with a chance to berate the government for its inaction in Assam and Punjab. Additionally, the BJP was apprehensive about the intentions of Indira Gandhi—they feared the country might be heading towards another Emergency, considering the legislation concerning disturbed areas that gave summary powers to government forces.

In June 1984, things finally came to a head when Indira Gandhi ordered the army to storm into the Golden Temple in Amritsar where the militant leader of the Damdami Taksal (a religious group), Jarnail Singh Bhindranwale, was holed up. The militants were flushed out and Bhindranwale and his associates were killed in the operation, but it led to a lot of angst in the Sikh community. The Sikhs were offended that their holiest shrine had been sullied with an army operation. Six months later, on the last day of October 1984, Indira Gandhi paid the price for this when her Sikh bodyguards shot and killed her at her official residence.

Rajiv Gandhi, her eldest son, was hurriedly sworn in as the prime minister of the country even as anti-Sikh violence erupted in the streets of Delhi. It is estimated that around 3,000 Sikhs were killed and properties belonging to members of the community were destroyed. The marauding mobs were led by members of the Congress party and Rajiv Gandhi callously said that 'when a big tree falls, the ground underneath shakes'. Elections were soon announced, and what followed was what can only be called an annihilation of the BJP at the hands of the Congress. The Congress won 414 seats in the Lok Sabha (including seats from Assam and Punjab, where elections were held a few months later)—its largest ever haul. The BJP, on the other hand, only managed to win only two seats—one each in Gujarat and Andhra Pradesh. Nobody was surprised at the performance because after the assassination of Indira Gandhi, national security had become the biggest concern for voters and they chose the Congress. In fact, this call for the maintenance of national security had become a major electoral issue all through the 1980s, with the voices of those demanding Khalistan getting louder by the day.

Although the BJP won a mere two seats, it had contested from 224 seats. Around 108 of the party's candidates lost their deposits even though the party accounted for 8 per cent of the total votes cast across the country. It also came second in about a hundred constituencies. There was a pall of gloom in BJP's ranks even as Advani said that this was not an election for the Lok Sabha but a 'shok sabha' for Indira Gandhi. The party had begun its new journey barely four years ago with a lot of promise. And even rank outsiders like former law minister M.C. Chagla had graced the first plenary and declared that the BJP was a viable alternative to the Congress and that in Vajpayee he saw a prime minister in waiting. What had hit the top echelon of the BJP leadership was that even parties like Janata Party (which had been emasculated after the ex-Jana Sangh members left them) had secured ten Lok Sabha seats. The Lok Dal of Charan Singh had also managed to win three seats.

The party bosses now began to rethink their strategy, with Vajpayee himself posing questions to the members at the national executive meeting in April 1985. Was the party's defeat because of the decision to merge Jana Sangh with the Janata Party and then withdraw from it barely three years later? Should the BJP go back now and revive Jana Sangh? There were no easy answers but the national council meeting of the party that met in Gandhinagar in October 1985 resolved that nationalism and national integration would be a major preoccupation of the party in the future, along with the defence of democracy and value-based politics. The BJP realized that, in times of crisis, the citizens were concerned with nothing more than keeping the nation together. However the party did not give up Gandhian socialism and positive secularism.

An official committee set up under the chairmanship of Vice President K.L. Sharma to review the working of the party found that the decisions to merge the Jana Sangh into the Janata Party and to later exit the Janata Party were in accordance with the situation prevailing then. 'We are very proud of our Jana Sangh heritage,' the report said. The committee, however, found a lot of lacunae in the working of the BJP. There was evidently a communication gap between the leadership and the grassroot-level workers in the party. The committee also commented on the lack of political training for workers on political, economic, ideological and organizational matters.

Among the other findings of the committee were the failure of the party to mobilize public opinion in Punjab effectively to combat terrorism, and the inability of the party to capture power in Himachal Pradesh in 1982 and Delhi in 1983. This, the committee said, had dampened the enthusiasm of the workers. It also found that the BJP had not taken up any agitation on issues at the national level. 'Basically, the committee politely said that the party was going nowhere. Since Vajpayee was the president of the party, it was his indictment,' says a BJP insider who wishes to remain anonymous.

The committee also made a range of recommendations on how to deepen and broaden the base of the party and impart momentum and direction to the BJP. One of the major recommendations was to convert the party from a cadre-based to a mass-based organization. This would entail the induction of many more members into the party. It was envisaged that the cadres of the party would bring in the new members but the former had an additional responsibility of leading the masses and getting them involved in the programmes and agitations of the BJP. In order to make the organization more robust, the Sharma Committee called for organizational elections every two years and recommended that the youth should comprise 20 per cent of all party committees. Moreover, the composition of the party committees had to be such that 20 per cent of the office bearers would get changed every year. In order to make the party organization even wider, the committee also recommended establishing kisan and labour cells which would take up issues pertaining to farmers and industrial labour respectively. The establishment of study groups for undertaking in-depth studies on subjects like foreign relations, economy, rural development, and science and technology was also recommended. So as to impart a sense of purpose to the members of the party, the Sharma Committee recommended that a week between 6 April and 13 April should be celebrated as foundation week and the period between 23 June and 7 July as national integration fortnight (this period marked the birth and death of Syama Prasad Mookerjee). Similarly, the interval between 5 September and 2 October was to be celebrated as antyodaya week. This period marked the birthdays of Deen Dayal Upadhyaya and Mahatma Gandhi.

After the systematic soul searching recommended by the Sharma Committee, there was a change of guard at the helm. Vajpayee stepped down and Advani took over as the new president. This was the beginning of a fruitful tenure for Advani as the party underwent a lot of changes. One of the first things that Advani did was to induct newer members into executive positions. Hitherto, the party had had one general secretary—Advani himself. When he became president, he appointed four general secretaries—Murli Manohar Joshi, Kedar Nath Sahni, Pramod Mahajan and K.L. Sharma, who had drafted the committee report. Joshi, till then not known in public circles, was a physics doctorate from Allahabad University where he taught as well, and had been a RSS member since a very young age. He had taken part in the cow protection movement in 1953-54 and the Kumbh Kisan Andolan of UP in 1955. He spent the entire period of the Emergency in jail. Elected as an MP from Almora in 1977, Joshi became the secretary-in-charge of the central office and later the treasurer of the BJP. Kedar Nath Sahni was an old war horse who had been in the RSS since the 1940s, having served as a pracharak in Kashmir and Punjab. After Independence, his sphere of work had been relocated to Delhi where he served as both the mayor and the chief executive councillor. K.L. Sharma had joined the RSS in 1942 and become a pracharak in 1946. All of them were veteran RSS members.

The fourth general secretary, Pramod Mahajan, also had an RSS background, but he was barely thirty-five years old. He was known to actively promote the party in Maharashtra and was reputed to be extremely efficient and have a widespread grassroots network. As a youth leader, he had spent time in jail during the Emergency. Two years later, another young RSS activist, K.N. Govindacharya, was inducted as political secretary to Advani. Known to be a master of strategy and electoral arithmetic, Govindacharya had been active in JP's student movement in Bihar in the mid-1970s. Four vice presidents were also appointed: two of them—Kushabhau Thakre and Sunder Singh Bhandari—were hardcore RSS men.

With the appointment of Advani as the president of the BJP, the relations between the party and the RSS—which had turned frosty when Vajpayee was at the helm—began to mend. In the past six years, however, the RSS had not been sitting quietly. As the BJP was promoting Gandhian socialism, the RSS had taken up the task of 'Hindu awakening'. In 1983, the RSS helped the VHP launch an Ekatmata Yatra to rouse people's faith and devotion towards Bharat mata and Ganga mata. Four processions from four starting points, including Hardwar and Gangasagar, converged at Nagpur before setting off to their destinations in Rameshwaram, Somnath and Kanyakumari. In 1985, when the RSS completed sixty years of its formation, it held nationwide awareness programmes. It had also held prantik shibirs in Karnataka and Maharashtra which were attended by 25,000-35,000 people. The RSS continued its mobilization efforts in the remaining years of the 1980s: in 1988, through the Jana Sampark Abhiyan conducted on the occasion of the birth centenary of the RSS founder Hedgewar, 150,000 families were contacted and 76,000 meetings were held. Advani, after taking over the reins of the party, also changed its tactics: his speeches became strident and focused on banning cow slaughter, maintaining a uniform civil code and abrogating Article 370 (that gave Jammu and Kashmir special status) of the Constitution. His speeches were reminiscent of those of the Jana Sangh era.

In the meantime, Rajiv Gandhi started his tenure as prime minister on the right note. A former Indian Airlines pilot, Rajiv was the antithesis of his younger brother, Sanjay, who had died in a plane crash in 1980. The centenary of the formation of the Congress party in 1985 coincided with the beginning of Rajiv's tenure and the new prime minister raised the country's hopes by declaring his determination to finish off the 'brokers of power and influence' who had converted a mass movement (the Congress) into a feudal oligarchy. Slowly but surely, he also began to dismantle controls that had shackled the economy.

But Rajiv was a political novice and had very little experience in administrative matters. He gathered his buddies around him and drafted them into official work. Soon, he began to falter and evidence of this first arrived in the form of the government's reaction to the Shah Bano affair. A sixty-two-year-old daughter of a police constable in Madhya Pradesh, Shah Bano had been divorced by her husband in 1975 after forty-three years of marriage. After the divorce, she approached the court asking for maintenance from her husband because she had no other source of income. The husband refused to pay, saying that he had remarried and Shah Bano was not his liability. The case was heard in the Supreme Court which cited Section 125 of CRPC and granted Shah Bano maintenance. But this judgement incensed orthodox Muslims who claimed that it was contrary to the Koran; they threatened to take to the streets in protest. Rajiv Gandhi, who had inherited none of his mother's toughness, capitulated and soon used the brute majority of the Congress party in the Lok Sabha to ram through a legislation that superseded the apex court's judgement. Liberal Muslims—especially women—were upset at the retrograde legislation but Rajiv Gandhi's implicit belief was that mullahdom and orthodoxy were the deliverers of the votes; he viewed the Congress as the Muslim community's spokespersons.

The BJP got a chance to mount protests against the prime minister's actions, claiming that this was a good example of the pseudo secularism of the Congress party that was determined to stall the progress of Muslims. At its national executive committee meeting held in Chandigarh in the first week of January 1986, the BJP passed a resolution condemning the law passed by the government as 'a retrograde step and surrender to bigotry and obstructionism'. It also pointed out that the move ran counter to the directive principles of the Constitution that required the state to move towards a uniform civil code.

But it was the Bofors scandal that sounded the end of Rajiv Gandhi's political career. In March 1986, the Government of India signed a deal with Bofors of Sweden for the purchase of 410 155 mm field howitzer guns at the cost of $285 million. A year later, in April

1987, the Swedish radio alleged that Bofors had paid kickbacks of $10 million to top Indian politicians to secure the order. A series of investigative reports brought the focus on a Delhi-based Italian middle man, Ottavio Quattrocchi, who was close to the Gandhi family. Soon, the corruption scandal dominated the headlines even as Rajiv Gandhi's government tried to sweep it under the carpet. Rajiv's finance minister, V.P. Singh, who had been made defence minister for coming down sharply on top businessmen for alleged economic offences, was sacked from his post and the party after he started his crusade against corruption in defence deals in October 1987. He had questioned a deal the government had made to purchase submarines, apparently to the discomfiture of Rajiv Gandhi, and was purportedly perusing the Bofors files. V.P. Singh soon became a rallying point for Opposition forces baying for Rajiv Gandhi's blood even as Bofors became a byword for corruption.

As if this were not enough, Rajiv Gandhi stumbled into yet another controversy: he signed a peace deal with the Sri Lankan government which was caught in an ethnic conflict between the Sinhalese and the Tamils. The deal was to disarm Tamil rebels in return for which the Sinhalese forces would withdraw into the barracks. But the LTTE—the main Tamil rebel group—was incensed because they had not been involved in the talks. This forced Rajiv Gandhi to rush forces to Sri Lanka to disarm the Tamil guerillas who, it was believed, had been armed by the Indian government in the first place. The whole affair showed the ineptitude of Rajiv Gandhi as Indian forces were pushed into bloody warfare in a foreign land. At its peak, 100,000 Indian troops were waging war in Sri Lanka, though they were officially keeping peace in the island nation. More than 1,100 Indian soldiers lost their lives in the peacekeeping operations, much to the chagrin of the people of India.

By the beginning of 1988, it was becoming increasingly clear that Rajiv Gandhi would not get re-elected in the elections slated for next year. To compound the Congress problems, a drought the previous year was causing public angst. Sensing an opportunity, the Opposition began to regroup. The National Front was formed with seven Opposition parties coming together, but the BJP and the Left were not part of this coalition. The president of the Telugu Desam Party (TDP), N.T. Rama Rao was the president of the front and V.P. Singh was the convener. Later in the year, on 11 October 1988, V.P. Singh's Jan Morcha (formed after he was ousted from the Rajiv Gandhi government), the Chandrasekhar-led Janata Party and two factions of the Lok Dal (led by Devi Lal and Ajit Singh respectively) merged to form the Janata Dal. With the elections approaching, there was an effort to form an alliance between the Janata Dal and the BJP—this with a view to combine the Opposition vote. There was, of course, no question of a merger between the two parties; after the Janata fiasco a decade ago, this was not even a distant possibility. Moreover, the BJP had earlier taken a decision to never give up its identity. This, in fact, had also been a key recommendation of the Sharma Committee.

According to Advani's autobiography, V.P. Singh was at first averse to the idea of forming an alliance with the BJP, dubbing it as a communal party. He later relented but wanted an alliance only in Madhya Pradesh, Rajasthan, Gujarat and Maharashtra, where the BJP was strong; Singh did not want to risk aligning with the BJP in UP and Bihar, fearing the loss of minority votes. Advani writes that his party did not agree, and wanted a national alliance or nothing at all. In the end, the BJP and Janata Dal entered a seat sharing and joint campaigning arrangement. The battle cry was anti-corruption and key leaders highlighted how the security of the nation had been compromised by bribery in high places, even in national deals. Rajiv Gandhi could not withstand the Bofors-centered campaign and the Congress party's tally in the 1989 elections fell from 414 in the previous polls to 193. The Janata Dal won in 141 seats and the BJP got 85 berths in the Lok Sabha, mustering 11 per cent of the votes nationally. 27 of the 85 seats came from Madhya Pradesh, 13 were accounted for by Rajasthan, while 12 candidates won from Gujarat. Bihar and UP returned eight seats each, Maharashtra accounted for ten seats, Delhi elected four BJP MPs, while Himachal Pradesh returned three BJP candidates.

A National Front government headed by V.P. Singh came to office on 2 December 1989. The BJP was invited to join the government, but Advani said that his party would be content giving outside support. Similarly, the Left also supported the government from outside. V.P. Singh, who had started his career as a Congress loyalist to Sanjay Gandhi, wanted to make his mark in history. After a few months in office, he brought out the Mandal Commission report that had been gathering dust for the last ten years. The commission had recommended that reservations in college admissions and jobs in the government—applicable only to scheduled castes and scheduled tribes—be extended to other backward castes (OBCs). These OBCs primarily were Yadavs and other intermediate castes that had benefitted from the green revolution in the 1970s. With increased income, they now sought higher education and social status and wanted empowerment through positions in the government. V.P. Singh wanted to cultivate this class that formed a significant part of the electorate—especially in North India. In fact, two Yadavs had already become chief ministers—Mulayam Singh in UP and Lalu Prasad in Bihar. But his attempt to introduce reservations led to violent protests in North India where youth immolated themselves on the street.

The applecart was suddenly upset and other political parties were thrown into a tizzy. 'It was generally the view of political parties that society ought to be divided and the BJP was concerned that a wedge was being created in Hindu society,' recollects R. Krishnan, a senior journalist then. 'There was pressure on the BJP to do something dramatic,' he remembers.

In a move to create unity among the Hindus, BJP President L.K. Advani hurriedly launched a yatra from Somnath in Gujarat to Ayodhya in UP which was believed to be the birthplace of Lord Ram. The purpose was to offer kar seva and build a temple. Ayodhya was a part of the BJP's agenda outlined in the election manifesto, and even before at the meeting of its national executive committee at Palanpur in June 1989, a resolution had been passed on the matter. The yatra, which was taken on a motorized van decorated like a Ram rath (chariot) went through many parts of the country. However, while passing through Bihar, Chief Minister Lalu Prasad Yadav had Advani arrested on the grounds that the rath yatra was stirring communal tension between the two major communities. The rath yatra was halted but the BJP withdrew its support from the V.P. Singh government. At a vote of confidence in Parliament, V.P. Singh could not cobble together the required number of seats (as even his own party had split in the run up to the vote), and the government fell on 10 November 1990. It had been in power for less than a year.

chapter 7

The Ayodhya Movement

The distance between Tirunelveli and Ayodhya is over 2,500 kilometres, but the recent history of the Ram Janmabhoomi movement starts in Tirunelveli, in a remote hamlet in Tamil Nadu. In February 1981, nearly 1,000 of the 1,200 Dalits of this village converted to Islam in protest against social discrimination by higher caste Thevars. As the news trickled out of the village, it was clear that, although the mass conversion was a protest against the higher caste atrocities, it had been catalyzed by third parties. Groups that had benefitted from petro dollars—a euphemism for the money flowing in from Arab countries—were the prime suspects.

It was during this time that the BJP had been launched but the then party bosses had vowed that it would be an outfit subscribing to the ideology of Gandhian socialism. The VHP, which had been founded in the mid-1960s but had been limited in its various activities, decided to take up what they averred was a new threat to Hinduism. This was also around the time when troubles in Assam and Punjab had begun and the VHP—with active support from the RSS—decided to fight what they perceived to be a threat to national integration. The VHP decided to mobilize Hindus with the aim of consolidating Hindu sentiment. To achieve this, the VHP formed a Dharma Sansad (a kind of religious parliament) in 1982 to provide a Hindu perspective on social and political matters. The body comprised sadhus and saints of diverse Hindu sects who, for the first time, came together on one platform. At the same time, the VHP began strengthening its organizational structure, aiming to be the political leader of the Hindus. Even as this was on, the VHP deliberated within its ranks to find a cause that would have the potential to unify Hindus. It did not have to look far—an issue had been lying dormant for the last three decades and had the potential to mobilize a large number of Hindus, at least in the northern states.

According to a popular legend, in 1528 CE the invading troops of the first Mughal, Babur, led by his general, Mir Baqi, invaded the holy Hindu city of Ayodhya and built a mosque named the Babri Masjid. The story goes that the mosque was built after demolishing a temple which stood at that place and where Lord Ram was believed to have been born (according to some other versions, the masjid was not built by Babur's generals but by the sultans of Jaunpur who had ruled the area a little earlier). The destruction of the temple must have caused angst for the local Hindus but that is not recorded in history. In fact, there is an argument that states that there is no historical evidence to prove whether or not a temple really was demolished to build a mosque and that these stories gained currency only in the second decade of the nineteenth century. It later entered the British gazetteers. The *Gazetteer* of the Province of Oudh published in 1877 says: 'It is locally affirmed that at the Mohammedan conquest there were three Hindu shrines with devotees attached at Ayodhya... [They] were the Janmasthan, Swargaddwar and Treta ke Thakur. On the first of these, Emperor Babur built a mosque which still bears his name. The Janmasthan marks the place where Ram Chandar was born.'

What, however, is known is that the first communal clashes happened here in 1853 during the dying days of the reign of the Nawabs of Oudh whose jurisdiction extended to Ayodhya. In 1859, the British administration put a fence around the site of the mosque, denominating separate areas of worship for Hindus and Muslims. The complex had two courtyards ringed by a wall and separated by a railing. In the outer courtyard there was a small wooden platform with an idol of Ram that the Hindus worshipped. The status quo continued till Independence, although in 1934 there were again local communal disturbances on the issue.

After 1947, many Muslims left the region and migrated to Pakistan, causing a resurgence among some sections of the Hindus. Many of them thought that now that the country was independent of the British and the Muslim rulers, it was time to 'liberate' the birthplace of Lord Ram. In late November 1949, there was religious friction in Ayodhya as some people started to openly air this view. A month later, on the intervening night of 22 and 23 December, a small idol of Ram Lulla—the infant Ram—mysteriously made its way inside the mosque. The next morning, there was commotion in Ayodhya about how Ram Lulla had appeared in the masjid. As word spread, large crowds gathered to see the infant Ram and worship him. Word soon reached Delhi and Jawaharlal Nehru, committed to India's secularity, sent orders to UP to have the idol removed. But the district administration would not hear of it. The district magistrate of Faizabad, an ICS officer, K.K. Nayar, wrote: 'Removing the idol is fraught with the gravest danger as it would lead to [a] conflagration of horror.' Nayar was himself believed to have been party to the smuggling of the idol of Ram Lulla into the mosque, and is said to have been assisted by the city magistrate of Faizabad, Guru Dutt Singh, and a group of sadhus led by Abhiram Das.

Immediately afterwards, petitions were filed both by Muslims and Hindus in the court. The government then locked the doors of the Babri Masjid, saying that the matter was sub judice. However, a caretaker was appointed and entrusted to look after the structure. Devotees were not allowed inside but a priest was permitted to enter via a side door and perform regular prayers. K.K. Nayar, who later resigned from government service, joined the Bharatiya Jana Sangh and was elected to the Lok Sabha in 1967.

In 1984, the VHP's Dharma Sansad with 500 sadhus in attendance met at New Delhi's Vigyan Bhavan. 'We cannot even light a holy lamp at Ram's birthplace. This is shameful in a country where 80 per cent of the denizens are Hindus,' the Sansad declared. It demanded: 'Give Ayodhya back to us.' VHP's choice of Ram as a symbol to fight the Hindu cause was not coincidental—Ram is a revered deity all over North India and the story of his life, as encapsulated in the Ramayana, is widely known. In fact, every regional language has its own version of the Ramayana. In India, Ram Rajya was a byword for good governance and this symbol has not only been used by the Bharatiya Jana Sangh but has also been referred to by none other than Mahatma Gandhi. Legends and myths about Ram have become part of the Hindu subconscious and he is hailed as 'maryada purshottam'—the ideal man. The VHP realized that the cause of Ram would move Hindus across the nation and, in any case, there was already a local issue of considerable importance that they could take up in his name.

In pursuance of this objective of mobilizing Hindu opinion, the VHP started a rally from Sitamarhi in Bihar which is the birthplace of Sita in late September 1984. The rally, with thousands of people, reached Ayodhya twelve days later. The VHP wanted to take the rally from Ayodhya to Lucknow and Delhi but the assassination of Indira Gandhi made the organization press pause on its plans. The VHP now wanted to go one step further and build a temple of Ram at his birthplace.

In January 1986, a petition filed in the district court in Faizabad requested that the locks of the Babri Masjid be opened so as to allow Hindu devotees to worship Lord Ram. On 2 February 1986, the district judge ruled that there was no formal order to place the lock on the masjid and ordered the lock to be opened 'forthwith'. In his order, he also noted that 'for the last thirty-five years, Hindus have had unrestricted right of worship at the place'. A day later, the Muslims protested and formed the Babri Masjid Action Committee to fight the move that allowed Hindus to pray at the site. They also moved the court for restoration of the status quo. The battle for Ayodhya had started in earnest.

All this coincided with the ascent of L.K. Advani in the BJP. He decided that this was a golden opportunity for the party to revive its fortunes. The Ram Janmabhoomi issue came up for the first time at its national executive committee in June 1989. The party passed a lengthy resolution on the subject, condemning the 'callous unconcern which the Congress party in particular and other political parties in general betray towards the sentiments of the overwhelming majority in the country—the Hindus'. The resolution went on to add: 'Ever since the temple was destroyed, Hindus have been longing to see the resuscitation of the temple at the site which they hold as extremely sacred. During the 1857 war of independence, the Muslims responding to the sentiments of the Hindus had accepted their claim over the Ram Janmasthan but the vile British in pursuance of their policy of divide and rule, scuttled the settlement.' The resolution added: 'Lately the Congress government has unleashed a virulent campaign against the BJP and VHP which has been representing the Hindu point of view in the negotiations with the government. The BJP holds that the nature of the controversy is such that it cannot be sorted out by a court of law. A court of law can settle issues of title, trespass, possession, etc. But it cannot adjudicate whether Babur did actually invade Ayodhya, destroy a temple and build a mosque in its place.'

The BJP national executive also cited the remarks of a British judge, Colonel F.E.A. Chamier, who had heard a petition on this matter way back in 1886, to buttress its point: 'It is most unfortunate that a masjid should have been built on the land especially held sacred by Hindus but as that occurred 356 years ago, it is too late to remedy the grievance.' The party also noted that, on 3 March 1952, the civil judge of Faizabad while hearing a petition had observed that: 'At least from 1936 onwards the Muslims have neither used the site as a mosque nor offered prayers there and the Hindus have been performing the puja at the disputed site.'

The BJP at the same meeting also likened the issue of Ayodhya to Somnath, where an ocean-front temple of Lord Shiva had been destroyed (and then rebuilt) many times by invading armies, including those of Mahmud of Ghazni in the eleventh century, Aurangzeb in the seventeenth century, and others in between. Somnath was located in the territories of the Nawab of Junagadh and, after Independence, Home Minister Sardar Patel decided that the Government of India would rebuild the temple with the blessings of Mahatma Gandhi. Education and Culture Minister Maulana Azad wondered whether the temple should be handed over to the Archeological Survey of India (ASI) but Sardar Patel put in the files: 'The Hindu sentiment in regard to this temple is both strong and widespread. The restoration of the idol would be a point of honour and sentiment with the Hindu public.' However, since it was a Hindu cause, the cost of rebuilding the temple was defrayed by donations collected from the public. Incidentally, Pandit Nehru believed that the government's official involvement in the Somnath project violated its commitment to secularism. When the jyotirling was formally installed at Somnath, President Rajendra Prasad participated in the function despite being advised not to by Nehru. By this time, both Gandhi and Patel had passed away. Advani says, 'In many ways, the Ayodhya movement was the continuation of the spirit of Somnath', in an attempt to explain his party's decision to take this matter forward.

In the meantime, the VHP had begun its objective of Hindu mobilization and mass reawakening in earnest from October 1985 by starting local rath yatras that crossed many parts of states like UP. The organization also engaged an architect—Chandrakant Sompura, whose grandfather had modelled the Somnath temple—to draw up blueprints for the temple of Lord Ram at his birthplace. In January 1989, the VHP Dharma Sansad met again in Allahabad where the Kumbh Mela was being held and decided to hold Ramshila pujans at as many temples in the country as possible. This involved consecration of bricks—or Ramshilas, as they were called—that would be used for the construction of the Ram temple. The first brick was consecrated at the famous temple at Badrinath. By the end of October 1989, the VHP claimed that 275,000 consecrated bricks had reached Ayodhya in an exercise that had involved sixty million people. On 9 November 1989, the foundation stone for the temple was laid at a site close to the Babri mosque. This was done with the permission of the government. The foundation stone was laid by a Dalit: this was a calculated move—the VHP (and thereby, by extended logic, the BJP) was trying to woo lower caste Hindus who had so far viewed the two outfits as representing only higher caste interests. Realizing that the Ayodhya issue was becoming an emotive one, even Rajiv Gandhi dispatched his home minister, Buta Singh, to participate in the shilanyas (foundation laying) ceremony. Later, Rajiv Gandhi started his electoral campaign from Faizabad, which was Ayodhya's twin city and talked of Ram Rajya.

In late January 1990, the VHP organized a meeting of the Margdarshak Mandal—a smaller body to decide on the organization's plan of action—which said that the construction of the temple should begin at the earliest, on 1 February. The construction of the temple at the spot at which Lord Ram was born would necessitate the removal of the mosque, and VHP's president, Ashok Singhal, called upon Muslims to find an alternative site. He also called on every Hindu family in the country to help by sending one member to Ayodhya. Ashok Singhal, a hardcore RSS man, had spent time as a pracharak in Kanpur, but in the late 1970s and early 1980s had been prant pracharak in Delhi. This was when he was deputed to the VHP, where he conjured up plans for energizing the organization. Singhal was one of the 150 full-time pracharaks sent to the VHP from the RSS. In addition, the VHP had independently inducted 100 full-timers on its own, training them under mahants of religious bodies in Hardwar.

Although the VHP's plan was to begin the construction of the temple on 1 February, it was postponed at the request of A.B. Vajpayee and the then prime minister V.P. Singh—the government wanted a four-month cooling off period to solve the problem. V.P. Singh pointed out that there were a lot of apprehensions being voiced among Muslims. But, in June 1990, after the four-month period was over, the VHP felt that there had been no progress by the government to solve the matter and it announced a Sant Sammelan in Hardwar where a Sri Ram Kar Sewa Samiti was set up with the objective of beginning work on the temple on 30 October 1990.

Around this time—7 August 1990—V.P. Singh issued the Mandal missive, and the BJP, finding itself on the back foot, decided to intensify its efforts in the Ram Janmabhoomi issue. To time their offensive with with the VHP's, which had resolved to start building the temple on 30 October, BJP President L.K. Advani, as we know, decided to tour a large part of the country on a Ram rath. The original plan was for Advani to undertake a padyatra—inspired by Mahatma Gandhi's Dandi March that had culminated in a salt satyagraha—but his lieutenant, Pramod Mahajan, pointed out that the progress of the yatra would be very slow. Advani then thought of a jeep yatra, but Mahajan recommended a mini bus that would be converted to look like a Ram rath. The rath yatra plan was announced on 12 September 1990. Though the yatra was meant to mobilize opinion in favour of the Ram temple, Advani also wanted to raise larger issues in order to generate more traction. According to him, the fundamental questions that he wanted to raise were: what is secularism and what is communalism? Can national integration only be achieved by constantly pandering to minority communalism? Can the government not reject the cult of minoritism?

Somnath was chosen as the starting point of the yatra—the reconstruction of the shrine on the rubble of loot and plunder was the first chapter in a journey to 'preserve the old symbols of unity, communal amity and cultural oneness'. The liberation of Ram Janmabhoomi would be the second chapter. However, liberals thought that this was a blatant attempt to communalize the polity and divide the people of India into Hindus and others.

On 25 September 1990, with Pramod Mahajan by his side (who had done the detailed organizational planning), Advani embarked on the yatra. Activists of the VHP and saffron-clad men accompanied him. After travelling to Saurashtra and others parts of Gujarat, the yatra entered Maharashtra and travelled through central India. Large crowds greeted the procession at every step, with supporters ringing temple bells, beating thalis and shouting slogans of 'Jai Sri Ram'. At some places, charged-up followers applied tilak to the Ram rath while at other places, those moved by the movement smeared dust from the path of the rath on to their forehead. That said, there was a severe communal backlash, with skirmishes being reported in Gujarat, Karnataka, Andhra Pradesh and Uttar Pradesh. In a bid to diffuse the situation, V.P. Singh tried to get Hindu religious leaders to negotiate with Muslim leaders when the yatra reached Delhi. But this move failed, forcing him to call an all-party meeting to reach a consensus on the matter. The BJP boycotted the meeting but the remaining parties called for the maintainance of status quo. V.P. Singh also sought a compromise, seeking the good offices of

Atal Bihari Vajpayee, and suggested that building the temple could begin on 30 October but on land that was undisputed.

The angst of the minority communities, who apprehended the move as one designed to marginalize them in the country, was especially high in Bihar and Uttar Pradesh. Here, the government in power was V.P. Singh's Janata Dal, headed by Yadav chief ministers who believed that the mandir issue had only been raised to foil the Mandal Report's recommended reservations. On the morning of 23 October, Advani was arrested in Samastipur and the rath yatra was disbanded. At the same time there was a crackdown in UP.

However, in spite of the crackdown and heavy police deployment in and around Ayodhya, about 1,000 devotees entered Ayodhya, managed to climb the Babri Masjid and hoist a saffron flag atop the structure on 30 October. Lakhs of people had collected around the masjid; the atmosphere was charged. Pitched battles were fought between the karsevaks on the streets of Ayodhya and even on the terraces of houses. Police firing was ultimately ordered, as a result of which many died. In an interview, taken twenty-three years later in 2013, the then chief minister of UP, Mulayam Singh, said that ordering the police to open fire was a painful decision but there was no option because it was a matter of the country's unity. He said that, according to his estimates, 1.1 lakh people had collected at the spot that day.

The number of people who were killed in the firing is disputed: the VHP claimed that thirty-six devotees had died on 30 October and 2 November, when there was a subsequent round of firing. It also claimed that twenty-five more were killed in other parts of UP. But two months later, the new prime minister, Chandrasekhar, said that according to official records only fifteen devotees had been killed. The VHP took out asthi kalash yatras (processions with the ashes of those who had died). This triggered more communal tension and led to riots which left 200 dead. Curfew had to be imposed in twenty districts of UP. Incidentally, a few years before this—in 1984—the VHP had spawned an affiliate called the Bajrang Dal. Comprising young men, the Bajrang Dal was like the infantry brigade in the forward lines of the mobilization effort. Many of its members were drawn from the ranks of the unemployed and lower middle classes. The organization was led by Vinay Katiyar, a former president of the Akhil Bharatiya Vidyarthi Parishad (the student's wing of the RSS).

V.P. Singh's successor Chandrasekhar, who headed a minority government, took the initiative to solve the Ayodhya tangle in right earnest. He urged his law minister, former Jana Sangh MP, Subramaniam Swamy, to negotiate with the VHP and the BJP. Due to his personal rapport with them, Swamy was able to get the two organizations—which were planning a nationwide stir on 9 December—to pause. In an article in the *New Indian Express* on 4 December 2012, Swami wrote: 'He [Chandrasekhar] told me to assure the VHP that our government would get removed the Babri Masjid with the consent of Muslim leaders through discussions.' In January 1991, Chandrasekhar himself initiated talks with Muslim leaders. The talks could not be carried through because the government fell soon thereafter with the Congress pulling the plug. What ensued were mid-term elections in the midst of which the Congress's prime ministerial candidate Rajiv Gandhi was assassinated.

The election results were interesting. The BJP improved its tally, winning 120 seats as compared to the 85 seats it won in the previous elections. The saffron outfit also became the second largest party after the Congress (which secured 232 seats). The Janata Dal was down to 59. Of the total number of 120 seats that the BJP secured, a whopping 51 came from Uttar Pradesh; clearly, the mobilization for the Ram temple had led to a groundswell of support for the party. The party also won 20 seats from Gujarat, which was a more impressive result than even UP, because Gujarat in total has only 26 seats, versus 85 in UP. The denizens of Gujarat had also been charged by the Ayodhya movement, partly because the Somnath temple was located in the state. Madhya Pradesh and Rajasthan returned 12 seats each for BJP while the party won five of the seven Lok Sabha seats in Delhi. The party secured 20 per cent of the total votes polled across the country, but that the support base was concentrated in a few states is clear from the fact that 185 of the party's candidates lost their deposits. BJP had contested a total of 468 seats.

Elections to the UP assembly, which were held in the same year, brought the BJP to power in this crucial state, with the party winning 221 seats in a house of 425. This tally was up from the 57 seats that the party had won in 1989. Obviously, the chant of 'Jai Sri Ram' had seeped into the minds of the voters. The BJP's vote share was up from 18 per cent in 1989 to 31 per cent in 1991.

With the establishment of the BJP government in Lucknow, the organizers of the VHP were jubilant. Along with the other sadhus and saints (who had become part of the rath yatra cavalcade) they mounted pressure on the state government to take forward the Ram Janmabhoomi agenda. But the BJP senior leadership was circumspect. Although the party's tally had increased in the Lok Sabha, the BJP was being increasingly seen as a single-agenda party —one that wished to build a Ram Mandir. This was seriously affecting the prospects of expanding the party's reach outside the core areas where the temple had become a big issue.

Around this time, L.K. Advani completed two terms as the BJP president and, according to the party's constitution, stepped down. He was succeeded by Murli Manohar Joshi. The new president wanted to make his own mark on the party and not live under the shadow of his predecessor, and soon began to look for a new agenda to augment his own popularity. He did not have to search far. Ever since 1989, the situation in Kashmir had deteriorated, with militant strikes occuring on an almost daily basis. Kashmiri Hindus were at the receiving end of this terror and many fell to the bullets of the extremists. A large number of Kashmiri Hindus had to migrate out of their home state to other parts of India, leaving their valuables behind. They had become refugees in their own land. Joshi decided to raise national consciousness on this subject and focus people's attention on this question of national integration. Having seen first hand the success of Advani's rath yatra, Joshi also decided to take the same route and, on 11 December 1991, started a 15,000-kilometre ekta yatra. The yatra that would take him through many states was to culminate at Srinagar's Lal Chowk where the BJP president wanted to unfurl the Indian tricolour on 26 January 1992 in a symbolic gesture that would demonstrate that Jammu and Kashmir was an integral part of India. Wanting a clean break from Advani, Joshi did not seek help from Pramod Mahajan, who had meticulously planned the rath yatra. His choice was a novice member of the party, Narendra Modi, who had been active in the Gujarat segment of the rath yatra. A five-year-old inductee into the BJP from the RSS, Modi had impressed everybody with his superb organizational skills.

The ekta yatra progressed as planned but then was held up by landslides on the way to Srinagar. Militants, too, were issuing threats. In the end, Joshi, along with fifty-odd party men, was airlifted to Srinagar where he did unfurl the tricolour on the appointed day. But it was under such tight security cover that it took the sheen off the event and was seen as an anti-climax.

With the passage of months, the pressure on the UP chief minister, Kalyan Singh, intensified. The VHP demanded that all legal and other obstacles in the way of constructing the temple be removed by 18 November, which is when they wanted to start work on the building. But Kalyan Singh was a little reluctant; given that the central government was being run by the Congress party, it could, on the pretext of a collapsing law and order situation, dismiss his government. The VHP was adamant however, and began inviting kar sevaks to Ayodhya for temple construction. By now, the BJP was also back on board and L.K. Advani and Joshi began different yatras in UP with a view to motivating people to participate in the building of the temple. Between them, they visited thirty-eight districts. Meanwhile, the UP government had taken over 2.7 acres of land adjoining the mosque and sought to build amenities for pilgrims. But both the Allahabad High Court and the Supreme Court ruled that no permanent structure could be built on the site. Towards the end of November, events started rapidly escalating. More than 20,000 kar sevaks reached Ayodhya and, with each passing day, their numbers swelled. Within a few days, almost two lakh people had gathered there. A major contingent was from Maharashtra, Gujarat, Karnataka, Andhra Pradesh and, of course, the rest of UP. There were a lot of women, Dalits, tribals and members of the backward castes. Several kar sevaks came from rural areas.

The date of the formal kar seva was set for 6 December which was Gita Jayanti. The gathering was expected to stir trouble but Kalyan Singh swore in an affidavit filed before the Allahabad High Court that the kar seva would be symbolic. According to the plan, kar sevaks would go down to the river Sarayu, that was not more than a kilometre away, pick up a fistful of sand and drop it into a pit that had been specially dug for that purpose. This was close to the site of the shilanyas (foundation stone) in 1989. At the same time, a hundred sadhus would hammer the specially erected concrete platform overlooking the mosque.

But on 6 December, events did not unfold as promised. By mid-morning, the area surrounding the Babri Masjid was overflowing with kar sevaks who were straining at barricades put up around the mosque. The mood was clearly belligerent. According to eye witnesses, from 11 a.m. onwards, top leaders like L.K. Advani,

Murli Manohar Joshi, Ashok Singhal, Vinay Katiyar and Mahant Avaidyanath began arriving at the disputed spot. But after looking around for a few minutes, they left. At mid-day, a crowd of kar sevaks broke the cordon and rushed towards the mosque. Some of them carrying iron rods, pickaxes, shovels and crowbars managed to scale the mosque and appeared atop the domes. Although they tried knocking at the domes for an hour, the kar sevaks were unable to make a single dent to the structure. At this time, through the public address system, an appeal was made to those on the domes to come down because the structure could crumble. The kar sevaks complied within half an hour. Around this time, some young men rushed out of the structure carrying a huge trunk that was believed to contain the idol of Ram Lulla and his ornaments. Some kar sevaks, meanwhile, worked at the base of the mosque. Using sharp-edged steel rods, they started digging into the thick walls of the structure at plinth level systematically from both sides, and managed to create holes in the walls. Thereafter, thick ropes were looped through these holes, and hundreds of kar sevaks pulled the ropes with all their strength. The mosque collapsed, one dome after the other. By evening, the mosque was gone and the crowd was celebrating in delirious ecstasy.

As the mosque was being pulled down, the police, heavily outnumbered, stood by, many of them actually enjoying the scene. In Delhi, Prime Minister Narasimha Rao, who had believed that the kar seva would pass off peacefully, had been getting reports since noon that things were getting out of hand and the security force was unable to intervene. He had obviously not read the writing on the wall. Later that evening, the Kalyan Singh government was dismissed and President's rule was clamped upon the state.

The next morning, the kar sevaks put up a makeshift canopy where the mosque had stood and installed the idol of Ram Lulla there. An FIR was filed against the act of vandalism and, a few days later, the case was transferred to the CBI. The BJP state governments in Madhya Pradesh, Rajasthan and Himachal Pradesh were also dismissed.

The aftermath of the demolition was furious, and communal riots broke out in many parts of the country. In Mumbai, 660 people were killed in riots; in Surat, around 100 people perished; and about 140 died in Bhopal. Trouble broke out in parts of Pakistan and Bangladesh as well.

A commission under Supreme Court judge M.S. Liberhan was set up to probe the demolition. It took a long time to complete its report—and was tabled in the Parliament in November 2009. The commission said that the demolition of the Babri Masjid was 'neither spontaneous nor unplanned'. The report also stated that 'the Sangh Parivar is a highly successful and corporatized model of a political party and as the Ayodhya campaign demonstrates has developed a highly efficient organizational structure. While the structure or the methods of the Sangh Parivar for aggregating a substantial public base may neither be illegal not strictly objectionable, the use of this garangutan whole for the purpose of the Ayodhya campaign was clearly against the letter and spirit of the Indian law and ethos.' The Liberhan Commission also lambasted the Kalyan Singh-led UP government and said that 'the state government had systematically and in a pre-planned manner removed inconvenient bureaucrats from positions of power, dismantled and diluted the security apparatus and infrastructure, and lied consistently to the high court and the Supreme Court and the people of India to evade constitutional governance and betray the confidence of the people.'

chapter 8

Sputtering to Power

Whatever might be its stance in public, within months of the demolition of the Babri Masjid, the BJP realized that it had gone overboard on the Ayodhya issue. It was now being seen as a party with a single agenda—the construction of the Ram Mandir—which meant that the electorate did not see the BJP as a party of governance. Moreover, the riots and disturbances that followed the demolition had spiralled out of control; in Mumbai, for instance, simultaneous RDX blasts rocked the financial capital of the country in March 1993, leaving over 300 dead and making many wonder where India was headed post Ayodhya.

As if this was not enough, it dawned on the BJP that the party had been robbed of its prime preoccupation. Though the temple was yet to be built, the public presumed that the matter had been resolved. The liberation of Ram Janmabhoomi—on which votes had been garnered earlier—meant that it could not be used as an electoral issue anymore.

When fresh elections were held in Uttar Pradesh in 1993—after President's rule—the BJP got only 177 seats in a house of 425. This was down from 221 seats that the party had won in 1991 before the Babri Masjid had fallen. The percentage of votes of the BJP had gone up marginally to 33 per cent in 1993 versus the 31 per cent in 1991. In fact, the biggest gainer was the Bahujan Samaj Party (BSP), whose tally went up to 67 in 1993 from 12 in 1991. The percentage of votes of the party had also gone up impressively from 10 per cent in 1991 to 28 per cent in 1993. Though called the Bahujan Samaj Party, the BSP's thinly-veiled agenda was to empower Dalits in the state. Clearly, BSP's massive Dalit mobilization had worked more effectively in the long term in UP than the repeated use of the issue of liberating Ram Janmabhoomi.

What was more unnerving to the BJP was the move by the central government to delink religion and politics in 1994 by passing an amendment to the Constitution. It did not take much to figure out that the union home minister, S.B. Chavan's proposal for the 80th Amendment was targeted at the BJP. In addition to this, the law minister had also proposed a Bill to amend the Representation of the People Act 1951 to provide for deregistration of political parties if their activities did not confirm to the tenets of secularism or democracy. To make matters worse, the move was coming from the Narasimha Rao government—the same Narasimha Rao who was perceived to have right-wing sympathies due to his failure to act in time to prevent the demolition of the Babri Masjid. Madan Lal Khurana, BJP's national general secretary, told the press: 'Separating religion and politics is impossible in the Indian context. It's like taking the soul out of India.' Eventually, the two Bills, which were introduced in the Parliament on 29 July 1993, could not be passed due to severe opposition from not only the BJP but also the Left parties, who saw it as a political move to garner more votes.

The signs of concern could be discerned at the national executive meeting of the BJP held in Jaipur on 31 July 1993. Advani, who had again become the president of the party, betrayed his fear that the BJP was being targeted when he said: 'Religion is not wrong, abuse of religion is wrong,' adding, 'Already there are provisions in the law to prevent such an abuse. What is now sought to be done by the ruling party is to gag ideological debate.' A few months later, at the executive meeting held in New Delhi on 18 December 1993 and convened after the results of by-polls in five states, Advani was sounding both tentative and confident. He told his party colleagues: 'BJP is now the principal pole of Indian politics. Ever since Independence evaluation has been based on how the Congress has fared: Has it won or lost? Now the test is on how the BJP has fared.' In the same breath, however, Advani added: 'The BJP has not fared well, let it be candidly acknowledged.' Out of the five states in which the BJP had major stakes, the party had suffered electoral setbacks in Himachal Pradesh and Madhya Pradesh; they had formed the government in Delhi and Rajasthan. In UP, however, Advani noted, 'The increase in popular base has not translated into seats'. He then went on to assert that in the five states put together, the BJP had secured 36 per cent of the votes versus the Congress's 26 per cent. This, Advani claimed, proved in this case that the 'loser stands first', and that BJP ideology had received strong support and that there had been a 'substantial enlargement of the party's popular base'.

A year later at its national executive meeting in Bombay on 17 December 1994, Advani was sounding vastly more confident. Commenting on the results of the state assembly elections in Karnataka and Andhra Pradesh where the Congress had lost, Advani said: 'A major poll battle has ended. The Congress has been decimated in the southern states which had put them in power barely three-and-a-half years ago.' He went on: 'The Congress has committed three grave sins. It has compromised national interests for the sake of electoral gains and endangered the nation's security. Secondly, it has been compromising social interest and resorted to sordid political expediency and this has intensified caste and communal tension. Thirdly, it was been compromising economic interests of the masses leading to all round corruption.' It was clear to independent analysts that the failure of the Congress was a factor that the BJP could potentially exploit.

Three months earlier in its national executive meeting at Patna on 15 September 1994, Advani had been virtually ecstatic. He said that three announcements made by Prime Minister P.V. Narasimha Rao in the preceding months reflected the point of view represented by the the BJP. Firstly, on 15 August, the PM had announced from the rampart of Red Fort that the only talks that India could have with Pakistan were on when the latter would vacate Pakistan occupied Kashmir (PoK). This was the first time that the government had taken a tough stand on the issue. Secondly, Advani pointed out that, while addressing a Congress rally in Delhi, the prime minister had said that a Ram temple should be constructed in Ayodhya, although, while saying so, he had made no reference to a mosque. Advani added that it was an open secret that the Shankaracharyas had been promised that the temple would be constructed at Ram Janmabhoomi itself. Advani also referred to the opening up of diplomatic relations with Israel—a matter that had been a strict no-no since Independence—and pointed out that this is what the BJP had been suggesting for a very long time. Advani ended by saying, 'BJP's agenda today. Country's agenda tomorrow.'

With the next general elections approaching, Advani, for all his bravado, realized that the party, which had increased its support base due to the Ayodhya movement, had few prospects of coming to power as long as he was at the helm of affairs. 'He was perceived as a hardline Hindu and, therefore, his appeal would not touch all sections of society,' says journalist R. Krishnan. 'Moreover, Hindutva could not bring the party to power although affiliate bodies of the parivar like the VHP were raring to move forward on the temple agenda,' he adds. In fact, on 27 February 1995, on the day of Shivaratri, VHP men converged at Benares to liberate the Kashi

Vishawanath temple which had been destroyed by Mughal Emperor Aurangzeb who built the Gyan Vapi mosque in its place. (However, 100 years after its destruction, Maratha queen Ahilyabai Holkar had the Shiva temple rebuilt next to the mosque.) The VHP now wanted to remove the mosque and extend the temple. But the response to the VHP call was limited and soon the programme had to be given up. For the BJP, this was another sign that the temple agenda would work no more.

At the end of his presidential address at the BJP national council meet held in Mumbai on 11-13 November 1995, Advani suddenly announced: 'We will fight the next elections under the leadership of A.B. Vajpayee and he will be our candidate for a prime minister... For many years, not only our party leaders but also the common people have been chanting the slogan, "Agli baari, Atal Bihari". I am confident that the BJP will form the next government under him.' Advani's words were greeted with stunned silence, followed by raptures among those present. Vajpayee protested and said that Advani should lead the party, but the latter refused and endorsed Atalji as BJP's next prime ministerial candidate.

In the course of his long address, Advani had also made a strong pitch to dispel the impression that the BJP was only a Hindu party, stressing that the 'BJP is unequivocally committed to genuine secularism'. He recalled how at the inaugural session of the party in December 1980, former law minister and distinguished jurist Mohammed Currim Chagla—who had attended as a guest speaker—had said that 'to say that the BJP is a communal party is absolutely absurd and without basis'. Advani recalled that Chagla had gone on to extol: 'Go round the country and tell the people that you are not a regional party, and the only party that can replace the Congress.'

As if this was not enough, Advani thundered that other parties were running 'a slander campaign that BJP is anti-Muslim and that if the BJP comes to power, it will make India a theocratic Hindu state'. Advani went on to question the secular credentials of these critics and said that 'we regard them as pseudo secularists'. The BJP president added that that there were two kinds of pseudo secularists—those who subscribed to the Marxist view that religion is the opium of the masses, and those for whom secularism is an euphemism for vote bank politics.

Advani went on to 'give some suggestions to Muslims': concentrate on education, trust the Hindus who have made India a secular country and free yourselves from the clutches of vote bank peddlers. He also claimed that Hindutva was a unifying principle—a collective endeavour to protect and re-energize the soul of India.

Around this time, the BJP was not sure whether it would ever be able come to power on the basis of the existing electoral system in India. This doubt had surfaced in the Jana Sangh in the late 1960s, and the sentiment was again being expressed by Advani in 1995. He demanded a review of the constitution of the party and suggested that a commission be set up for comprehensive assessment, specifically to explore the possibility of changing the 'first-past-the-post' (FPTP) system of elections—a system by which the candidate getting the highest number of votes is elected, even though he might have got a minority percentage of the votes. The BJP wanted the proposed commission to look at the German list system of elections by which 50 per cent of the candidates are elected by the present FPTP model but the other 50 per cent are elected as per the percentage of votes garnered by the party. So if a party gets an aggregate of, say, 20 per cent of votes, then it can nominate MPs/MLAs for 20 per cent of the seats. The BJP also wanted to redraw the internal map of India on the principles of development and administration to create similar sized states. The internal understanding within the BJP was that these reforms would give a boost to the party's chances to come to power at the federal level.

With Vajpayee declared as the PM candidate, the party began to concentrate on the failure of the Congress government so as to garner anti-incumbency votes. The BJP realized that this was a potent way to gather support—possibly even more powerful than the Ram Janmabhoomi movement. The Narasimha Rao government—a minority government—gave ample opportunity for the Opposition party to take potshots at it. As a minority government, it had made many compromises to remain in power, and charges of corruption were surfacing all round. In fact, in July 1993, the government had to face a no-confidence motion that it was able to surmount with the help of the MPs of the Jharkhand Mukti Morcha (JMM). These MPs were alleged to have been bribed by Narasimha Rao and, after his tenure as prime minister, he had to face trial and was, in fact, convicted and handed a three-year prison sentence. Rao, however, did not serve the term because the high court reversed the ruling.

In fact, Rao was also charged by the CBI for the St. Kitts forgery that he had resorted to when in office—though, ultimately, these charges could not be proven. Rao—along with a god man, Chandraswami, and some others—was accused of forging documents to show that Ajeya Singh, son of V.P. Singh, had a bank account in St. Kitts, a tax haven in the Caribbean Islands. The idea was to embarrass V.P. Singh. 'There were also numerous other scams—the fertilizer scam, the sugar scandal—that were exposed. Rao's tenure was the first time that allegations arose about the auctioning of posts of chief executives of public sector companies,' points out R. Krishnan. There was also the securities scam, which involved stock broker Harshad Mehta who had borrowed money from banks—which he never returned—to boost the stock markets. Mehta alleged that he had gone to the prime minister's house to personally pay one crore rupees to him under the guise of a donation to the Congress party. But the amount was really a bribe to let him off. After the term of Narasimha Rao, the residence of his telecom minister, Sukh

Ram, was raided and suitcases full of cash were recovered. He had got the money as quid pro quo for helping a private party land a contract. The negative image of the Congress emerging from this mess made the party an unattractive proposition to the voters and this, by implication, had the potential of benefitting the BJP.

Rao's term is, however, best known for the process of liberalization that he initiated shortly after coming to power in 1991. In a sense, this was forced on him: India's foreign exchange reserves had hit rock bottom and the previous prime minister, Chandrasekhar, had to pledge India's gold—that had been airlifted to Washington—for a loan from the World Bank. The public was very agitated because they perceived that the sovereignty of India had been compromised. People were ready for strong action from the new government to set the economy in order. Narasimha Rao appointed economist and non-politician Manmohan Singh as finance minister and asked him to liberalize the economy. With one stroke of the pen, Singh delicensed industrial production, giving freedom to companies to produce whatever they wanted and in whatever quantities they desired to. The rupee was sharply devalued vis-a-vis the dollar to make Indian currency reflect market reality across. At the same time, the process of issuance of equities by companies was made simpler and the stock market was opened to foreign institutional investments. The rupee was made convertible on the trade account and the tariff wall was dismantled by reducing customs duties on products imported by the country. This, in effect, meant that the protection afforded to domestic production was removed.

As an Opposition party, the BJP gave a guarded welcome to liberalization. On the one hand, liberalization that meant an open economic regime reflected the philosophy of the BJP and was the need of the hour. But as a major Opposition party, the BJP could not go all out and endorse the policies, although it was appreciative of the fact that the Congress wanted to turn a new leaf and step away from the disastrous Nehru-Mahalanobis model which it blamed for bringing the country to its knees in 1991. It was similar to the dilemma that the Jana Sangh had confronted when Indira Gandhi had nationalized banks; with public mood swinging in her favour, the Jana Sangh could not oppose the move.

Initially, there had been widerpread support for dismantling the permit quota raj. Indeed, industry had been pushing for an open economy for years. However, once the policy of liberalization was implemented, it started drawing criticism. With a free economy, industry was nervous that domestic manufacture would be wiped off. At the same time, labour unions were also skeptical as they stared at the prospect of large-scale unemployment. On its part, the Narasimha Rao government had gone easy on the reforms after the initial enthusiasm of two years because of the opposition they faced from powerful interest groups within the country.

This gave an opportunity to the BJP which, by 1995, had started asking why the process of economic reforms had gone awry. The party insisted that the 'steady worsening of the nation's economic health' now matched the deterioration of the country's political health. In the last four years (1991-95), the BJP said, prices had soared, poverty had increased, the rupee had tumbled and national debt had grown. 'BJP averred that the liberalization policies of Narasimha Rao were much too radical and that in the name of liberalization and globalization, foreign banks and unscrupulous elements were benefitting,' says Jagdish Shettigar, who was the convener of the BJP's economic cell in those days. 'We were for swadeshi and economic nationalism. We were a little wary of external liberalization because that allowed indiscriminate entry of foreign companies into India, much to the detriment of domestic companies.' The party was also berating the Congress for failing to live up to its promise of a 'tryst with destiny' and not being 'able to end poverty and ignorance and disease and inequality of opportunity'.

When the results of the general elections for 1996 were announced, the BJP came out on top; for the first time, they had won the largest number of seats in the Lok Sabha. The part secured 161 seats and garnered 20 per cent of all votes. This made its tally greater than that of the Congress that won 140 seats (despite a higher percentage of votes at 28 per cent). President Shankar Dayal Sharma called the BJP to form a government even though the numbers were far short of the majority of 272 required in the house of 543. Thus, Atal Bihari Vajpayee became the first BJP prime minister of India on 16 May 1996.

Over the next few days, the party tried hard to forge a majority, but its opponents proved smarter. Thirteen days later, Vajpayee resigned and a broad left-of-centre coalition called the United Front came to power under H.D. Deve Gowda, who was the chief minister of Karnataka and a Janata Dal member. That government lasted from 1 June 1996 to 21 April 1997, dissolving due to tensions between coalition partners and the Congress—with whose outside support the government had been formed. A day later, the coalition was reinstated with a new prime minister, I.K. Gujral (who had once been a close associate of Indira Gandhi in the Congress party), at the helm. This government lasted eleven months—from 21 April 1997 to 19 March 1998.

General elections were held once again, and this time, too, the BJP won the maximum number of seats in the Lok Sabha—182, securing 25 per cent of the votes. This was a good 5 percent above the proportion of votes that it had polled in the elections held two years ago and was seen as an indicator that the people wanted to give a chance to the party to form a government. The Congress's seat tally remained at 141 even as its vote proportion fell by two-and-a-half per cent.

Atal Bihari Vajpayee again became the prime minister and assumed office on 19 March 1998. Besides the old allies like Samata

Party, Akali Dal and Shiv Sena, this time round, the BJP was able to rope in a few new allies: the Telugu Desam Party (TDP), the All India Anna Dravida Munnetra Kazhagam (AIADMK) and Biju Janata Dal (BJD). This coalition—which was basically an anti-Congress front—was called the National Democratic Alliance (NDA) and had a thin majority in the Lok Sabha. The BJP again won 182 seats but the NDA had requisite numbers to form a stable government.

chapter 9

Aiming to Be a Great Power

The BJP government in 1998 came to office with a bang—almost literally. On the evening of 13 May 1998, Vajpayee hurriedly called for a press conference at his residence. 'Today, at 15:45 hours, India conducted three underground nuclear tests in the Pokhran range. The tests conducted today were with a fission device, a low yield device and a thermonuclear device,' the new prime minister said triumphantly. He had been in office for less than two months, having taken oath on 19 March.

Thus, India became the sixth country in the world to test a nuclear bomb and joined the elite club of countries with nuclear arsenal. Of course, nearly a quarter century earlier on 18 May 1974, in an operation named Smiling Buddha, the government under Indira Gandhi had conducted a nuclear test as well. But the Pokhran test was conducted on a much larger scale and created a no-nonsense image of the BJP government. 'It established the macho portrait of the country and said loudly, "Don't mess with us",' says Rajeev Saxena, a bank manager and BJP sympathizer. The nuclear test was also in line with BJP's disdain for Nehru's foreign policy legacy based largely on peace. The party held the view that a nation's status in the world was decided by its might. In fact, the country had been enfeebled by pacifism and this did not reflect India's ancient heritage. Almost every Indian God was armed, macho and masculine, and even ancient Indian epics like Ramayana and the Mahabharata reflected the country's military might.

It now seems that a few years earlier, in 1995, the then prime minister, Narasimha Rao, had decided to conduct a nuclear test. But word reached the US whose satellites picked up signals that India was readying itself for a test. They put pressure on the Narasimha Rao government and the plan was given up. One of the first things that Vajpayee did after coming to office was start consulting scientists like A.P.J. Abdul Kalam (later to become president of India) and others; by the end of March, Vajpayee gave the green signal to the project, on the condition that it be conducted in the shortest possible time. Extreme secrecy was maintained and the operation was planned so meticulously that the US spy satellites picked up no indicators that such a test was underway.

Not surprisingly, the tests generated extreme reactions worldwide. The United Nations Security Council (UNSC) passed a resolution on 6 June condemning the test and China demanded that the international community exert pressure on India to sign the Non-Proliferation Treaty (NPT) and eliminate its nuclear arsenal. Japan clamped economic sanctions on India, freezing all new loans and grants, and the US, Canada, UK and EU followed suit. However, countries like Russia and France endorsed India's right to defend itself. Also, needless to say, Pakistan was furious and within a fortnight—on May 28—performed a nuclear test as well. This, at one stroke, brought parity between India and Pakistan and quashed the advantage that India had over Pakistan in conventional weapons. 'But this did not matter because, in India, the image of the Vajpayee government was strong and unshakable. Moreover, the sanctions had no real impact,' says Amit Dasgupta, then a serving diplomat.

The main adverse impact of the nuclear test was that relations with Pakistan became a trifle strained. There also was growing criticism in the Western world regarding Vajpayee's confrontationist foreign policy. Ever since the early 1990s, Vajpayee had been discussing foreign policy issues with a retired IFS officer and the head of the foreign policy cell of the BJP, Brajesh Mishra. Mishra, who was now principal secretary to the prime minister (later, he would be appointed as the national security advisor), advised him to make attempts to ease relations with Pakistan. India, after the nuclear tests, was seeking the status of a 'great power' and this necessitated an end to the Indo-Pak deadlock. As a result, in late 1998, Vajpayee started pushing for a full scale diplomatic peace process with Pakistan. The result was that the historic bus service between Delhi and Lahore was kick-started in February 1999. Vajpayee travelled in the bus to Pakistan and was received by Pakistani Prime Minister Nawaz Sharif at the Wagah border. They proceeded to Lahore for official talks to initiate the peace process and to solve the Kashmir issue and other territorial disputes. At the end of the two-day talks, the Lahore Declaration was announced on 21 February 1999, which committed to more dialogue, expanded trade relations and mutual friendship, especially in the context of the fact that both the nations were nuclear powers. The two countries also agreed to peacefully resolve the Kashmir problem.

Vajpayee came back to India victorious. After triumphantly testing a nuclear device, the new prime minister had managed to successfully engage with the Pakistanis—a feat that the Congress governments in the last couple of decades had failed to accomplish. There was euphoria all around. 'The Pakistanis were happy that a government headed by the BJP, that seemed to be against that country [Pakistan], had taken the lead in normalizing relations,' says a diplomat who does not wish to be identified. He, however, points out that Vajpayee, though representing the BJP, did not completely disregard the Nehruvian approach to foreign relations, and therefore often publicly stressed stress on global disarmament and peace. At the same time, however, the Vajpayee government established the National Security Council (NSC) in April 1999 to analyze military, economic and political threats to the nation and advise the government regularly on the same. The establishment of the NSC instituted a comprehensive review of India's national security system—something that had been done for the first time since Independence.

The BJP was jubilant. At its national executive meeting held in New Delhi on 1 and 2 May 1999, the party noted that India had emerged as a strong nation during the Vajpayee regime: 'The nuclear initiatives have ensured that India is stronger than a year ago. The various diplomatic initiatives culminating in the PM's historic bus journey have set the pattern for better relations with neighbours including Pakistan.'

But this euphoria was not to last long. Possibly even as Vajpayee was confabulating with Nawaz Sharif in Lahore, the Pakistani army under the leadership of General Pervez Musharraf had other plans. The Pakistani army, which dominates the politics of the country in many ways and never seems to favour peaceful relations with India, was plotting an offensive. The evidence for this came the following summer when the Indian armed forces discovered, to their dismay, that Pakistani troops masquerading as Kashmiri militants had occupied strategic heights in Kargil and other parts of north Kashmir on the Indian side of the unguarded line of control (LOC). The infiltration had happened in the dead of winter when temperatures plummet to below minus 50 degrees. The National Highway connecting Srinagar and Leh in Ladakh passes through Kargil and since the occupied heights overlooked the highway, the infiltrators could cut off Leh from the rest of the country. The infiltration extended to about 160 kilometres, which showed that it had been planned well.

This offensive cast a pall over the image the Vajpayee regime had been trying to project, and critics immediately began to berate the PM for foolishly extending an olive branch to Pakistan while it had been planning on attacking India. Nawaz Sharif claimed that he was unaware of the operation and that it was the handiwork of his top army commanders. Two years later, however, Pervez Musharraf said that he had briefed Nawaz Sharif about the operation beforehand. In May 1999, the Indian forces launched Operation Vijay to evict the Pakistanis, which came to an end on 26 July when it achieved its objective. More than 500 Indian soldiers were killed in the process, as the battle had been fought in a most hostile terrain. At one point, apparently, Nawaz Sharif had planned to use the nuclear capabilities of Pakistan against India, but he was called to Washington by US President Bill Clinton and asked to refrain from doing so. By this time, however, Sharif had lost control over his forces, and when he asked his troops to withdraw, the Pakistani Northern Light Infantry did, but the irregulars refused.

At its national executive meeting held between 15 and 17 April, the BJP passed a resolution saying that it was conscious of the serious threat to India's internal and external security: 'Pakistan has continued with its futile but dangerous anti-India policy. It is a country that has proclaimed jihad as an aspect of its international policy. But the party compliments the government for the resolute steps to keep the country safe and secure.'

By the time the Pakistanis had been cleared from the Kargil area, the Vajpayee government had fallen after Jayalalitha's party, AIADMK, had withdrawn its support from the NDA. In the ensuing vote of confidence in Lok Sabha, the government lost power by only one vote. But Vajpayee continued as the caretaker prime minister, and won the next election, only to be formally reinstated on 13 October 1999. Many called the polls The Kargil Elections.

But there was more trouble brewing. On 24 December 1999, Indian Airlines flight IC 814, travelling from Kathmandu to Delhi, was hijacked as it was flying over Varanasi. After detours to Amritsar, Lahore and Dubai, the flight finally landed in Kandahar in Taliban-controlled Afghanistan where the hijackers finally made their demand: release thirty-two militants held in various Indian jails.

The Vajpayee government went into a tizzy. Releasing the militants would compromise the government's image but holding them would gravely endanger the lives of the 150 passengers left on the plane. Twenty-seven passengers had been freed at Dubai, along with the body of a passenger—Ripan Katyal—who had been killed. On the other hand, pressure was being mounted on the government by the relatives of the passengers, the media and the other political parties to quickly resolve the crisis. In the end, the Vajpayee government capitulated; after negotiations, it was agreed that three militants would be released. Foreign Minister Jaswant Singh personally escorted the three militants to Kandahar and got the Indian hostages released on New Years' Eve. (It is to be noted here that the three militants proceeded to commit countless acts of terrorism after their release: Masood Azhar was the mastermind behind the 26/11 attack on Mumbai and founded the Jaish-e-Mohammed terrorist group, while the other two were involved in the abduction and killing of American journalist Daniel Pearl.) The abject surrender, as the public saw it, did not help Vajpayee's image.

▪

Even after the Kargil and Kandahar disasters, Vajpayee was reluctant to give up on his mission to maintain good relations with India's neighbours. Moreover, the international community—the UN and the US—was keen that the Indian government take the process forward. The party was also on board. At its national executive meeting in Delhi on 5 January 2001, the unanimous resolution was that 'good relations' and 'peaceful coexistence' with neighbours including Pakistan should be built. An opportunity came their way a year later when, at a private luncheon, Advani, Vajpayee and the then foreign minister, Jaswant Singh, reasoned that it was the Pakistan military that was coming in the way of the peace process in a bid to stall the civilian government there. Now that General Pervez Musharraf was in command (he had taken over after a coup) he would not be disinclined to explore the option of peace between the two countries. Moreover, this would create a place for Musharraf in history. Thus, an invitation was sent to the General and a summit meeting was slated at the historic capital of Agra from 14 to 16 July 2001. Musharraf agreed, and the meeting started on a pleasant note, but soon ran into rough weather. India wanted to discuss a whole gamut of issues with Pakistan that included cross-border terrorism. There was great concern in the country regarding militants that were being trained in Pakistan and smuggled across the border into India. In fact, while the summit was on, there was violence in Kashmir and eighteen people were killed in the crossfire between Indian soldiers and Islamic militants. On the eve of the summit, too, Indian and Pakistani troops had exchanged fire—the first such instance in 2001.

However, Pakistan held that Kashmir was the core issue between the two countries and wanted to focus only on that particular problem; cross-border terrorism did not figure on their agenda. Other issues that India wanted to discuss included economic cooperation between the countries, military confidence-building measures and Indian concerns about prisoners of war (POWs) in Pakistan. Even as the talks between the two heads of states were on, the foreign ministers of both countries were preparing a draft statement that would be signed and released at the end of the summit. When the draft statement came up for consideration, the cabinet committee for security hurriedly convened in Vajpayee's suite in the midst of the summit. Advani pointed out that the draft did not refer to cross-border terrorism at all: therefore, it could not be accepted. Others present agreed, although Jaswant Singh had agreed to the draft with the Pakistani foreign minister. Thus, the Agra Summit ended in failure with not even a joint declaration to show for at the end. The Pakistani spokesperson told the press that a joint statement had been readied but how a 'hidden hand' had intervened to prevent it from being finalized and announced. The hidden hand was a veiled reference to Advani. Though the summit failed, Advani's intervention boosted the image of the BJP government, they had refused to fall for the Pakistani ploy to divert attention from real issues and be part of an unequal agreement.

A few months later, Parliament was attacked. On 13 December 2001, five armed terrorists infiltrated the Parliament House complex using a car that had fake Home Ministry and Parliament entry stickers. They then started firing indiscriminately, killing some of the security personnel before being shot dead. The gun battle exposed the vulnerability of Parliament and shocked the nation, coming barely three months after the 9/11 attack in the US. The next day, Home Minister Advani informed Parliament that his agencies had information that pointed to a neighbouring country and some terrorist organizations based there were to be responsible for the attack. This was a reference to Pakistan and the terrorist organizations, Lashkar-e-Taiba and Jaish-e-Mohammad. The same afternoon, the Pakistani ambassador was issued a demarche demanding that leaders of the two organizations be apprehended and the financial assets of the groups be frozen. The Pakistani forces were put on high alert the same day, indicating that they feared an attack; India had undertaken the largest military mobilization since 1971. Some suggest that this mobilization on the border was conducted with the express purpose of carrying out a pre-emptive strike on Pakistan, but the US, concerned that this could degenerate into a nuclear war, prevailed upon the Indian government.

The strong action (massing of the army on the borders) by the government delighted the BJP. At its national executive meeting held on 29 December in New Delhi, the party passed a resolution stating that national security should now be the major plank of BJP's agenda. It said: 'BJP welcomes steps taken by the government to put Pakistan on notice. The recall of the Indian high commissioner in Islamabad, drastic reduction in the size of Pakistan's mission in New Delhi, confining the personnel of the Pakistan mission within the limits of the Delhi Municipal Corporation, banning... flight facilities to Pakistani airlines and suspension of Samjhauta Express and the Delhi-Lahore bus service are some of the initial measures to warn Pakistan,' the resolution said. A month ago, at its national executive meeting in Amritsar on 2 November 2001, the party had expressed concern at President Musharraf's description of cross-border terrorism as a struggle for freedom, and had said that the international community should feel suspicious about the resolve made by Pakistan to counter terrorism 'in view of its track record'.

After the 1998 nuclear tests, the Vajpayee government decided to engage the US in talks as well. The ground realities in the subcontinent were changing. With the Indian economy opening up for business, American companies were suddenly interested in exploiting the Indian markets. India, in turn, wanted technology and investments from these companies. The county also wanted support from the US to counter the threat from Pakistan. Hence, there was great scope for better relations between the two countries and India pursued this with vigour. Two visits (of the then US President Bill Clinton to India in 1999, and Vajpayee to the US in 2000) led to greater engagement between the two countries. Brajesh Mishra was the architect of this Indo-US engagement. Vajpayee's visit to the US consolidated a shift in the Western country's policy towards Kashmir. In his speech to the US Congress, Vajpayee made reference to how 16,000 people had died in Kashmir due to Pakistan-sponsored terrorism. He also pointed out how the neighbouring country had adopted religious war as its official policy. Pakistan had, all through the Cold War era, been the priority of the US, but the ground reality of Islamic terrorism and the Taliban's presence in the country forced America to redefine its policy in South Asia. The 9/11 attacks, too, played a part in this change of outlook. Now, India and the US were on the same page in matters relating to combating Islamic fundamentalism.

Due to its pursuit of building closer relations with the US, there have been allegations made that the BJP government was now jettisoning the country's long-standing stance of non-alignment. Critics have also pointed out that India was seeking a three-way axis with India-Israel-US as a way to counter Islamic forces and the threat from Pakistan. Brajesh Mishra, addressing the American Jewish Council in the US, had pointed out how the three countries would have to face terrorism head-on—implying, thereby, the need for greater engagement with Israel. Closer relations with Israel, with whom diplomatic ties had opened up in 1992 during the time of the Narasimha Rao government, also meant that India's old West Asian policy of cozying up to the Arabs was now somewhat downplayed.

India also started working towards maintaining closer defense relations with the US, and joint military exercises were held with all three wings of the forces. Closer ties between the defense and intelligence wings of the two countries were also encouraged. When the US declared war on international terrorism after 9/11, the Vajpayee government offered India's air bases and logistical support to the US for the purpose. (The US, however, did not avail the offer.) The BJP, at the national executive meeting in Amritsar referred to earlier, approvingly mentioned that the 'American government with the help of other nations has adopted the policy of chasing terrorists to their homes across many countries and continents.' The party was raring to go and added that 'it is right for the time being for India that it has decided not to strike beyond the borders, but if the situation warrants and circumstances are such, there is nothing that should come in the way to finish terrorism by striking it inside and outside for national security.'

In line with its aim to make India a great world power, the Vajpayee government also increased the defence budget. From Rs 35,277 crore in 1997-98, it grew to Rs 65,300 crore in 2003-04. Though tilting towards the US, the Vajpayee government did not restrict its acquisitions to the Western Bloc: contracts were signed with Russia for supply and local manufacture of the Sukhoi 30 (advanced multi-role aircrafts) and for the supply of 310 T-grade tanks. In fact, Russia, after the disintegration of the USSR, was also looking for a fruitful relationship with India. Among other things, this was also to boost their local defence industry that was starved of orders. The government in India also did not mind accepting Russia's hand in friendship; Vajpayee was pragmatic enough to realize that it was in the best interests of the country to continue the decades-old relationship. As a result, Russian President Vladimir Putin visited India twice while the NDA government was in power. In 2000, during Putin's first visit, the two countries made a declaration on strategic partnership that provided a long-term perspective to the bilateral relations based on geostrategic realities and economic opportunities. In 2009, during Putin's next visit, two defence deals and one civil nuclear energy agreement were signed.

Intrestingly, Vajpayee had a more difficult time cultivating a relationship with China, as was evident from his first visit to the country as foreign minister in Morarji Desai's government. While Vajpayee was in Beijing, the Chinese army invaded Vietnam and stated that this was to teach a lesson to the Vietnamese the same way that India had been taught in 1962. Vajpayee again visited China in 2003; this time, however, the reception was better. Although the

Chinese perceived him as someone not particularly pro-China, the bilateral relations got a bit of a boost as because of an agreement the two countries signed to upgrade the level of talks on the border issue. This was the first time the Indian government recognized Tibet as a part of China, and the Chinese agreed that Sikkim was a part of India.

Therefore, whether or not India became a great power under Vajpayee, the BJP government was certainly able to put India's international standing a notch above what it was before.

chapter 10

The Party in Power

In late April 1998, barely a month after he took over as the prime minister, Atal Bihari Vajpayee was addressing captains of industry under the auspices of the Confederation of Indian Industry (CII). He said: 'We simply cannot afford to play politics with the nation's economy anymore. The time has come to insulate the nation's economy as much as possible from the turmoil in the democratic polity... Swadeshi does not mean that the government does not value foreign investment and foreign companies. Permissions [to foreign companies] will not be withdrawn or narrowed in scope. The government is a continuing entity.'

This assurance had been prompted by several factors. Firstly, after three governments in a short span of two years (including his own government of thirteen days), Vajpayee knew that there were a lot of apprehensions in the minds of businessmen about the stability of policies. Secondly, even though the BJP was seen as a party that was in favour of an open economy, doubts were raised regarding this after the establishment of the Swadeshi Jagran Manch (SJM) with the blessings of the RSS in November 1991 in Nagpur. A combination of Sangh Parivar affiliates—the Bharatiya

Mazdoor Sangh, Akhil Bharatiya Vidyarthi Parishad, Bharatiya Kisan Sangh, Akhil Bharatiya Grahak Panchayat and Sahakar Bhandar—had established the SJM. Their agenda: the promotion of Swadeshi industries as an antidote to liberalization, privatization and globalization (LPG) that had been promoted by the Narasimha Rao government. The SJM contended that the Congress government was bowing to pressure from the multinational lobby and perpetuating economic imperialism.

By the time Vajpayee came to power, seven years had elapsed after the first flush of liberalization. In fact, from 1995, the Rao government itself had started going slow on reforms. This was in response to the opposition it was facing from within. Indian industry had lobbied for de-licensing and opening up the economy. But once this was done, they started crying hoarse about how they would get wiped off by unequal competition from overseas companies. At the same time, in knowledgeable circles, there was the realization that having kick-started economic reforms there was no way that one could go back on them. Holding on to status quo was not an option—going forward was the only way out. In fact, the time was ripe for pushing through second generation reforms. 'Vajpayee realized this and went forward, managing the opinions within [his government],' says journalist R. Krishnan.

One of the first things that Vajpayee did was to announce the new telecommunications policy (NTP) in March 1999. By this, the department of telecommunications, which was both a policy-maker for the sector and operator of fixed telephone services, was divested of the latter responsibility. A new government-owned corporation called Bharat Sanchar Nigam Limited (BSNL) was set up which was more accountable to the public and took on the job of running telephone services across the country. Cellular phone operators whose services were not being expanded fast enough (because their operations were not viable) were allowed flexibility to move to a revenue-sharing regime from a fixed licensing fee regime. In 2002, the Videsh Sanchar Nigam Limited (VSNL), which had a monopoly on international long distance calls, was privatized.

The first privatization actually came in January 2000, when the Modern Food Industry that produced bread was sold off to Hindustan Lever. This move was followed by some protests among workers but nothing more happened. This emboldened the government and, in the next budget session, the finance minister formally announced a new privatization policy that would allow for the strategic sale of public sector companies. The department of disinvestments that existed in the Government of India was upgraded to a ministry. This was to strengthen the minister of disinvestment who would otherwise face hurdles from ministries in charge of enterprises that were sought to be divested. In the end, thirteen hotels and twelve other companies were sold off between January 2000 and June 2002. But trouble hit the government's shores in 2002 when two oil companies—Hindustan Petroleum and Bharat Petroleum—were going to be sold off. The Supreme Court intervened and prevented the deal, the reason being that both the companies were multinationals that had been nationalized by the government in the 1970s. The takeover had been completed on the condition that they would not be sold off again.

Addressing members of the BJP's national executive, Party President Bangaru Laxman (at the behest of Vajpayee) said: 'Critical voices are being heard within the party and among the adherents of our ideological fraternity (sic) that the party has abandoned its long standing commitment to Swadeshi and effected an U-turn by adopting reforms. This is wrong. BJP always wanted [the] end of license permit raj and wanted a system where the government was merely a facilitator. Moreover, Swadeshi in today's concept does not mean blind adherence or opposition to liberalization and globalization. It means seizing the opportunity to further national interests, taking advantage of opportunities and resisting challenges.'

But not everyone in the BJP or the government was convinced about privatization and proof of this was amply demonstrated in the case of BPCL and HPCL. The privatization of these companies was opposed by none other than the petroleum minister and old RSS loyalist Ram Naik. He soon found support from minister George Fernandes (an old socialist who had sent away Coca Cola and IBM from India in his old avatar as industry minister in the Janata government of 1977) and IT Minister Pramod Mahajan. Soon, Advani was also expressing his opinions against the privatization of the two companies, and at a cabinet committee convened to discuss the sale of HPCL and BPCL, Vajpayee could not convince Ram Naik to find a 'middle path' for their sale. Vajpayee pleaded that their privatization should not be halted, only to be told by Urban Development Minister Ananth Kumar that there were a lot of disputes about valuations of companies being sold and this was a problem.

Incidentally, Ram Naik, in his former role as heavy industry minister, had had a run-in with Arun Shourie, the divestment minister, over allowing Suzuki to raise their stakes in Maruti Udyog and buying into the company. Naik had also gone through the approval given in principle by the cabinet in February to the sale of HPCL and BPCL, but while discussing the nuts and bolts had come up with many objections. There were also objections raised to the sale of some other public sector undertakings like Engineers India Limited, where workers protested in large numbers, and the National Aluminum Company (NALCO), where minister Uma Bharti and Orissa Chief Minister and NDA partner Naveen Patnaik, in whose state the company's plants were located, agitated. In the case of National Fertilizers, Akali Dal minister S.S. Dhindsa, in charge of the ministry, was not in favour of privatization. In some cases, Vajpayee was able to ram through the sale in the face of opposition from Ram Naik but, in the case of BPCL and HPCL, the prime minister had to hold back. 'Vajpayee was convinced about divestment and sales and had deliberately appointed the aggressive and bull-headed Arun Shourie for the job. But, beyond a point, Vajpayee could not take it forward,' says R. Krishnan, who used to cover economic ministries for a major daily at that time. 'But even then I would say that Vajpayee delivered a lot, considering that he was not elected to office on the mandate of economic reforms,' he adds.

Harry Dhaul, a power producer and president of the Independent Power Producers Association of India (IPPAI), concurs: 'His government did more for power sector reforms than any other government. With the private sector coming into the area, there was need for an independent power sector regulator to ensure a level playing ground, and the government created the institution of a regulator. The age-old Electricity Act that governs the sector was also amended.'

The government also approved of private participation in the development of ports and paved the way for the construction of world class airports. A decision to go ahead with Delhi's metro rail was taken during the Vajpayee regime. But if there is one thing for which Vajpayee will be remembered for posterity, it is his commitment to the construction roads. Stylishly branded as the golden quadrilateral project, this national highway development programme launched in January 1999 proposed to link the four cities of Delhi, Mumbai, Kolkata and Chennai by a four-to-six-lane road network. Other major cities like Pune, Bengaluru, Ahmedabad, Kanpur and Surat were also to fall on the network that would cover 5,846 kilometres. The project got completed in the tenure of the next government but this was the most ambitious road construction project since Sher Shah Suri built what is now known as the Grand Trunk Road in the sixteenth century. Though Vajpayee was initially criticized for what was described by some as a pipe dream and blamed for throwing away good money, in the end he proved his detractors wrong with the successful implementation of the project which boosted business through rapid and cheap transportation. The initial project completion date was December 2003 but, in the beginning, it was bogged down by delays in land acquisition, arrangement of funds and finalization of contracts.

■

When a party comes to power, the government becomes relatively more important and the party is relegated to the background. This is but natural because all the top leaders of the party troop into the government, leaving only lesser-known members to take care of the party's affairs. This, of course, should not be how a disciplined party works, but that is what happened in the case of BJP. The top leaders—Atal Bihari Vajpayee and L.K. Advani, along with Murli Manohar Joshi, Pramod Mahajan, Sushma Swaraj, Arun Jaitley, Uma Bharti and many others—became ministers in the government. BJP's most successful chief minister, Bhairon Singh Shekhawat, became the vice president of India. Other important leaders of the party who had played a yeoman's role were rewarded and made governors. This included Sunder Singh Bhandari, Bhai Mahavir (two of the earliest members of the Jana Sangh), Kedarnath Sahni, K.L. Malkani, and many others.

The party president when the BJP came to office as the leader of the NDA was Kushabhau Thakre. A member of the old guard, he had built the party's base in Madhya Pradesh but he was much too rigid and had no national status. He was followed by three lightweight presidents. Bangaru Laxman, who took over from Thakre after the latter had completed his four-year term in 2000, had no real claim to fame other than the fact that he was a Dalit. The party merely wanted to emphasize that it represented all sections of society. A member of the state legislative council of his native Andhra Pradesh for one year in the mid-1980s, he was pushed into the government as a Rajya Sabha MP from Gujarat. He was a minister of state for some time under the Vajpayee administration, but was not considered important enough to be awarded the portfolio of a cabinet minister. The next president, Jana Krishnamurthy, although an old RSS swayamsevak and one of the founding secretaries of the BJP, had no political importance other than the fact that he belonged to Tamil Nadu where the party had been unable to plant roots. After being president of the party, he was inducted as law minister in the Vajpayee ministry. Venkaiah Naidu, who was the minister for rural development in the Vajpayee ministry, took over the party's reins from Krishnamurthy. A student leader who was active in the Jai Andhra movement in Andhra Pradesh that opposed the first Telangana movement in the early 1970s, Naidu had potential but was not powerful enough to be an effective party president in 2003.

'The government is—to use a simile—where all the honey is. So, like bees, less ideologically inclined members swamped to the corridors of power,' wryly comments an old RSS member who does not want to be identified. He admits that he, too, was interested in a Rajya Sabha berth but outsiders manoeuvred their way into the corridors of power. Of course, one of the reasons for this was that the government was of a coalition of parties. Therefore, parties other than the BJP had to be given positions of importance. Some of the constituents of the NDA like the Telugu Desam Party were able to drive hard bargains and get representation more than commensurate with their strength in the Lok Sabha. 'This meant dilution of the BJP's agenda, which I understand the hardliners did not like,' points out Paranjoy Guha Thakurta, a senior journalist and analyst. Indicative of this, BJP President Venkaiah Naidu became well known for his phrase: 'BJP ka jhanda, NDA ka agenda (we carry the BJP flag but implement the NDA agenda)'.

▪

Regardless of the seats that had to be given to other members of the NDA, Vajpayee, interested in running his government as smoothly as possible, roped in specialists who he thought could deliver their targets. One of his close associates was Jaswant Singh, who served as the finance, external affairs and defense minister. A former army major, Jaswant, though a BJP man, had no RSS background, rendering him 'less eligible' in the eyes of hardcore party men. For these members who idealized a life of simplicity, Jaswant Singh's lifestyle was seen as 'luxurious'.

Even Arun Shourie, although ideologically hardcore, was a non-politician; thus, he was looked at with suspicion. But Vajpayee had roped in Shourie with a purpose. He averred that only a stubborn person like Shourie could carry out the task of disinvestment without getting derailed by opposition from within and outside.

Then there was Yashwant Sinha, a former IAS officer who had joined the BJP as late as 1996. But Sinha was important enough in the eyes of Vajpayee to be his government's finance and foreign affairs minister. Of course, the fact that he had administrative experience, first as an IAS officer and then as the finance minister in the Chandrasekhar government, helped convince Vajpayee about the usefulness of appointing him in the top slots.

Soon, there grew a feeling within the party that Vajpayee had created a coterie around him and operated through them. For instance, it is said that after the hijacking of IC 814, Vajpayee took a decision to free terrorists in consultation with Brajesh Mishra and Jaswant Singh, keeping L.K. Advani out of the loop. This did not please Advani at all, especially as it was a matter concerning his own home ministry. 'Brajesh Mishra was in total control of the Prime Minister's Office, and Vajpayee himself would not get into the details, leaving it to the concerned persons,' says former Union Home Secretary K. Padmanabhaiah (who was in charge of bringing about an accord with the National Socialist Council of Nagaland who were seeking full sovereignty during the Vajpayee era). 'Vajpayee was a very keen listener and would allow everyone to speak, and pronounce policy directions in very few words,' he adds.

▪

Lobbyists and fixers have been a constant feature in the corridors of power ever since the 1960s. After the demise of the license/permit raj, it was expected that this tribe of lobbyists and fixers would become extinct. A few years after the initiation of reforms, it was clear that this hope had been misplaced. With liberalization resulting in more wealth creation in the private sector, the lobbyists donned a more sophisticated avatar. Some ministers and officials of the Vajpayee government were not immune to the influence of these fixers. It was alleged that sometimes when decisions were delayed, the reasons were other than those formally stated. The twists in the process of the privatization of VSNL and the inordinate delay in the sale of Indian Petrochemicals Limited (IPCL) is attributed to corporate rivalry that had spilled over to the blocks and bhavans of the secretariat. The name of Ranjan Bhattacharya, a businessman and the foster son-in-law of A.B. Vajpayee, who used to stay with the prime minister, began to be bandied around as an important influencer of deals.

The government's most embarrassing moment came when party president Bangaru Laxman was caught on tape accepting bribes to push a defence deal through. He took the bribe from Mathew Samuel, a special correspondent for the news magazine *Tehelka*. Samuel, along with reporter Aniruddha Bahal, took part in the now famous sting operation, Operation West End, where Samuel posed as a defence dealer seeking to sell thermal binoculars to the army. Laxman had to immediately step down from the presidency of the party and was later convicted under the Prevention of Corruption Act. The incident was a massive setback for the BJP because of the blatant fashion in which the party president was found accepting a bribe. Earlier on, the government also had to face charges for buying coffins for the dead soldiers of the Kargil conflict at exorbitant rates in a scandal that was called Coffingate. The defence ministry at that time was under George Fernandes who was not a BJP representative, but the flak had to be taken by the BJP because the government was led by Vajpayee, a BJP man.

Apart from accusations of corruption, the BJP was also facing problems internally. Intoxicated by power, BJP party men who occupied positions in the government now distanced themselves from the organization. This comes out clearly in what then President Venkaiah Naidu told the national executive on 18 July 2003 at Raipur a few months before the general elections: 'You will recall that in the meetings of the national executive in the initial years of the government, many members used to feel the need to have greater interaction between the government and the party.' Naidu said that this had been rectified. 'Now the level of interaction has exceeded expectations. Ministers have increased their involvement in the party's activities by coming to the party office regularly, taking up the party's programmes and interacting with party workers.'

But clearly this was not enough, and evidence of this came a year later when the new president, L.K. Advani, addressed the national council on 27 October 2004 at Delhi after the NDA had been voted out of power. Advani identified (along with other problems) the fact 'that we could not motivate the karyakartas sufficiently and uniformly' as a reason for the defeat. He also noted that there were 'innumerable complaints about the style of functioning of party functionaries during the time BJP was in power at the centre. There have been charges of arrogance, aloofness, cronyism, overdependence on money power and even corruption.' A succinct description indeed of the party when it was in power!

chapter 11

The Northern Conquest

The Jana Sangh and the BJP have always been closely linked with the RSS, but in public perception, the name Arya Samaj is never taken in the same breath as these parties. Yet, it is the Arya Samaj which played a great role in establishing and grounding the fortunes of the Jana Sangh in its early years in Delhi and areas of central UP which were the first citadels of the party.

In his lifetime, Dayananda Saraswati, who originally hailed from Saurashtra, extensively toured parts of the country to spread the message of the Arya Samaj, an organization he founded in Bombay in 1875. Deeply disturbed by the ritualism which had crept into Hinduism, Dayananda sloganeered: 'Go back to Vedas.' He felt that latter-day texts had weakened the ideological basis for the religion and made its adherents weak. In fact, Hindus had become so weak that they could not resist foreign invasions and attacks on their religion, which had led to continuous conversions to other faiths. Part of this renaissance movement was not only to persuade Hindus to live according to the Vedas but also to reconvert those who had been Hindus earlier but had converted to Islam or Christianity. He also asserted that Hindi should be the lingua franca of the country.

The states most deeply affected by his philosophy were Punjab (with Lahore as its headquarters) and the United Provinces.

Dayananda did not live long enough to see the fruits of his labour, but after his death, his followers carried his work forward earnestly through Arya Pratinidhi sabhas and the educational Dayanand Anglo Vedic (DAV) Trust. The latter set up schools and colleges to initiate students into the culture of the Arya Samaj and, as the name indicated, sought to impart the best of Vedic and English education. The movement developed deep roots in Hindu society in undivided Punjab. Sikhs kept away as their gurus had been ridiculed by Dayananda. In Punjab's political economy, the Arya Samaj represented urban, middle-class Hindus, especially the Khatris. Lala Lajpat Rai, one of the primary political leaders of Punjab, was also an adherent of the Arya Samaj, as was Ghadar Party revolutionary Bhai Parmanand, who had served a sentence in the cellular jail in the Andamans. Boys from many Arya Samaj families joined the RSS when it became active in the province in the last decade before Independence. In fact, the RSS grew very quickly in Punjab and acted as a counter to the National Guards of the Muslim League that had become very active in the 1940s.

DELHI

There was a huge influx of Hindus from west Punjab after the Partition of 1947. Over four lakh refugees are estimated to have taken shelter in Delhi, most of them choosing to settle down in the capital city. Many of the refugees had been followers of the Arya Samaj and a smaller number had also seen the RSS at work. When the Jana Sangh came up in 1951, many such refugees became supporters of the new party. In fact, many of the early leaders of the Jana Sangh who lived in Delhi had a dual Arya Samaj/RSS background. This included Balraj Madhok, Bhai Mahavir and Kedarnath Sahni.

Incidentally, the Arya Samaj already had a strong base in Delhi. This was due to the work of leaders like Swami Shraddhanand, who had set up a highly popular educational institution at Kangri near Haridwar. In the early 1920s, Swami Shraddhanand took up the task of reconversion in all earnestness, targeting Malkana Rajputs of western UP. This created many enemies for him and, in December 1926, he was killed at his home in Delhi by a Muslim. Though many found fault with Swami Sharaddhanand's work, there were others who applauded him. 'This was the culture of the Arya Samaj: reform society but do not be apologetic about what you do. It challenged and fought, and did so passionately,' says an adherent, Satnam Arora. Two days after the killing of Swami Shraddhanand, a condolence resolution was passed by the Congress party at its session in Guwahati. Mahatma Gandhi was instrumental in getting this done.

The adherents of the Arya Samaj already in Delhi also formed the support base of the Jana Sangh. Little wonder then that in the first elections in Delhi in 1951—when there was an assembly in the capital city—the Jana Sangh garnered 22 per cent of the votes. In the general elections, the party barely got a little over 3 per cent of votes cast across the nation, illustrating how Delhi had become a stronghold for the Jana Sangh. Ten years later, in 1962, the vote percentage polled by the Jana Sangh in Delhi had gone up to 32 per cent in the general elections. (There are no comparable figures for assembly polls because the assembly had been scrapped in the city.)

It may be noted here that DAV institutions that had been first set up and nurtured in west Punjab by Lala Hansraj—who had become a legend in his lifetime—were shifted to Delhi and other north Indian towns after 1947. This meant that the influence of the Arya Samaj kept growing. 'Delhi was the spring board from where the Jana Sangh spread to northern India and the philosophy of the Arya Samaj went a long way in determining the world view of the

Jana Sangh,' says political journalist Pankaj Vohra, who has studied the party's journey closely.

UTTAR PRADESH

The party's early base in UP—mainly in towns like Agra, Kanpur and Varanasi—was also due to the combined influence of the RSS and Arya Samaj. Deen Dayal Upadhyaya came under the influence of the RSS while studying at Sanatan Dharma College in Kanpur in 1937 and Atal Bihari Vajpayee had studied in Arya Samaj institutions before joining the ranks of the RSS. Nanaji Deshmukh, an RSS pracharak who had worked hard to establish the Sangh's network in UP in the late 1940s and was based in Gorakhpur, was appointed as the first secretary of the Jana Sangh for the state. To him goes the credit of setting up Jana Sangh units in every district of the sprawling state.

The early supporters of the Jana Sangh in UP were Brahmins and Baniyas, and the influence of the party did not extend to the Jats, OBCs and Dalits in its early years. The Jats were with Charan Singh who was first in the Congress and then broke away to form his own Bharatiya Kranti Dal in the late 1960s. The OBCs were partly with the Congres, which was at its peak in those years, but its support base was being chipped away by the socialist parties led by Ram Manohar Lohia. In Delhi, too, the Jana Sangh's base centred around Baniyas and Arya Samaj followers but did not extend to outer Delhi which overlapped with the rural hinterland that was populated with Jats. 'The Brahmin population of UP is significant and the combination of Nanaji Deshmukh and Atal Bihari Vajpayee made sure that they hitchhiked their wagon with the party,' Pankaj Vohra says. Nanaji Deshmukh had superb organizational abilities and used this to spread the roots of the party in India's most populous state.

Though the base of the Jana Sangh deepened in UP, it was

only in its avatar as the BJP that it could get a significant number of supporters. In fact, it was the Ram Janmabhoomi movement which attracted a huge section of the OBCs and Dalits to the party. Kalyan Singh, the chief minister of UP when the Babri Masjid was demolished, was an OBC politician. The battle for OBC votes was, however, two-way in the state: the Janata Dal led by V.P. Singh and Mulayam Singh Yadav were competing for the same support base. What benefitted the BJP was the upper-caste-lower-caste combination: Brahmin voters were swayed by Vajpayee, and OBC voters were influenced by the presence of Kalyan Singh in the party.

There was another party that was strengthening in UP but targeting a different support base. This was Kanshi Ram's Bahujan Samaj Party that appealed to the Dalits—20 per cent of UP's voters are Dalits, whereas OBCs comprise nearly 35 per cent. Yadav votes account for 9 per cent and Brahmins are 10 per cent. Upper caste Rajputs and Thakurs make up for another 7 per cent.

A regional parties in UP grew in significance, the BJP found its prospects dwindling. At the beginning of 2013, a year before the 2014 general elections, the BJP had been reduced to an insignificant position in the state compared to what it was at the height of the Ram Janmabhoomi movement in the early 1990s, due to the increasing influence of the BSP and the Samajwadi Party. The latter, founded by Mulayam Singh Yadav, was the breakaway from the Janata Dal. In the assembly elections to the state in 2012, the BJP just got 15 per cent of all votes cast and won 47 of the 403 seats it contested. In contrast, the SP secured 224 seats and 29.13 per cent of the votes, and the BSP won eighty seats and 25.91 per cent of the votes. Five years earlier, in 2007, the BJP won 51 seats, securing 17 per cent of the votes cast. In 2002, the party had secured 20 per cent of the votes and won 88 seats. Thus, the secular vote percentage of the BJP in UP had slowly decreased over time: in the first decade of the twenty-first century, the battle for UP had essentially been between the SP and the BSP, who alternated in power, with both securing 25-29 per cent of the votes each. It seemed as if the BJP lost both the OBC (after capturing a significant part during the time of the Ram Janmabhoomi movement) and Dalit votes to the two parties and was restricted to battling for its traditional vote bank of Brahmins and Baniyas with the Congress party. This was hardly surprising, because the BJP leadership showed no determination to come up with a new agenda designed to recapture the OBCs. In the 2004 general elections, the BJP just managed to win 10 of the 80 Lok Sabha seats in the state. But in 2009, this had gone up to 20. Of course, as the recent 2014 Lok Sabha elections have shown, the BJP has once again made a significant splash in the heartland of the cow-belt states using Narendra Modi as the mascot. The party went to the Lok Sabha polls in UP emphasizing the OBC origins of Modi in order to recapture the OBC vote. Their strategy worked wonders: the BJP won 73 out of the 80 seats in the state.

In 2000, the BJP-led NDA government bifurcated UP and created the state of Uttaranchal. Six years later, the state was renamed Uttarakhand. But the creation of the new state—with a majority population of either Brahmins or Rajputs—has benefitted the Congress party the most. The Congress party's vote share in UP has now fallen to the range of 8-12 per cent. But in Uttarakhand, the Congress's vote percent is between 30-33 per cent. The BJP is also a strong player in this new state with its vote share adding up to 25-33 per cent, but both the BSP and SP are non-players. The BJP and Congress have been alternately in power in the state. It may be noted that it has been decades now since anyone from the BJP or the Congress became the chief minister of UP.

MADHYA PRADESH

In Madhya Pradesh, the Jana Sangh took a different route to success, achieving it much earlier than it did in UP. The credit for this went to the RSS and a particular individual who was outside the Sangh Parivar fold—Vijaya Raje Scindia. The maharani of the former princely state of Gwalior, she contested the 1957 Lok Sabha polls from Guna on a Congress ticket and won. She had been requested to contest by none other than Jawaharlal Nehru, who was worried about the monopoly of the Hindu Mahasabha in the territories of the erstwhile Gwalior state. In next election held in 1962, Vijaya Raje (now Rajmata after her husband passed away in 1961) once again earned a berth in the Lok Sabha on a Congress ticket. But this time she contested and won the Gwalior seat. However, allegations began surfacing that people close to the princely family were supporting the Hindu Mahasabha in the region. Five years later, in 1967 when the Congress was on the decline, Vijaya Raje Scindia switched sides. In the process, she created history by simultaneously contesting for the Lok Sabha seat on a Swatantra Party ticket and the assembly seat on a Jana Sangh ticket. She won both the seats but decided to give up the Lok Sabha seat. She then formally joined the Jana Sangh and helped the party establish a base in the area. Following her example, many erstwhile princes (small princely houses abound in Madhya Pradesh) came to back the Jana Sangh. After the Jana Sangh metamorphosed into the BJP, she continued with the outfit as its vice president.

There were other reasons too for the Jana Sangh gaining prominence in Madhya Pradesh. Situated in Central India, not far from Nagpur, the RSS had been active in the area from almost the very beginning. The early Jana Sangh growth was fuelled by the RSS network in the region, especially around Indore and Dewas. In these areas, RSS shakhas had started operating before 1930, barely five years after the organization was founded. The man playing a key role in this region was Kushabhau Thakre who, many decades later, became the president of the BJP. Thakre, who had joined the

RSS in 1942 and belonged to Dhar—located in the princely state of Indore—was first deputed to Neemuch and then put in charge of the Ratlam division, covering Ratlam, Ujjain, Mandsaur and Jhabua, among other areas. Even after Thakre, popularly known as the 'Bhishma Pitama' of the BJP, had relinquished his official position in Madhya Pradesh, he continued to be the de-facto boss and had three disciples whom he had groomed personally. These three—V.K. Saklecha, Kailash Joshi and Sundarlal Patwa—also became chief ministers, though the relationship between them is believed to have been strained. Factionalism within the party, however, was kept under check by Thakre. Incidentally, the Jana Sangh also attracted the Jains, a large number of whom were in the trading business.

In the area that has now become Chattisgarh, progress of the Jana Sangh was slow but helped by the Vanavasi Kalyan ashrams, a Sangh Parivar enterprise that had been working in the area since 1952 to counter the influence of Christian missionaries. The ashrams actively preached that Hanuman was the Hindu tribal God, and achieved a fair amount of success in their mission to re-convert.

Madhya Pradesh was one of the states where the influence of the Jana Sangh spread the fastest. In the 1957 elections to the state assembly, the party won 10 seats and got nearly 10 per cent of the votes cast. Ten years later, in 1967, the party won 78 seats and polled a significant 28 per cent of all votes cast.

By 1990, when the BJP started mobilizing support for the Ram temple and broadened its base to target the OBCs, their vote percentage climbed steeply to 39 per cent, giving the party 220 seats. It was at this time that OBC representatives like Uma Bharti came to the forefront. In the 1993 elections, after the demolition of the Babri Masjid, the party held on to its vote share, securing 39 per cent of the votes. However, the number of seats it won fell to 117 because the Congress was able to garner a bigger chunk of the votes:

41 per cent versus the 33 per cent in 1990. The BJP held on to its vote percentage in the 1998 elections to the state assembly, getting 39 per cent of the votes.

It is interesting to note that the Mandal politics of reservation for OBCs did not gather any steam in this state, the reasons for which are two-fold. Firstly, the OBCs were scattered and no leader and outfit tried to mobilize them properly, and secondly, the main OBC leader in the state, Uma Bharti, was part of the BJP and an active participant in the Ram Janmabhoomi movement.

In 2000, Madhya Pradesh was bifurcated, but the BJP's vote share was maintained; it got 38 per cent of the votes in the 2008 assembly elections. In 2003, it had got 42 per cent of the votes. The vote shares were also maintained in the new state of Chhattisgarh that was carved out of Madhya Pradesh. In 2003, the BJP got 39 per cent of the votes and in 2008 it secured 40 per cent of all votes polled. The consistently high proportion of votes secured by the party in both states unequivocally establishes that the BJP is in a good position here. The 2013 assembly poll results confirm these trends: in both the states, the incumbent BJP governments of Shivraj Singh Chauhan in Madhya Pradesh and Raman Singh in Chhattisgarh returned to power.

Also noteworthy is the fact that, even though the BJP holds its own in these states, the Congress party remains significant. On an average, the Congress secured a marginally lower percentage of votes than the BJP, but this also meant that the BJP, although in a good position, could never disregard the Congress. The Congress party was able to maintain its position because of the development policies pursued by Digvijaya Singh, who was the chief minister for two terms in MP between 1993-2003. (Incidentally, Digvijaya Singh, an ex-royal, revealed in a recent interview that he had been invited to join the BJP when he was entering politics in the late 1970s.) Due to these pro-development policies that countered the BJP's strategy of consolidating Hindu votes, the Congress has remained in the race in MP, unlike in Uttar Pradesh where it has completely collapsed. In the Lok Sabha polls of 2009, the BJP won 25 seats compared to the 10 in UP. In the 2004 elections, Madhya Pradesh returned sixteen BJP MPs out of a total of twenty-nine offered by the state. In Chhattisgarh, their performance was even better: in both the 2004 and 2009 Lok Sabha elections, the party secured 10 Lok Sabha seats each. This is stupendous considering that the state elects only eleven MPs.

RAJASTHAN

In Rajasthan, the early growth of the Jana Sangh was halting because of its refusal to cater to the feudal agenda of the ruling Rajput class that lost land in the wake of the abolition of jagirs. This influential class—angry with the Congress—shifted its allegiance to the Swatantra Party. Thus, the Swatantra Party was more successful than the Jana Sangh in Rajasthan. As a result, in 1962, the Jana Sangh won 15 seats against the 36 seats won by the Swatantra Party, and in 1967 it won 22 seats against the Swatantra Party's 48-seat tally. The Swatantra Party's best-known mascot was Maharani Gayatri Devi of Jaipur.

The Jana Sangh, however, came to fore in the state after it merged with the Janata Party in 1977, and broke up in 1980 to form the Bharatiya Janata Party. The party's establishment was largely due to the efforts of one man, Bhairon Singh Shekhawat, who had been a Jana Sangh MLA 1952 onwards. When the Janata Party came to power, he became the chief minister from June 1977 to February 1980. In 1990, when the V.P. Singh government was in the centre, Bhairon Singh again became the chief minister of the BJP government with the support of the Janata Dal. When elections were held in Rajasthan after the demolition of the Babri Masjid,

BJP was able to return to power, whereas it lost in UP and Madhya Pradesh. In fact, the vote percentage of the BJP increased from 25 per cent in 1990 to 38 per cent in 1993 and the increase can be partially explained by the collapse of the Janata Dal. Bhairon Singh, who remained a key player in the BJP, continued as chief minister till the end of 1998. After that, he became the vice president of India.

In 2003, the second BJP chief minister to take office was Vasundhara Raje, the daughter of Vijaya Raje Scindia. After losing one term, the BJP came back to power in Rajasthan at the end of 2013 with Vasundhara Raje at the helm. Since the mid-1990s, the BJP's vote share has remained in the range of 33-38 per cent in a state that has been largely bipolar, with Congress as the only other contender. The key to power in Jaipur rests with the Jats—the predominant caste of peasants who comprise about 9 per cent of the electorate—and the Gurjars—traditional herdsmen predominant in the eastern plains and southern plateau. Neither of these castes is fully with the BJP. The Rajputs—comprising 2-9 per cent of the state's electorate, depending on which region you go to—have alternately swung between the BJP and Congress. The Brahmins, who have held the levers of power in the state for a long time, comprise about 8 per cent of the voters.

HARYANA

The BJP's failure to captivate the Jats and the other peasant castes has not only restricted the party's march but kept it out of any power matrix in Haryana. The BJP has never been able to get more than 9-10 per cent of the votes in the state and the seat tally in the assembly has been in single digits. The influence of the party is restricted to urban areas, where there is a significant population of Brahmins and Banias. Among the top leaders of the BJP who hail from Haryana is Sushma Swaraj. Although she began her career from her state, her political growth was guided by the BJP's strength in other states, including Delhi and Madhya Pradesh.

PUNJAB

In Punjab, the BJP is conspicuous by its absence. This is not surprising. Considering its Arya Samaj background, the Jana Sangh has always been opposed to the creation of a Punjabi suba, which it saw as a Sikh state. The Sikhs always kept away from the Jana Sangh because of the Arya Samaj's apathy towards the Sikhs and their lack of appreciation for the reform agenda of the Sikh gurus. Moreover, the large Sikh/Jat population of Punjab did little to help the Jana Sangh first and then the BJP. The party's vote base among Hindus accounts for only 5-9 per cent of the electorate. However, ever since the formation of the NDA, the strategic alliance of the BJP with the Akali Dal, a Sikh party, has helped the saffron outfit, albeit marginally. The BJP tally in the Punjab assembly has never crossed 18—the number of seats it won in 1997. In the last assembly elections in 2012, the party won 12 seats. In most elections, the party's tally has been in single digits. The Akalis have aligned with the BJP only because the party is locked in competition with the Congress in Punjab. There is nothing that binds the Punjabi-speaking Akalis and the Hindi-speaking BJP, except the opponent—the Congress.

HIMACHAL PRADESH

The hilly state of Himachal Pradesh, that was carved out of the undivided state of Punjab and merged with thirty small princely states in 1966, has alternately veered towards the Jana Sangh and the BJP from the very beginning. In 1967, the Jana Sangh polled 14 per cent of the votes, which increased to over 35 per cent in 1982.

Like in Rajasthan, the metamorphosis of the party into the BJP helped it improve its tally in a state that has a very high proportion of high-caste voters. Brahmins, Rajputs and Banias comprise 56 per cent of the total population. The BJP has consistently maintained a vote proportion of over 35 per cent in Himachal since then. Again, power alternates between them and the Congress. Himachal Pradesh has never seen Mandalization: not surprising since OBCs just form 10 per cent of the population in the state. Thus, political competition is confined to the upper castes alone.

BIHAR

In Bihar, the BJP has fared better than in Punjab, Haryana and Rajasthan, but has not managed to establish a base like it did in Madhya Pradesh. In fact, till date, there has never been a BJP chief minister in Bihar, although the party had, until recently, formed an alliance with the Janata Dal (United), that is in power in the state at present. This alliance had been in existence since 1996.

The Jana Sangh's early rise in Bihar was due to the efforts of Kailashpati Mishra, who joined the RSS in 1944 when he was just twenty-one. He belonged to the landowning Bhumihar caste that forms the party's main support base. By 1967, the Jana Sangh had already built up a vote base of 10 per cent (as can be seen from the results of the state assembly elections in that year). This climbed to 13 per cent in 1998. In the last assembly elections in 2010, the party secured 16 per cent of the votes.

Unlike Himachal, in faction-ridden Bihar, where various castes compete fiercely for votes, Mandal politics largely overshadowed everything else—including the Ram temple mobilization that was not able to translate convincingly into votes for the saffron party. Lalu Prasad's Yadav-Muslim combine was able to keep the BJP at bay. The influential Bhumihars, who, besides being landholders, are a part of the bureaucracy and professions like teaching and medicine, are numerically insignificant, comprising not more than 5 per cent of the population. 'Other than the Bhumihars, the Brahmins also support the BJP. Two-and-a-half decades ago, they formed a part of the support base of the Congress. After the decline of Lalu Yadav, nowadays a part of the Yadav community also supports the BJP,' says senior journalist and political analyst Uttam Sengupta. In 2004, the BJP won five seats to the Lok Sabha from Bihar and this number went up to 12 in 2009. Bihar has a total of 40 Lok Sabha seats.

In Jharkhand, the breakaway state from Bihar, the BJP has had better luck. Since the formation of the state in 2000, Jharkhand has seen nine years of rule under BJP chief ministers. In fact, the first five years of the state was under two different BJP chief ministers—Babulal Marandi and Arjun Munda. Both of them are tribals. 'This allowed state patronage to be extended to Sangh Parivar outfits which have set up Vanavasi Kalyan centers and Saraswati shishu sadans to promote their philosophy amongst tribals and other groups,' Sengupta explains. In the 2009 elections, the BJP won eight seats out of 14 in Jharkhand, although in the 2004 elections, they just managed to win one seat.

chapter 12

Western Consolidation

MAHARASHTRA

Considering that the RSS kick-started from Nagpur and was led by Chitpavan Brahmins, the first stronghold of the organization—and its political affiliate, the Jana Sangh, and then the BJP—should have been Maharashtra. But this is not what happened. For starters, Nagpur—where the RSS is headquartered—in central India is far from Mumbai (earlier Bombay). This location allowed the RSS to expand its network relatively easily in central India, and accounts for the stronghold that the Jana Sangh and BJP built in Madhya Pradesh. In 1960s Maharashtra, the politically important areas lay in its western region—the areas south of Pune and extending to Satara, Sangli and Kolhapur—and the politics revolved around the farming class of Marathas. Y.B. Chavan, the Congress boss of the state, had forged equations in such a fashion that the party had a monopoly over these Maratha votes. In such a scenario, the Jana Sangh and later the BJP had no substantial role to play in the electoral politics of the state. The Jana Sangh—till it existed—had never won any Lok Sabha seats in the state and the best assembly tally was 14 seats.

Then a saviour came and lifted the BJP out of its morass. This was not a party insider but a leader from the outside. In 1984, for the first time, the BJP entered into an alliance with the Shiv Sena, jettisoning the Janata Party. The alliance was largely due to the efforts of a young, upcoming BJP leader, Pramod Mahajan, who was able to sell the idea within the party and also to the Shiv Sena supremo Balasaheb Thackeray. Against the backdrop of the assassination of Indira Gandhi, the combine came a cropper in the Lok Sabha polls and performed slightly better in the assembly elections held the next year (1985). The BJP got 20 seats in the legislative assembly which had been its best ever performance till that point.

The Shiv Sena, which was a force in Mumbai after assiduously cultivating the city's 'Marathi manoos' for a decade-and-a-half, now decided to foray into the rural hinterland of the sprawling state. This decision coincided with the Ram Janmabhoomi mobilization movement post 1986 and the Shiv Sena joined hands with the BJP to organize the Ram Yatra in Nashik and celebrate Shiv Jayanti. The Shiv Sena, being a confrontational organization, aroused a lot of hostility from the minorities in the course of the yatras. The result was that riots broke out in many places like Nanded, Beed, Panvel and Aurangabad. Around this time, the general public was getting disenchanted with the Congress. Feudal dynastic politics had become rampant within the party, whose leaders leveraged the cash-rich sugar cooperatives to increase power and wealth for their own kith and kin. These cooperatives were set up after Independence to empower sugarcane farmers to get good renumeration for their produce. The cooperatives followed a system of elected leadership and were soon captured by politicians.

In this newly emerging scenario, the Shiv Sena was able to make inroads into rural Maharashtra where people were feeling disempowered. Their first success came in Marathwada, a backward region in south-east Maharashtra which was a part of the Hyderabad state during the time of the Nizams. Here, Hindu mobilization was possible, largely because of the misrule of the Nizams and the imposition of an alien culture upon the people of the region during their rule. The Shiv Sena took up the Hindu cause very stridently and with great success. By 1988, the BJP was under pressure from affiliates such as the VHP to become equally forceful and collaborate more intensively with the Shiv Sena.

For the 1989 Lok Sabha and the 1990 assembly polls, the BJP and Shiv Sena tied up again. The agreement was that the BJP would be the senior partner in the parliamentary polls; in the assembly polls, the roles would reverse. Balasaheb Thackeray, the founder and supremo of the Shiv Sena, was the star campaigner of the combine for both the elections. Thackeray did not mind this because it helped his own party, too; the Shiv Sena was seeking to be a Hindutva party, shedding the earlier image of a Marathi party. In the Lok Sabha elections, the BJP got 10 seats, and bagged 42 seats in the assembly elections. The BJP was well on its way to creating a solid vote bank in Maharashtra, though the BJP-Shiv Sena alliance was not yet a winning combination. The Congress party had won more seats both in the Lok Sabha and the assembly than the alliance. But five years later in 1995, when assembly polls were held, the Shiv Sena won 73 seats and the BJP got 65. Their tally of 138 was more than the Congress's 80 seats. For the first time, the BJP formed the government in Maharashtra albeit as a junior partner. Manohar Joshi of the Shiv Sena became the chief minister. The Shiv Sena-BJP government continued till the end of 1999, even as charges of misadministration and corruption began to be levelled against them.

In the next election in 1999, the combine was voted out of power but that had more to do with the changing social dynamics of the state. Before the elections, Sharad Pawar, who was a tall figure in the political firmament of Maharashtra and represented the interests of the powerful Maratha lobby, left the Congress after differences with Sonia Gandhi. He now formed his own outfit called the Nationalist Congress party (NCP). Because of this, the 1999 assembly polls became a four-party affair. The Congress secured 65 seats, the Shiv Sena 69 seats, the NCP 58 seats and the BJP 56 seats. A coalition government led by Congressman Vilasrao Deshmukh came to power, obviously without the BJP and Shiv Sena. In 2004, there was an encore; again, there was a four-way battle, with the BJP getting 54 seats. Again, the government was formed by the Congress-NCP coalition. The situation repeated itself in 2009, when the BJP won 49 seats. The BJP was stuck with a vote share fluctuating between 13 and 14 per cent. The party had stopped growing in Maharashtra and its dependence on the Shiv Sena was also not working anymore. Balasaheb Thackeray had died and the Shiv Sena was facing internal problems. Thackeray's nephew, Raj, had broken away from the party to form the Maharashtra Navnirman Sena (MNS) even before his death.

The Shiv Sena, headed by Bal Thackeray's son, Uddhav, is now facing a direct threat from the MNS that is growing stronger every year. This has created huge problems for the BJP which has been forced to make a choice between the Shiv Sena and the MNS. Though it chose the Shiv Sena as its partner for the 2014 elections, BJP's bosses know that the MNS leadership is more vibrant. However, the Shiv Sena, being an older, more experienced party, has a better organizational network. It may not be out of context to point out that BJP's problems in the state have also been compounded by differences within its leadership. Former deputy chief minister of the state, Gopinath Munde, is locked in a dispute for supremacy with former BJP president, Nitin Gadkari.

GUJARAT

Gujarat, which was carved out of what is Maharashtra today, presents a rather interesting political picture. It has now become the strongest fortress of the BJP and even the prime minister of the new BJP government hails from the state. But being the land of Mahatma Gandhi and Sardar Patel, Gujarat (although it came into existence in 1960, much after the demise of the duo) was under the influence of the Congress party, for a long time. In 1975, just on the eve of the Emergency, an Opposition government that included the Jana Sangh came to power after the Nav Nirman Andolan took the wind out of the sails of the Congress party, accusing it rampant corruption. After the failed Janata Party experiment in the centre, the local bosses of the Congress—back with a bang—conjured a plan to create a new support base for the party. This was born out of the realization that the Brahmin-Bania high caste support base could abandon the Congress at any point as they had in the 1975 election. As part of this strategy, a Kshatriya-Harijan-Adivasi-Muslim (KHAM) combination was built and the Congress government of Madhavsinh Solanki started reservations for OBCs in 1980 to cater to these communities. This was much ahead of the Mandal reservations that were introduced in the north a decade later. These reservations led to a severe backlash from the upper castes and Gujarat was soon rattled by anti-reservation riots. Unmindful of this, the Congress went to the assembly elections in 1985 under Solanki and won a record 149 seats in a house of 182. This is an achievement that has not been bettered even by Narendra Modi. The Congress in this election got a staggering 55 per cent of the votes cast.

Buoyed by his success, Solanki now pushed for more reservations, leading to another bout of riots. Particularly affected by the reservations was the upcoming community of Patels who, in the mid-1980s, had just got economically empowered after the green revolution of the previous decade. Now this farming community with money at their disposal wanted to educate their young in colleges, especially in the fields of engineering and medicine. Some of their community members also wanted government jobs. But the reservation of seats in colleges and jobs hit them hard. Traditionally, the Patels, who comprised about 20 per cent of the voter strength of the state, always opted for the Congress. Now they wanted to review their position.

It is at this time that Advani took over the reins of the BJP and soon thereafter began building the party's base in Gujarat and mobilizing support for the Ram Janmabhoomi movement. 'At that time, the BJP was a party looking for supporters and the Patels were a community looking for a party that would take up their cause. The fit was perfect and the Patels shifted to the BJP,' says political analyst Rajiv Shah.

In the 1985 state assembly elections, the BJP had got a mere 11 seats and secured only 15 per cent of the votes. When the assembly elections were held again in 1990, the Congress's vote proportion tumbled to 31 per cent and seats to a mere 33. The BJP was up to 67 with a vote proportion of 26 per cent. But another party, the Janata Dal, secured 29 per cent of the votes and 70 seats. This was not surprising considering that in New Delhi the Janata Dal government of V.P. Singh was in power. As a consequence, a Janata Dal-BJP government came to power in Gandhinagar. Unlike New Delhi, where the BJP had supported the Janata Dal government from outside, here, the BJP joined the government. The coalition fell apart in Gujarat soon enough—after the BJP withdrew support from the Janata Dal government in New Delhi—but the state government did not fall. The Janata Dal chief minister managed to break the Congress party and, with their MLAs, continued in power. This setback notwithstanding, the BJP intensified its mobilization zealously. As mentioned earlier, Advani began his march to Ayodhya from Somnath, traversing many districts of Gujarat and converting the local population to the cause of the Ram Janmabhoomi. Gujarat, in the eleventh century, had seen many incursions by Mahmud of Ghazni who had raided and plundered the Somnath temple, and memories of this incident remained in Gujarati subconsciousness through contemporary Gujarati literature of the late nineteenth and early twentieth century. 'All this made Hindu mobilization relatively simple,' says Rajiv Shah.

In the 1995 assembly elections, BJP got 121 seats and polled 42 per cent of the votes. This enabled them to form the government for the first time in the state. The chief minister was Keshubhai Patel, mainly because the party ran with the support of the Patels. But soon, internal dissensions raised their ugly head and BJP leader and RSS man Shankar Singh Vaghela, who thought he had a better claim to the chief minister's post, broke the party by taking a large number of MLAs with him. The government nearly fell and Keshubhai was hurriedly replaced with a Vaghela confidant by Vajpayee, after which Vaghela returned. On Keshubhai's insistence, Narendra Modi, who was the organizational boss of the party and directly responsible for the mobilization in Gujarat, was banished to the Delhi central office of BJP. Patel argued convincingly that Modi had been playing intra-party politics that had led to the Vaghela episode. After a year, Vaghela formed his own party and his own government with Congress support. The government did not last too long and mid-term polls were held in 1998. The BJP was back, securing 117 seats and 45 per cent votes. Keshubhai became the chief minister once again.

Due to his poor performance, compounded by troubles in the aftermath of the earthquake of 26 January 2001, Keshubhai was replaced by Narendra Modi in October 2001. Modi, an RSS pracharak, had lived many years out of the organization's regional headquarters in Ahmedabad and was a shrewd administrator.

The events that took place in Gujarat in 2002 are well-known nationwide. On 27 February, coach S6 of the Sabarmati Express was burnt down at Godhra station and fifty-nine passengers—many of them kar sevaks returning from Ayodhya—died. What followed shocked the nation and the world as riots broke out in the major cities of Gujarat like Ahmedabad and Baroda, killing more than 1,000 people, most of them Muslim. The violence took over three months to completely die down. The riots also, rather oddly, increased the BJP's support base and the popularity of the sitting chief minister, Narendra Modi: in the assembly elections held in December 2002, the BJP got almost 50 per cent of the votes polled and secured 127 of the 182 seats. With this mandate, Modi went around assiduously courting business groups to invest in the state and in the process established Gujarat and himself as being extremely business-friendly. As a result, there was an encore of the election results in the 2007 assembly polls: the BJP got 117 seats and 49 per cent of the votes. The performance was repeated in 2012. Thus, the BJP has reached an unassailable position in Gujarat, getting nearly 50 per cent of the votes in three successive elections. However, in the process, the party has begun to play a subordinate role in the state. Modi has loomed larger than life and the party has become a one-man show.

KARNATAKA

BJP's foray into Karnataka makes for an interesting story. Although numerous RSS shakhas have been in existence in coastal Karnataka for decades and have spread their influence greatly, the BJP was never able to convert this influence into votes. This had much to do with the caste matrix of Karnataka. The most dominant castes from a political perspective are the Lingayats (who comprise about 17 per cent of the population) and the Vokkaligas (who stand at a lower 15 per cent). Both these dominant castes were with the Congress before 1980, and the Lingayats—who had grown out of a Shaivaite reformist movement in the twelfth century—dominated the scene. They had taken early leads in education and they had religious mutts that enabled them to leverage a political advantage. The Vokkaligas—the cultivator class dominating the south Karnataka districts—became prosperous much later but demanded their share of the political pie as well.

In the early 1990s, the Lingayats started supporting the BJP—not the entire community but a part of it. At the same time, the Vokkaligas began shifting to the Janata Dal. But the Congress was not decimated, because large sections of both the communities remained with the party. In 1994, the BJP won 40 of the 224 assembly seats, securing 16 per cent of the votes. The Congress won 34 seats and 27 per cent of the votes. The real winner was the Janata Dal, which won 115 seats and 33 per cent of the votes. The boss of Janata Dal was H.D. Deve Gowda, a Vokkaliga, who was to become prime minister in 1996.

In the next assembly elections in 1999, the BJP's tally went up marginally to 44 seats, securing 21 per cent of the votes. The BJP leader at this time was B.S. Yeddyurappa, a Lingayat. It was the Congress, however, which won a majority of the seats (132), while the Janata Dal—which had split into two—could get only 28 seats. The new chief minister was S.M. Krishna, who was also a Vokkaliga. Obviously, the Vokkaliga votes had deserted the Janata Dal and hitched their fortunes to the Congress.

In the 2004 elections, the BJP came out on top with 79 seats and 28 per cent of the votes. However, although it was the party with the largest number of seats, it could not form the government. The Congress (with 65 seats) and the Janata Dal (with 58 seats) combined to keep the BJP out of power and formed the government under Congressman Dharam Singh. But, in 2006, the Dharam Singh government fell because H.D. Kumaraswamy (son of Deve Gowda) broke up the Janata Dal and took forty-two MLAs with him. With the support of the BJP, he formed the government. The arrangement between the Janata Dal breakaway faction and the BJP was that they would share power. Kumaraswamy would be chief minister for one-and-a-half years and the next one-and-a-half years of the term would be under the chief ministership of Yeddyurappa. However, when it was time to vacate his seat, Kumaraswamy refused to step down, leading to a crisis. The government fell and President's rule was imposed on the state. The electorate was disgusted at this naked display of power and showed their displeasure in the 2008 assembly elections, awarding the BJP 110 seats, the Congress 80 seats and decimating the Janata Dal to 28 seats.

The BJP came to power with B.S. Yeddyurappa as chief minister and with this began an ugly game of power. At 110 seats, the BJP was 3 seats short of a majority and they began their government with an operation codenamed Kamala, designed to poach upon elected representatives of other political parties and get the support of independents and defectors from Congress and Janata Dal. But the party and the chief minister hit a roadblock in the form of the Reddy brothers of Bellary. These brothers were miners who had become associated with the party through a quirk of fate.

In 1999, Sonia Gandhi decided to contest elections from Bellary, one of the most backward places in Karnataka. The choice of Bellary had to do with the fact that it had never failed to elect a Congress candidate since Independence. To give Sonia a run for her money, BJP's Sushma Swaraj decided to contest from Bellary, too. The BJP had no organizational base in Bellary in those days and had to offer cadres from other districts to work for Swaraj. In order to get local support, Swaraj had to enlist the help of the Reddy brothers, who were upcoming businessmen in the area. Sushma lost the election but gave Sonia Gandhi a tough fight. The BJP came to power in New Delhi and the Reddy brothers joined the BJP.

During this time, there was a huge demand for iron ore from China where there was an unprecedented demand for steel. Bellary produced low grade iron ore but such was China's hunger that it did not mind even low quality ores. Using their political clout, the Reddy brothers, who by now had become major financiers of the party in Karnataka, began mafia-like activities in the state. The hills of Bellary were denuded and forest land was encroached upon to mine for iron ore. The district administration and forest officials were helpless against the clout of the Reddy brothers who had now begun to dictate terms to Chief Minister Yeddyurappa. In the end, the BJP high command was so embarrassed by this saga of corruption, land scams and nepotism in Karnataka that, in July 2011, the party forced Yeddyurappa to step down. But Yeddyurappa had been given enough leverage in Karnataka and he had built his personal power base. He agreed to step down only if his follower, Sadananda Gowda, was made the chief minister. The BJP bosses complied and Yeddyurappa continued to call the shots from outside. A few months later, Yeddyurappa fell out with Gowda and sought his removal. The BJP high command gave in to his demand once again and made Jagadish Shettar the chief minister. But Shettar was a Lingayat like Yeddyurappa and, very soon, the latter began to feel that the chief minister was chipping away at his caste base. It was Yeddyurappa's turn to quit the party, and in December 2012, he left the BJP and formed his own political outfit, the Karnataka Janata Paksha (KJP).

Given this state of affairs in the BJP, it was not surprising that in the assembly elections in May 2013, the party was voted out of power. It secured only 40 seats while the Congress bagged 122 seats. The Janata Dal got 40 seats as well, and the KJP—that undercut the votes of the BJP—secured 6 seats. The Congress was back in power. Incidentally, during its tumultuous five-year tenure, the BJP government also oversaw the passage of a strident bill against cow slaughter, and right-wing youth were given a free reign to conduct moral policing in the state. Jagdish Shettigar, an economist who as a ten-year-old joined the RSS in coastal Karnataka in the late 1950s, said: 'The RSS has lost moral authority over the BJP in the state. What we see is the worst form of corruption.'

GOA

The BJP is slowly becoming strong in Goa as it is situated close to both Maharashtra and Karnataka. The present state government—in office since March 2012—is that of the saffron party. Being a small state, Goa has only 40 seats in the assembly, making majorities unstable as defection of a few MLAs can lead to changes in the government.

After Goa was liberated from the Portugese, it became a union territory and in the first election in 1963, the Maharashtrawadi Gomantak Party (MGP) under Dayanand Bandodkar was elected. The party represented majority non-Hindu interests and the MGP continued in power till 1979. After that, the Congress came to power and the BJP opened its account in 1994 as a junior partner in an alliance with the MGP. The MGP gradually weakened and the BJP took over its support base. In October 2000, the BJP's Manohar Parrikar became the chief minister of the union territory, and he remained in power till 2005. The party was again re-elected in 2012.

chapter 13

Combating the East and the South

Hindu nationalism first struck roots in the Indian subcontinent in Bengal. Reflecting this phenomenon is the novel *Anandamath* by Bankim Chandra Chattopadhyaya, who graduated from the Calcutta University in 1857 and joined the British magistracy. The novel is about the rebellion in parts of Bengal against its medieval Muslim rulers. 'Vande Mataram'—India's national song—which fired generations of freedom fighters in the twentieth century is very much a part of this novel. Thus, it is surprising that after Independence, the ideology of Hindu nationalism could not grow roots in West Bengal. This is in spite of the fact that Bengal, Punjab and Sindh were the three states most perniciously affected by Partition. As noted in an earlier chapter, it was the plight of Bengali refugees from East Pakistan that moved Syama Prasad Mookerjee to start the Jana Sangh. With the death of Syama Prasad, the party disappeared into oblivion in West Bengal and, even in its new avatar as the BJP, could never be resurrected.

The dismal state of the BJP in the state is best captured by election results. In the last assembly elections in West Bengal in 2011, the BJP contested 289 seats and the party's candidates lost their deposits in 285 seats. This was not an isolated result: ever since the first general elections, Jana Sangh and BJP candidates never got more than 6 per cent of the votes in the state, sometimes even as less as 2 per cent. The only exception was 1991, when BJP got 11 per cent of the votes but even then 240 of its 290 candidates lost their deposits. In 1998 and 1999, when the BJP was on the upswing nationally, the party won only one and two Lok Sabha seats respectively in the state. Tapan Sikdar won in both 1998 and 1999 from the Dum Dum seat in Kolkata, while in 1999, Satyabrata Mookherjee won from the Krishnanagar seat.

So, what explains this poor performance of the BJP? 'The party could never capture the Bengali imagination. Moreover, it could not catch the anti-Congress votes in the 1960s and the anti-Left votes in the later years,' explains Paranjoy Guha Thakurta, a political and economic commentator. He pointed out that the Ram temple mobilization did not work in West Bengal because Ram is not considered a god by Bengalis but only venerated as an honourable man. The party is seen as an outfit that represents the Marwaris and other north Indians and not as one representing the Bengali interest.

Bengal had a revolutionary tradition pre-Independence and had its roots in Hindu symbolism like worshipping Mother Kali—the Hindu goddess associated with empowerment—and Shakti, who is venerated as a figure of annihilation of evil forces; but with the advent of the 1940s, the revolutionaries who were fighting for freedom started gravitating towards the Communist party. This was not surprising because Bengal (especially the area around Kolkata) was industrialized early. This gave rise to trade unions and Communist parties which started attracting the erstwhile Hindu revolutionaries.

In the first decade after Independence, the Hindu Mahasabha had a presence in West Bengal. But in the state, like many other parts of the country, the party was seen as representing traditional, upper caste and somewhat reactionary Hindu consciousness that did not appeal to the greater masses. 'The British came to Bengal first. Therefore, Bengal was influenced by the western liberal tradition and the elite were influenced by the Brahmo Samaj. This prevented the rise of the Jana Sangh variety of ideology,' says political scientist Jyotirmaya Sharma, known as an authority on Hindutva.

Many of the Punjabi refugees who settled in Delhi patronized the Jana Sangh not merely because they were dislocated by Partition; they gravitated towards it under the influence of the Arya Samaj. Besides concentrating on social reform, the organization also put its faith in re-converting Muslims to Hindus. The Ramakrishna Mission order of Bengal can be roughly compared to the Arya Samaj and, in fact, had a taller leader than Dayanand Saraswati in the form of Swami Vivekananda. Although active in social reforms, the mission never talked of reconversions. Vivekananda himself was steeped in ancient Indian philosophy. So followers of the Ramakrishna Mission and Vivekananda did not automatically gravitate towards the Jana Sangh.

Unlike pre-Partition Punjab, in Bengal the entire Muslims community was that of converts. As Hindus, they had occupied a low social position in the caste hierarchy. Upper caste Hindus, though smarting under the aftereffects of the Partition, reasoned that division of Bengal was akin to lower castes rebelling against upper caste domination. Thus, they accepted Partition as a consequence of the evolution of society.

BJP has not been able to gather the anti-establishment votes in West Bengal in recent years like it has in many other states. In 2011, the Left front—after being in power for decades—was dislodged by the Trinamool Congress (TMC), which had earlier been a part of the NDA coalition but is now distant from the BJP. 'Every state has its own requirements. Even a national party has to tailor its policies to take care of the local conditions. The BJP failed to do so in West Bengal,' comments an IAS officer, who declined to be named. He pointed out that the demographic balance has been altered in the border districts of West Bengal due to continuous infiltration from Bangladesh in the last three decades. 'True, the infiltrators cross over for economic reasons, in search of employment. But what does it matter? This is an issue that the BJP should have been using for mobilizing support and this campaign would have caught the imagination of the people,' the IAS officer says.

ASSAM

In neighbouring Assam where the problem of influx of Bangladeshis has aroused greater passion, the BJP is relatively more successful than in West Bengal. Ever since 1992, the BJP has been getting some seats in the Lok Sabha from the state. In the general elections in 2009, BJP secured four seats even as the Congress-led UPA got a majority. In 2004, the BJP had secured two seats, which was the same number as in 1999. But the BJP has been more successful in parliamentary elections as compared to assembly polls. For instance, in 1992, the BJP got over 9 per cent votes for the Lok Sabha polls but only 6.5 per cent votes in the assembly. In 1991 assembly polls the party got 10 seats which, however, fell to five in the last assembly polls of 2011. The votes polled, however, rose to 11.5 per cent.

In Assam, too, the BJP could not fashion its policies in tune with popular aspirations. While the influx of migrants from Bangladesh is a major issue in the state, the political discourse in the state has revolved around the issue of Assamese identity. The Asom Gana Parishad (AGP), a party born out of the students' movement against foreigners, has struck a deeper chord with the people of Assam than the BJP. 'The BJP is seen as a North-Indian, Hindi-promoting outfit. It has failed to culturally integrate with the Assamese,' says a serving IAS officer from the state. It has also been pointed out that during the five years of the NDA government (1999-2004), nothing was done to seal the Indo-Bangladesh border and deport the illegal immigrants. 'This in spite of Advani being the home minister,' the IAS officer says.

ARUNACHAL PRADESH

However, the BJP has entered an unlikely state in the Northeast: Arunachal Pradesh, located on India's border with China and earlier called the North-East Frontier Agency (NEFA). The party started contesting elections in the state in 1995 but could get only 3 per cent of the votes. This went up to 19 per cent in 2004 by which time the party had nine legislators. In 2004, the party won both the seats in Lok Sabha from Arunachal Pradesh. In 2009, however, both the Parliament seats were lost and the tally in the assembly also came down to three. Now the RSS has decided to intensify its activities in the state.

ODISHA

The BJP story in Odisha is uneven. In 1990, the BJP won two seats in the legislative assembly in Odisha whose upper crust—the middle class and professionals—is almost entirely Hindu and are known to be devout. Five years later, the party won nine seats in the assembly, securing 8 per cent of the votes. In 2000, however, the party won 39 seats and garnered 18 per cent of the votes. The BJP's tally increased in the Lok Sabha, too: as prospects of a BJP government in New Delhi increased, the popularity in the state also got a leg up. BJP's prospects in the state further improved after a tie-up with Biju Janata Dal (BJD), a regional outfit headed by Naveen Patnaik, the son of the legendary Odiya leader and chief minister Biju Patnaik. United by nothing other than their anti-Congressism, the BJP and BJD entered into an alliance in December 1997. Naveen Patnaik became the minister for mines in Vajpayee's government in 1999. In 2000, both the parties came out victorious in the assembly polls and a coalition government was formed. Naveen Patnaik now became the chief minister. The coalition functioned well, although BJD consolidated its position better. In the next assembly polls in 2004, the combine was returned to power. In public perception in Odisha, BJD soon started being seen as the party representing the Odiya interest while the BJP was perceived as a party from North India. This was a strange phenomenon, because the mild-mannered Patnaik spoke no Odiya but turned out to be a consummate politician. Sacking many ministers who could be a threat to him, including his second in command—Bijaya Mahapatra—Naveen, who was seen as an inheritor of his father's legacy, acquired an anti-corruption, pro-poor image. BJP began losing ground in the state which has barely 6 per cent Muslims. With the national leadership of the BJP also impressed with Patnaik, they never allowed the local leadership to meddle with him. This stunted the rise of local leaders.

Odisha was gripped by anti-Christian violence in the tribal Kandamahal district in 2008 when two groups of tribals—one Hindu and the other Christian—clashed after the murder of a sadhu affiliated to the VHP. The state government received a lot of adverse criticism both nationally and internationally for this incident. The charge was that Sangh Parivar outfits like the Bajrang Dal had instigated the violence. In 2009, in the run-up to the general elections, Naveen Patnaik broke his eleven-year alliance with the BJP, blaming them for the Kandamahal violence. The election results showed that the electorate applauded Patnaik's decision. BJD came back to power on its own, securing 103 wins in 147 assembly seats; the BJP won just six seats. In the Lok Sabha, the BJP drew a blank. 'It is true that the people of Odisha are religious and proud to be Hindus but they do not favour the Sangh brand of Hindutva. This is the cause of grief for the BJP in Odisha,' explains journalist Sandeep Mishra.

'The BJP could never spawn local leaders who could take charge of the party locally. They have Bijaya Mahapatra, earlier the leader next to Naveen in BJD. But he has not been empowered because he did not come up the RSS route,' Mishra added.

ANDHRA PRADESH

Andhra Pradesh is another state where the Jana Sangh and the BJP could make little dent. This had much to do with the caste composition of the largely feudal state where different castes are aligned with different parties. The major castes are that of Reddys and Kammas. While the Reddys were aligned closely with the Congress party, the Kammas were supporters of the Telugu Desam Party. 'This left no caste for us to capture. That's why we have failed in Andhra Pradesh,' says a national leader of the BJP who does not want to be named. The Brahmins, the caste that has traditionally been the first to support the BJP everywhere in the country, are numerically very small, comprising less than one percent of the electorate in the state. 'The lower castes are aligned with the Congress or the BJP. So while the Kapus—the next caste after the Reddys and Kammas—are aligned with the Congress, the OBCs tend to support the TDP. The Dalits are with the Congress,' the BJP leader says. The BJP did try to woo the Kapus in the last decade but to no effect,' she adds. The efforts were half-hearted and the Kapus under film star Chiranjeevi first formed their own party and then went back to the Congress fold.

Many BJP insiders feel that the alliance that the party had with the TDP since 1998 did it in. In 1999, the BJP was able to win seven Lok Sabha seats from Andhra Pradesh; Kakinada, Rajamundhry, Tirupati, Karimnagar, Mehbubnagar, Narsapur, Medak and Secunderabad. 'But Chandrababu Naidu was overpowering. We were unable to grow in the state because of our alliance with his party. The BJP cadres have been very upset because of this,' the BJP leader said. In the next election in 2004, the BJP lost all the seats and the same happened in 2009—an indication of the negligible base of the party in the state. The best performance of the BJP was seen in the 1999 elections when it won 12 assembly seats but only 3.67 per cent of the votes. In 2004 and 2009, the party won two assembly seats each time and less than 3 per cent of the votes. Surprisingly, however, in 1984 when the BJP won only two Lok Sabha seats nationally, one was from Andhra Pradesh (the other being from Gujarat).

However, with the creation of Telangana and bifurcation of Andhra Pradesh in the beginning of 2014, the BJP is seeing better chances in the region. Telangana comprises a large part of the erstwhile Nizam's Hyderabad state where the RSS had been active in the 1940s. Due to the merger of Hyderabad state with Andhra state in 1956 to create the much larger state of Andhra Pradesh, the Hindu voice in Hyderabad state that had stood up against the Nizam in the 1940s dimmed and stymied the possible growth of the Jana Sangh and the BJP. The number of Hindu voices became a minority in Andhra Pradesh because Andhra interests dominated. However, old-time observers aver that the hidden agenda behind the creation of Andhra Pradesh was not to dim the Hindu voice but the Muslim voice that was dominant in Hyderabad state. It was also an effort by the Congress to finish off the Communist party which was very strong in Andhra state. For the record, however, the Jana Sangh had made initial efforts to ramp up in Andhra Pradesh with their annual conference in 1965 held in Vijayawada. In the early 1960s, a Telugu was also appointed the president of the Jana Sangh. Bangaru Laxman, a BJP president who later had to resign after being caught on camera accepting a bribe, was elected MLA from the Telangana area. Analysts expect that within a few years, the BJP will become a major force in the newly created state. It was with this understanding that the party supported the Congress on the Telangana issue and helped pass the relevant bill in the Lok Sabha.

KERALA

Many analysts think that with the existing composition of population, Kerala should have been a happy hunting ground for the BJP. This is especially as the RSS has been present in the state ever since 1942 when three pracharaks were sent to Kerala to initiate activities in Trivandrum, Cochin and Calicut. One of the three was Dattopant Thengdi, who made it big as a trade union leader of the Bharatiya Mazdoor Sangh (BJP's trade union affiliate) many years later. The Sangh Parivar also floated two dozen social educational and cultural organizations in the mid-1960s but the saffron party has not been able to make any dent in this southern state. A Virat Hindu Sammelan was also convened in 1982 in Kerala but to little effect.

Christians and Muslims comprise 40 per cent of the population in Kerala. The Muslims are with the Muslim League while the Christians have traditionally favoured the Congress party. The upper class and the lower caste Hindus have, however, patronized the Communist party. The BJP thus has not been able to get a captive vote base: their vote percentage in the state hovers around 6 per cent. It may be noted that in the early years of the Jana Sangh—in 1967—the party had held its annual session in Calicut to highlight what it thought were the problems of Kerala. This included opposition to the creation of a Muslim majority district of Mallapuram.

'The BJP has some support in the capital Trivandrum and Kasargode in the north. But this support is not enough to win the seats,' says senior journalist Manoj Das. In the 2011 assembly elections, the party lost deposits in 133 of the 138 seats it contested from polling 6 per cent of the votes. In 2006, the party polled

5 per cent of the votes and then, too, had lost deposits in 133 of the 136 seats that it contested. 'Though in the Trivandrum area the Nair community members vote for the BJP, the party can't be said to be having a base among the Nairs in the state. Nor do they have support among the significant Ezhava community of Hindus,' elaborates Das. In recent years, the BJP has been trying to rope in sections of the Christian community to support the party. The Syrian Christians are especially being targeted. In the run-up to the 2014 general elections, Narendra Modi, other than addressing rallies in Kerala, also met with some church leaders. A former IAS officer, K.J. Alphons, famously known as a demolition man in his earlier avatar at the Delhi Development Authority (DDA), has also joined the BJP in Kerala. But since the ethos of Kerala is so different from the rest of the country, it might be a while before the party can make waves in the state.

TAMIL NADU

Similar is the situation in Tamil Nadu whose political culture and social ethos is very different from that of the cow-belt states of North India. Dravidian politics was focused on securing justice for the backward classes who were being discriminated by the Brahmins. During the period when the DMK emerged and came to power in the late 1960s, the Hindi issue had become big in Tamil Nadu. English was to be the official language for the first fifteen years of the Republic and the situation would be reviewed after that. In North India, many political outfits including the Jana Sangh pressed for the adoption of Hindi as the national language and in Tamil Nadu there was a virulent anti-Hindi movement. Little wonder that the Jana Sangh, and later the BJP, could not strike any chords in the state. 'The Dravidian politics was based on Tamil cultural nationalism. Hindu cultural nationalism as promoted by the BJP had no place in this politics,' points out journalist R. Krishnan.

After the establishment of the Dravidian parties, politics in the state took a new turn. With non-Dravidian parties, notably the Congress, having been reduced to an insignificant position, caste politics became the basis for contests between the different Dravidian parties. In this scenario, the BJP was absolutely irrelevant. But in 1996, the party made some inroads into the state after a tie-up with the AIADMK in the 1998 general elections. BJP won two Lok Sabha seats that year: M. Mantham won the Nilgiri seat whereas Kumaramangalam Rangarajan emerged victorious in the Tirucharapalli seat. In the 1999 elections, the BJP changed partners and tied up with the DMK and was able to emerge victorious in four Lok Sabha seats. Besides the two seats mentioned above, the party also won the Coimbatore seat from where C.P. Radhakrishnan was elected and Nagarcoil from where P. Radhakrishnan won. It goes without saying that the BJP candidates won because of the piggyback riding as a result of which votes were transferred to the party candidates. The BJP's performance has been consistently dismal in state assembly elections. The best results were in 2001, when BJP won four seats in the assembly. In 2006, this had fallen to zero and the party lost deposits in 221 of the 225 seats that it contested. In 2011, the party drew a blank once again, forfeiting the security deposits in 198 of the 204 seats from which its candidates had contested. The party garnered only 2 per cent of the popular votes.

Incidentally, Tamil Nadu has also seen a BJP national president: K. Jana Krishnamurthy, a lawyer originally from Madurai who was the party president in 2011. He was a member of the RSS since 1940. In 1998, he contested the Lok Sabha seat of Chennai (south) but lost narrowly. He was elected to the Rajya Sabha from a northern state and was cabinet minister in the Vajpayee government. P. Radhakrishnan was also made a minister of state in the Vajpayee government.

Other than the BJP, a controversial organization called the Hindu Munnani has also been working for the Hindu cause in Tamil Nadu. Founded in 1981 against the backdrop of the Meenakshipuram conversions (which was the starting point for the Ram temple movement), Hindu Munnani has been vehemently opposing Christian conversions and fighting radical Islamic right-wing groups. 'There is little chance of a Hindi belt party succeeding in Tamil Nadu where the people sympathize with the demand for separate homeland of Tamils in Sri Lanka. Parties like the BJP can never appreciate this feeling among Tamils, so how can they win seats in the state?' asks R. Krishnan.

chapter 14

Hardliners versus Softliners

The beginning of the end of the Vajpayee government was seeded at Gujarat's Godhra railway station. When coach number S6 of the Ahmedabad-bound Sabarmati Express started burning on the morning of 27 February 2002, it set off a chain of events that ultimately led to the defeat of the NDA alliance in the elections held two years later.

That fateful day, kar sevaks returning from Ayodhya were travelling in the train along with regular passengers. At the Godhra railway station—where the train at halted—the kar sevaks got into a fracas with Muslim vendors on the platform. The exact sequence of events that followed is unclear but soon it degenerated into stone pelting and extreme violence. In the end, coach S6 was burnt down and fifty-nine passengers perished in the fire. The reaction to the ghastly incident in Godhra was intense and widespread, leading to riots on a massive scale, mass killings and destruction of properties in many parts of Gujarat. The most severely affected were the cities of Ahmedabad and Vadodara. Over 1,000 people died in the riots, most of them Muslims. The riots received national and international attention and the BJP government that was in office in the state was accused of inaction and much worse.

The BJP government in New Delhi had been in power for over two years in February 2002, and the VHP and other Sangh Parivar affiliates were getting restive. They asserted that it was time that the agenda on which the party had built its support base and popularity be implemented. This was the construction of the Ram temple. The VHP decided that 15 March 2002 would be the day that the organization would begin work on building the Ram temple in Ayodhya. They wanted to go ahead with the plan in spite of the status quo injunction of the Supreme Court after the demolition of the Babri Masjid in 1992. The Vajpayee government was unwilling to intervene in the mahayagna planned by the VHP at the site in the last week of February as a prelude to the beginning of the actual construction work. Hundreds of kar sevaks were arriving at the ongoing mahayagna from various parts of the country, building up the tempo of the event. Though people were alarmed, the government's plea was that they were unwilling to intervene so long as there was no law and order problem. The VHP had also assured them that the mahayagna would be conducted peacefully. But the main Opposition parties including the Congress were not satisfied; they pointed out that the VHP had given a similar assurance ahead of 6 December 1992 when the Babri Masjid had been razed to the ground. Action should be taken before anything untoward happened, they suggested.

When the post-Godhra riots showed no sign of ending—though their intensity had reduced somewhat after three days—the Vajpayee government came under tremendous pressure to sack the then chief minister of Gujarat, Narendra Modi. This followed an indictment of what was happening on the ground by agencies like the National Human Rights Commission (NHRC) and even the Editors' Guild of India, besides other national and international civil society organizations. The removal of Modi was not an easy task considering that he was a party man and the government was that of the ruling BJP. Modi had been a full time pracharak of the RSS and had built the BJP's base Gujarat. Moreover, he was the first pracharak to be made chief minister without ever being even an MLA. Thus, he enjoyed huge support in the RSS, the Sangh Parivar and was popular among those sections of the BJP that believed that Modi had acted to the best of his abilities. In Gujarat, Modi was known as an acolyte of L.K. Advani, who was the home minister them, and was keeping the chief minister's flag flying high.

Vajpayee, in order to gauge how things were on the ground, flew down to Ahmedabad on 4 April 2002. However, by all reckoning, it was a visit that came too late, more than a month after the incident at Godhra. Nevertheless, Vajpayee visited riot relief camps and was visibly disturbed by what he saw there. After meetings with the state administration in the evening, he addressed a press conference. Flanked by Modi on one side, Vajpayee talked about how the government's main task was to follow '*rajadharma*': "The king or rulers cannot discriminate between people on the basis of birth, caste and religion… It is heart-wrenching that people must become refugees in their own country.' Quite unexpectedly, Modi reacted very strongly to the advice that he must follow '*rajadharma*' and said, '*Wohi toh nibha rahe hain* (that is what we are following).' The audience was shocked but the snubbed Vajpayee kept quiet. It was perhaps then that the prime minister made the decision to get rid of Modi. He made his mind known to his close circles but the information leaked out. As per the plan, Modi would offer to tender his resignation at the party's national executive meeting on 11 and 12 April and this would be accepted.

But events unfolded in an unexpected manner. On the flight to Goa from Delhi, tremendous pressure was exerted on Vajpayee by Advani who prevailed on the former not to accept Modi's resignation. When the national executive met at Goa and Modi stood up to offer his resignation, there were protests from the young leaders and the mid-level leaders of the party. '*Isteefa mat do, isteefa mat do* (don't resign, don't resign),' they thundered. In the end, the national executive passed a resolution stating that Chief Minister Narendra Modi, the state government and the state police had done their best while facing the challenge that was 2002. Since in a democracy there is only one way to put the issue to rest, and the people are the ultimate arbiters, it was decided that the people of Gujarat are the ones who must give their verdict on the matter. Accordingly, the national executive unanimously rejected Modi's offer to resign. They advised him to seek dissolution of the assembly, go to the people and seek their verdict.

Thus, Vajpayee was stymied and decided to change his tactics in order to get his stock up within the party. On the evening of 12 April, while addressing a public meeting in Goa, Vajpayee said: 'Wherever Muslims live, they don't like to live in coexistence with others, they want to spread their faith by resorting to terror and threats. If a conspiracy had not been hatched to burn innocent passengers of Sabarmati Express alive, the subsequent tragedy would have been averted. The subsequent developments were no doubt condemnable but who lit the fire? How did the fire spread?' Vajpayee continued to tread this hard line in the coming months and in a speech to the BJP Parliamentary Board (and reported in the press) on 1 December 2002, he pointed out that the 'Godhra killings were not adequately condemned by the Muslim community'. This was seen as a sort of justification for the post-Godhra riots. Later, in December, Modi won a fresh mandate in the elections, winning 127 seats in a house of 182. This was seen as a vindication of the support he had from the people of Gujarat. Many years later the chief minister of the state Narendra Modi was given a clean chit by a Supreme Court appointed Special Investigations Team (SIT) and absolved on charges of any wrong doing.

But in June 2004, shortly after the BJP lost power nationally, Vajpayee lamented in a TV interview: 'The impact of Gujarat riots was felt nationwide. This was unexpected and hurt us badly. Modi should have been removed after the incident.'

A retired secretary to the Government of India who was heading a key department during that time—but does not want to be named—says that there was tension between Vajpayee and Advani ever since the former took over as prime minister, and things came to a head over Gujarat. 'You can say it was a tussle between the softliners like Vajpayee and hardliners led by Advani. To complicate things, the RSS and other Sangh Parivar affiliates were in the fray as well; Vajpayee had kept them in check for far too long. After Gujarat, the hardliners won,' the former official says. Even the NDA allies like the TDP, headed by Chandrababu Naidu, and JD(U), run by Nitish Kumar, which could have forced Vajpayee to oust Modi kept quiet. This was born out of the realization that the hardliners in the party had gained ascendancy and would not tolerate the ouster: they would rather let the government fall than ask Modi to go.

When the NDA formed the government in 1999, Vajpayee thought that a coalition government could not premise its decisions on hardcore BJP ideology. Thus, he built a coterie of softliners like Jaswant Singh and Brajesh Mishra who acted as a shield around him. This, however, led to the alienation of those who had a hardcore ideology, although Vajpayee and Advani had been associates for decades and had an excellent working relationship. Vajpayee was also shored up by NDA allies like DMK and Trinamool Congress. They made it clear that they would only support a government headed by Vajpayee. George Fernandes, who held important portfolios in the government, was also an important ally of Vajpayee from the NDA.

Many say that when Advani suddenly proposed that Vajpayee should be the prime ministerial candidate of the party in December 1995, it was not in a fit of generosity; neither was it because Advani perceived that Vajpayee was more popular. The Jain hawala scandal in which Advani's name had cropped up made him take this step. The Rs 64 crore hawala scam had broken out in 1991 after the arrest of militants operating in Kashmir. A diary recovered from them linked them to a hawala operator, S.K. Jain, who apparently had made payments to top politicians. Among the politicians alleged to have received payments was L.K. Advani, who was alleged to have received Rs 35 lakhs. The matter dragged on till a public interest litigation (PIL) filed in Supreme Court brought it into sharp public focus. On 16 January 1996, Advani was chargesheeted by the CBI. On being named, Advani quit his Lok Sabha seat and declared that he would not run for public office till he was cleared. 'Advani did not want to be party's prime ministerial candidate when he was on the dock and this was the real reason why he had proposed Vajpayee's name,' avers a BJP insider. There is a belief in some quarters that Advani was nudged by the RSS bosses to prop up Vajpayee. A year-and-a-half later, on 8 April 1997, the Delhi High Court acquitted Advani, ruling that the evidence presented proved nothing.

Party insiders say that after he was acquitted Advani felt that even if Vajpayee became the prime minister, the latter should at least have appointed him the deputy prime minister. But Vajpayee showed no such inclination, instead handing over the home portfolio to him. Those belonging to the Advani camp constantly pointed out to him that he deserved to be deputy prime minister if not the prime minister because it was he who was responsible for building the party and making it popular. They also stressed that Vajpayee had been virtually sidelined in the party after the Ayodhya movement and Advani had done him a great favour by rescuing him and bringing him to the centrestage. Advani, however, maintained his cool and never appeared to be disconcerted on this matter in public. 'Perhaps Advani had a better understanding of Vajpayee. Although they were rivals at one level, they were associates for ages and friends, too,' a party insider says. Party men who were not in the Vajpayee camp kept their pressure up and at one time tales were spread that Vajpayee was trying to initiate a bus yatra to Lahore and engaging with Pakistan merely because he wanted a Nobel Peace Prize. Vajpayee apparently heard these stories and one day remarked: 'So what if I get the Nobel Peace Prize, it will be for everyone in the government.'

Meanwhile, stories of Vajpayee's poor health were doing the rounds and found their way into the mainstream press too. The fact that Vajpayee had left the national executive meeting in Nagpur in 1999 because he was feeling uneasy, the way he had stepped out of the car with only one shoe during the Independence Day function in 1998 and how he had stumbled at a similar function in 1999 was touted as evidence of his failing health. Vajpayee's aides pointed out that the problem was only with his knees (he later had a knee replacement done). The prime minister himself said: 'I have no problem but if the media wants to indulge in speculation I cannot prevent it.'

Notwithstanding what he said, Vajpayee took all steps to ensure that the hardliners were sidelined. This is best illustrated by the case of old RSS ideologue K.N. Govindacharya who, in the early 1990s, was a very close associate of Advani and the RSS's representative in the saffron party. Known to be a key strategist and an expert in deciphering caste complexities and electoral politics, Govindacharya had planned the widening of the party base by roping in the support of OBCs who formed a major portion of Hindus. This would allow the party—then more or less restricted to the upper castes—to expand quickly. But Govindacharya got into a needless controversy by calling Vajpayee a '*mukhauta* (mask)' in an interview in the mid-1990s. By this he meant that Vajpayee was merely the soft face of the hardline party. Though he later said that he had been misquoted, the damage was done. Vajpayee was miffed and plotted for the removal of Govindacharya. After he came to power, Vajpayee insisted that Govindacharya not remain the secretary of the party and was relegated to the post of an inconsequential vice president. Vajpayee was upset with Govindacharya for another reason too: the latter was a critique of the policy of liberalization and had vocally batted for the Swadeshi policy. Finding the heat unbearable, Govindacharya sought a sabbatical for one year and withdrew from party activities.

Vajpayee was fine as long as Rajendra Singh, the only North-Indian and non-Brahmin to be the sarsanghchalak of the RSS, was the boss. Vajpayee knew how to manage Rajendra Singh, a former professor of physics at Allahabad University who had quit academia to become a full-time pracharak. The demands of Rajju Bhaiya (as he was popularly called) were simple. He was satisfied with a chance to address BJP MPs impressing upon them how to conduct themselves and taking forward the agenda of the Sangh. In July 1998, Rajendra Singh addressed BJP MPs where Vajpayee was also present, but this drew criticism because the saffron party was now in power.

Because of his ill health, Rajendra Singh abdicated his position in February 2000 and was replaced by K.S. Sudarshan. Vajpayee's problems began now: Sudarshan was a strong votary of the Swadeshi policy and was considered a hardliner even within the RSS. He soon began to criticize the BJP and NDA's policies of privatization. He also wanted an RSS nominee in the Prime Minister's Office (PMO) and wanted the wings of Brajesh Mishra to be clipped.

Vajpayee was able to keep the RSS at bay till Godhra happened but lost out after the Gujarat riots. It is instructive to note that the privatization of public sector undertakings that formed an important part of Vajpayee's agenda was stalled in September 2002. More importantly, in July 2002, at long last, L.K. Advani became the deputy prime minister. According to press reports on 24 October 2002, the RSS bigwigs had a high-level summit meeting with Vajpayee, Advani and then BJP president, Venkaiah Naidu, to rein in the government and correct its course. Primarily, the RSS was agitated over Vajpayee's economic policies, failure to 'counter' Pakistan and lack of action on the temple issue. They were also upset that the government had been unable to control terrorism which had reached the doorsteps of the Parliament. The RSS was represented by K.S. Sudarshan, RSS Joint General Secretary H.V. Seshadri, and Madan Das Devi at the meeting. The 'summit' meeting however 'did not lead to "reconciliation" between Vajpayee and the RSS', say the press reports.

Now the VHP started becoming more vocal on the temple issue. In the beginning of 2003, VHP General Secretary Giriraj Kishore called Vajpayee a 'pseudo Hindu' for not assisting in the construction of the Ram temple. A few months later, the VHP boss Ashok Singhal commented that Vajpayee was 'inebriated' with power and said that he should resign if he cannot bring in legislation for the construction of a Ram temple. In March 2003, RSS General Secretary Mohan Bhagwat also started talking about the Ram temple in what was a not so discreet hint to Vajpayee. He said: 'It appears that the time is fast approaching for us to become once again active in the Mandir movement.'

Murmurs were heard in the corridors of power beginning 2001 that the RSS was okay if Vajpayee could be nominated to the post of president of India which was falling vacant in 2002. The grapevine said that the RSS's preferred candidate for the post of the prime minister was former party president and HRD minister, Murli Manohar Joshi. The stories doing the rounds suggested that nothing happened because Advani was not willing to rock the boat. After Vajpayee, it was Advani who was second in the chain of command and without him taking active interest in deposing the prime minister, nothing could happen—and nothing did.

In 2002, the BJP government also passed a tough terror law—the Prevention of Terrorism Act (POTA), something that the hardliners had been campaigning for. POTA was passed in the Lok Sabha but could not be passed in the Rajya Sabha where the Opposition was stronger. Ultimately, it was approved by a joint sitting of the Parliament. The Opposition had argued that the provisions of POTA would be misused to jail political rivals and against members of the minority community. Under POTA, confessions made before the police are also permitted as evidence admissible in a court of law, unlike under the normal laws. The contention of the Opposition was that the police would misuse this law and torture suspects to plead guilty. The passage of POTA gladdened the hearts of hardliners in BJP and the Sangh Parivar.

With the elections not even a year away, the BJP officially started reflecting a hardline approach. On 4 April, at the party's national executive meeting at Indore, BJP President Venkaiah Naidu declared that: 'Cultural nationalism is our lifeline and Hindutva is the soul of India.'

The next year, the country went to polls earlier than scheduled. The party was confident that the government had performed well on all fronts and India was shining. The leaders had deluded themselves into believing that they would be re-elected. But that was not to be.

chapter 15

The Wilderness Years

RSS Sarsanghchalak K.S. Sudarshan set loose the cat among the pigeons in April 2005 by suggesting on a television programme—NDTV's *Walk the Talk*—that both Atal Bihari Vajpayee and Lal Krishna Advani should make way for younger leaders in the party. About Vajpayee, Sudarshan specifically said: 'I have been saying that he should go and let new faces emerge. He should stay as senior advisor only.' Referring to both Vajpayee and Advani, he commented: 'Age is a factor after all.' Vajpayee was officially seventy-nine then and Advani past seventy-six but Sudarshan's frustration was the result of the party's losing power in the centre once again and the implicit message was that the BJP had lost because it did not follow the path charted out by the RSS.

For a year before this, the BJP had been internally debating the reasons it was voted out of the government. Vajpayee continued to believe that it was the Gujarat riots of 2002 which had shown the exit door to the NDA government and wanted to revisit the matter of axing Modi at the party's national executive meeting on 22 June 2004 in Mumbai. But he was prevailed upon not to do so by Advani, Arun Jaitley and Venkaiah Naidu (who had the support of Sudarshan to not rake up the issue).

Advani, who had quickly taken over as the president of the BJP after losing power (Venkaiah Naidu had resigned, taking moral responsibility for the defeat) was grappling with his analysis of why the party had lost power. Addressing the party's national council on 27 October 2004 he said: 'In May 2004 we lost an election that we were confident of winning. The reasons for failure were many: while stressing on good governance the party had forgotten to be attentive to the human costs of rapid change. There was no cushion to communities overwhelmed by technology and market. Then we aroused expectations in the course of BJP's voyage from [the] fringe to the centre of political stage but could not fulfil the promise of a Ram temple,' Advani added.

A year later at the silver jubilee session of the party in Mumbai from 28-30 December 2005, Advani (still identifying the causes of failure) said: 'These days we often hear that India's political culture has been "Congressized". It is said that even the BJP has fallen victim to "Congressization". This charge cannot be outrightly denied. Perhaps the party has grown so rapidly that there are elements that have internalized the corrupt ethics of the Congress.' He went on to add: 'We have to reverse the distressing descent of some members into the disreputable and corrupt Congress culture.' At the same time, Advani also said: 'In the past six years, the BJP ignored the karyakarta, the Sangh Parivar and the core voter.' For good measure he also added: 'Shri Ram is not just a religious icon. He is also the symbol of the Indian ethos, culture and unity. He is the personification of our concept of cultural nationalism.'

If Advani was trying to appease the RSS and the hardcore ideologues—while looking for the causes of failure—this was because his position as a hardliner had been diluted after he went to Pakistan in June and made some controversial statements. On a visit to Jinnah's mausoleum in Karachi on 4 June, Advani said that

Jinnah was a 'rare individual' who had espoused the cause of secular Pakistan. Subsequently, in a speech to the Karachi Council of Foreign Relations, Economic Affairs and Law, Advani cited Jinnah's address in the Pakistan Constituent Assembly on 11 August 1947 and said that the founder of Pakistan envisioned a state that 'guaranteed equality of all citizens in the eyes of the state and freedom of faith for all citizens.'

These incidents had raised hackles back home in the RSS and VHP camps. In the eyes of the RSS, Advani had committed sacrilege by praising Jinnah. He had also given credence to the two-nation theory and diluted the concept of Akhand Bharat. VHP said that Advani was a traitor. However, Advani was only trying to be a good guest in Pakistan. Moreover, he was trying to follow the footsteps of the softliner Vajpayee who had tried to mend relations with Pakistan. Vajpayee had all but retired and it is possible that Advani, at long last, saw an opportunity to step into his shoes. But whatever might have been the case, all his explanations did not find favour with the RSS. Cornered, Advani offered his resignation from the post of the president of the party. However, he did not agree to give in to the RSS's demand for reviewing his statements on Jinnah and reiterated his views in his autobiography, *My Country, My Life*, asserting that: 'I have not said anything in Pakistan that I have to review and withdraw.' He was persuaded to stay back and continue but obviously the die had been cast. Though this had not been made public, insiders knew that Advani would be removed from the post sooner than later.

The VHP, which jumped into the fray a day after Sudarshan made a call to induct GenNext into the top leadership of the party, offered its own choices. VHP President Giriraj Kishore pushed for one of the three: Narendra Modi, the Gujarat chief minister; Uma Bharti, former chief minister of Madhya Pradesh; and Rajasthan chief minister, Vasundhara Raje, as possible bosses of the party.

Interestingly, when asked about it, Sudarshan mentioned the name of Sushma Swaraj, even though she did not have a Sangh pedigree. By that time, Modi had become the unquestioned boss of Gujarat and his speeches in the election rallies drew larger crowds than what Advani had drawn in the state. When Modi and Advani spoke at the same meetings, the former was applauded and the latter received a lukewarm response. This was in spite of the fact that Advani represented Gandhinagar, the capital of Gujarat, in the Lok Sabha.

In the months after Advani praised Jinnah, the party was riven with conflict with everyone shoring up their own positions. Yashwant Sinha, trying to get into the good books of the RSS, started virulently attacking the BJP government of Jharkhand led by Arjun Munda calling it corrupt and inefficient. Protestations by party members that public criticism of a BJP-led state government was not in order fell on deaf ears. Meanwhile, Sudheendra Kulkarni, a party intellectual close to Advani, brought out a paper called 'The State of the Hindu Movement' advocating a revised version of secular Hindutva—allegedly at the behest of Advani himself. The paper was circulated at the Thinkers' Meet at Bhopal on 23 March 2005. At the same time, Sudarshan himself chose an RSS function to publicly praise Indira Gandhi as an 'iron-willed leader' who dismembered Pakistan and always stood by her 'words and deeds'. This stymied Advani because he was planning a big function on the occasion of the twentieth anniversary of the Emergency that would be directed at criticizing the Congress party and the legacy of Indira Gandhi.

It was Rajnath Singh, a not-so-well-known BJP politician from eastern UP, who took over as the party president in December 2005 when Advani stepped down. Advani—as it transpired—had been given a temporary reprieve by the RSS bosses after the Jinnah episode and allowed to continue till the end of the year. Although Rajnath Singh had been the chief minister of UP for a brief while and the surface transport minister and agriculture minister in the Vajpayee government in two stints, he did not have a pan-India profile when he became the party president. However, he was a rare candidate for the post as he had a rural profile: he was a farmer's son who had steadily climbed the ladder of the Sangh Parivar—from being an ABVP activist in jail during Emergency to an MLA in 1977 to a minister in the Kalyan Singh government in 1991. As UP's education minister, he had made cheating and copying a cognizable offence—this established his reputation as a tough administrator. He also introduced Vedic mathematics in school syllabi and, much to the glee of the hardliners, had introduced chapters on Hedgewar and Deendayal Upadhyaya in text books. He had also made changes in the history syllabi to reflect the ideology of the Sangh Parivar. However, he was chosen not only because of his ideological approach but also because he hailed from UP. This was a state where the party had started sliding. In order to build a base in the south, three successive presidents—Bangaru Laxman, Jana Krishnamurthy and Venkaiah Naidu—had been inducted from that region. But this had not yielded results. Now there was a need to rebuild the party base in UP, so in came the leader from Mirzapur in eastern UP.

However, since Rajnath lacked pervasive influence, he could not control the party effectively. The next few years were marked by dissensions and faction rivalry. It is said that leaders like Arun Jaitley thought nothing of Rajnath and looked down on his penchant for consulting astrologers at the drop of the hat. Sushma Swaraj was pushing hard for her place under the sun using the women empowerment card as her weapon. Advani was still around; he was the leader of the Opposition in the Lok Sabha and this gave him considerable clout and exposure. Moreover, he was still the tallest leader in the party. A BJP insider says: 'The RSS was enjoying itself. It had succeeded partially in keeping Advani down, Vajpayee was in retirement mode and Nagpur kept propping up mid-level party leaders who were not from the Delhi establishment.'

To compound the BJP's problems, the country was in the midst of unprecedented economic growth. This was largely due to the global boom and its impact was being felt in India too. But the fact is that the UPA-led government with Manmohan Singh as prime minister had much to do with boosting the country's morale. Singh had served a successful stint as finance minister under the Narasimha Rao government and had played a major role in changing the economy of the country. Moreover, the UPA government also followed up on the reforms of the NDA government and this resulted in higher economic growth. Rajnath Singh's BJP continued harping on the 'bad economic situation' and 'rising inflation' at its successive national executive committee meetings but this had little impact—unsurprisingly, considering that the economy was clocking a high growth rate that reached 9 per cent.

Simultaneously, the BJP started falling back on its old staple of issues of terrorism, infiltration of people from the western and eastern borders and began declaring with more frequency how the Congress party was playing the politics of appeasement of minorities. On 6 April 2006 (the day of Ram Navami), the party started two Bharat Suraksha Yatras. The two yatras were slated to reach New Delhi on 10 May 2006. One of the yatras began from Dwarka (the capital of Lord Krishna) and was led by L.K. Advani. The other yatra was led by Rajnath Singh and started from Jagannath Puri. The two yatras covered seventeen states and 11,500 kilometres and the avowed objective was to raise consciousness about the need to safeguard national security from jihadi and left-wing terrorism. Another purpose of the yatras was to focus on the need to defend national unity and save it from divisive policies of minorityism that were being taken recourse to by the government in power. It also sought to mobilize opinion on corruption and to fight against erosion of values.

Along with its focus on terrorism which was growing, the BJP was also seeking to focus on its traditional agenda of Ram. Therefore, it energetically took up the Ram setu issue and sought that the Ram setu be declared a world heritage site and that all activities that could destroy it be ceased. 'A government displaying complete ignorance about its history, culture and tradition, literature and not accepting the great heroic characters like Ram and great saints like Valmiki who have shaped the ethos of the nation since times immemorial do not deserve to stay in office,' the BJP declared in a political resolution passed at its national executive meeting in Bhopal on 21 September 2007. At this time the central government was moving forward on the Sethusamudram project that would involve dredging the area where the Ram setu exists. The dredging was to allow movement of ships but the BJP claimed that this was a man-made bridge made by Ram to send Hanuman's Vanar Sena into Sri Lanka to rescue Seeta who had been abducted by Ravan.

The reigning belief in the Congress after the 2004 election—not stated publicly—had been that the party had been elected to power because of minority votes going en masse against the BJP and other parties of the NDA coalition. This was a consequence of Gujarat 2002. Based on this belief, the party decided to focus on issues concerning Muslims. The Sachar Committee was set up in March 2005 to examine the issue of backwardness in the Muslim communities. The committee, headed by retired judge Rajindar Sachar and comprising other experts, reported that the state of Muslims in India was worse than that of scheduled castes and scheduled tribes. It also said that the overall percentage of Muslims in bureaucracy is just 2.5 per cent though Muslims constitute 14 per cent of the country's population. It recommended the setting up of an Equal Opportunity Commission for Muslims, the establishment of a mechanism to promote Muslim participation in public bodies, a recognition of degrees given by madrasas and bank assistance to minorities among many other measures.

The BJP was alarmed: it began to assert that the recommendations of the Sachar Committee that had been accepted by the government were a 'charter for social divisiveness'. It was also anxious about the move for job reservation for Muslims introduced by the Congress-run Andhra Pradesh government—although, as mentioned earlier, it was subsequently struck down by the courts who ruled that religion-based reservations were not permitted by the Constitution. The party said that the Congress was 'following the path of the Muslim League before Partition' and in its national executive meeting in Bhopal in September 2007 stated that the Muslim electorate was being 'wooed as an instrument of political power'. The BJP also charged that the Congress-led government was 'tackling terrorism not from the standpoint of national security but the desire to consolidate the vote bank'. It also pointed out that infiltration from the western and eastern border was continuing unabated.

But these protestations by the BJP were not having much effect. At its national executive meeting in New Delhi on 26 June 2007, L.K. Advani, delivering a special address, pointed out how the party had lost recent elections in UP which was a state 'that elected 80 MPs to Lok Sabha and had 403 assembly seats' and how this was 'a matter of concern'. The Samajwadi Party had lost in the elections but the Bahujan Samaj Party had won. Advani said that the obvious questions to ask was why did the BJP fail to project itself as the most credible and winnable alternative to the incumbent government of the Samajwadi Party. Also, why did a section of BJP supporters shift to the BSP and why was the BJP unable to get the support of other sections? Advani asked. The question, though generally asked, was also directed at Rajnath Singh because he hailed from UP. Good news, however, came in for the BJP in 2008 from Karnataka. For the first time the party won enough seats on its own to form a government in South India. This was a matter of great cheer because the party had, all this while, been branded as a North-Indian party. Earlier on at the end of 2007, Narendra Modi had won the elections once again in Gujarat to bring the BJP back to power. In 2005, the BJP-JD(U) combine had come to power in Bihar under the leadership of Nitish Kumar.

With the 2009 elections approaching, the party had to fall back on L.K. Advani and make him the prime ministerial candidate. Advani, of course, always fancied himself in that position and as far back as December 2006 had said that as leader of the Opposition he considered himself the prime ministerial candidate for the next election. Not all his colleagues were ready to back his claim at that time but after the withdrawal of Vajpayee there was no other taller leader in the party other than Advani. On 2 May 2007, Rajnath Singh announced publicly: 'After Atal there is Advani. Advani is the national choice. It is he who should be PM.' A few months later on 10 December, the BJP Parliamentary Board firmly announced that Advani would be the PM candidate for 2009. On 14 September 2008, the Election Management Committee of the party charted out its task. This was to 'highlight the personality of L.K. Advani in every nook and corner of the country and his spirited espousal of cultural nationalism for campaigning against pseudo secularism.' It was also decided to highlight his 'remarkable parliamentary career', 'comradeship with Atal Bihari Vajpayee' and 'consistent advocacy of good governance'.

Closer to the elections, the BJP seemed to be buoyant and perceived that it would win. Rajnath Singh, addressing the national executive on 6 February 2009 at Nagpur just before the elections, attributed this optimism to the fact that over the last five years, the Congress had been able to win only four elections to state assemblies on its own. Moreover, in the assembly elections held in six states 'in last November/December 2008, the BJP won 294 seats while Congress could win 244 seats'. Rajnath also pointed out the unprecedented success the party had achieved in Madhya Pradesh and Chhattisgarh where they had come back to power.

At the same meeting, however, L.K. Advani was more circumspect. Hailing 'onward to victory', Advani predicted: 'If people are happy with an incumbent government they give it a renewed mandate. But change is not guaranteed if they are unhappy. For the desired change to come about, the people must see a clear and credible alternative.'

In the event, however, BJP does not seem to have been seen as an alternative by the electorate. The party went to the 2004 election with the slogan of 'Indian Shining' and a 'feel good' factor. But in 2009, the electorate was feeling good after five years of Congress rule: even if this was largely due to the booming world economy. The BJP won 116 seats in Lok Sabha which was lower than the 138 seats it had won in 2004. The performance of the Congress improved dramatically: from 145 seats in 2004 to 206 seats in 2009. The BJP's percentage of votes polled fell from 22 to 19 per cent while the Congress's vote share improved from 26 per cent to 28 per cent. The saffron party was back in Opposition.

chapter 16

Rising from the Ashes

Shortly before the 2009 elections, RSS chief K.S. Sudarshan had to leave office on account of his ill health. The man chosen to replace him was a second generation RSS man—Mohan Bhagwat, a student of veterinary sciences who belonged to Chandrapur in south-east Maharashtra. Bhagwat's father had been the prant pracharak of the organization in Gujarat many decades ago. Mohan Bhagwat had been in the RSS since 1975 and was the general secretary when he was made the sarsanghchalak.

When the BJP was routed in the general elections, Bhagwat decided that the time had come to begin micromanaging the party. Although the RSS's influence had increased after 2004, Bhagwat decided to tighten the controls now. In typical RSS fashion, BJP president Rajnath Singh, who had led the party to defeat, was allowed to continue for a few months and then made to exit. In the same way, Advani was 'relieved' of his charge as leader of Opposition and leader of the BJP parliamentary board in Lok Sabha after some time. This was a clear message to Advani that he would not be the de jure prime ministerial candidate of the party for 2014. Sushma Swaraj, who was the deputy leader of the BJP parliamentary party, was elevated to Advani's place. Advani had to comply with the diktats of Bhagwat who was over twenty years younger than him and who was born when Advani was already an RSS karyakarta. In 2005, too, Advani had been removed from the post of president but that was at the insistance of Sudarshan who was almost as old as Advani. Thus, the pinch would not have been felt so intensely. However, Bhagwat, in an interview published on 28 August 2009 by various newspapers like *The Hindu* and *Mint*, said that the issue of the leadership of BJP had to be decided by the party members themselves. 'The party has to decide what is right for them [sic], we cannot decide,' he stated. At the same time, Bhagwat said that '55-60 years should be the average age of the leadership of the party'. Clearly, the RSS boss had spoken his mind. Nine days before Bhagwat's interview was published, another party stalwart and close associate of Vajpayee, Jaswant Singh, was expelled from the party. This was because he had allegedly praised Jinnah in a biography of the founder of Pakistan titled *Jinnah: India-Partition-Independence* that he had penned. There was considerable mud-slinging in the party around this time. Jaswant Singh also gave out interviews suggesting that Advani was a party to the release of militants in the Kandahar hijacking case. In TV interviews in 2008, Advani had denied involvement in this matter.

Incidentally, Advani did not think that the BJP had been 'routed' in the 2009 elections. Addressing the national executive of the party on 20 June 2009 at New Delhi, Advani said: 'We have not been routed.' He pointed out that this 'setback' was nothing compared to 1984 when the party had won just two seats. Moreover, he pointed out that the party had won 116 seats in the Lok Sabha. Although this was less than the 138 seats won in 2004, 'this was more than what the Congress had won in 1999'. The Congress's performance in the election was at its nadir in that year and the implication of this statement was that if Congress could recover from this situation and stay in power for two terms, the same could happen in the case of BJP. Advani, however, pointed out that 'it was a matter of concern that our party seems to be plateauing in some states which are our strongholds and has actually suffered big reversals in some others. Additionally, there are several big states where our political base continues to be small and our electoral presence narrower still.' Pointing out that 58 of the 116 BJP Lok Sabha members were first termers, Advani also called for evolving a system to encourage leaders at all levels. He was, however, happy that the third and fourth front that were planned for the elections had failed. He said that as a consequence of this, 'the BJP can rally all others around its pole to build a strong stable and superior alternative to the Congress.'

If Rajnath Singh, who had been inducted as president in 2005, had a low profile, the new man chosen by the RSS as the BJP president had virtually no profile at all! Nitin Gadkari's claim to fame was that he had been the PWD minister of Maharashtra in the Shiv Sena-BJP government and in that capacity had successfully implemented the Mumbai-Pune Expressway project. He also belonged to Nagpur, the city where the BJP was headquartered and had been a member of the RSS since his college days. He was also not the ordinary run-of-the-mill politician and had considerable business interests. If the RSS thought that the BJP could come to power under his leadership, they were highly mistaken.

But the continuous goof-ups of the ruling UPA government and the huge scandals that surrounded them offered a great opportunity to the saffron party. By 2011, buoyed by the terrible position the Congress found itself in, the BJP went full throttle against corruption. At its national executive meeting in Lucknow on 3 June 2011, the party declared that the 'present UPA government is the most corrupt government since Independence' and listed out the various instances of corruption, ranging from the licensing and allocation of the 2G spectrum, loot of common wealth in the organization of the Commonwealth games, the Adarsh cooperative scam and the impropriety in appointing an allegedly tainted official—P.J. Thomas—as chief vigilance commissioner. The appointment of Thomas happened even after the then leader of the Opposition, Sushma Swaraj—who was mandatorily a part of the selection team—had categorically refused to endorse his candidature.

The party declared at its national executive meeting at Lucknow on 3 June 2011 that 'the Manmohan Singh government had lost all moral authority, popular legitimacy and forfeited the right to rule the country' and that it had 'permitted the plunder of national wealth and brought shame and humiliation to India and Indians.'

At the same time the BJP was also apprehensive that the 'UPA government was taking one step after the other to destabilize the federal structure of the country.' To prove this the party pointed out that with the Right to Education (RTE) and the National Food Security Act, states would have to make more expenditure commitments without the support of the centre. The BJP also complained that the establishment of the National Investigation Agency (NIA) by the ministry of Home Affairs was contrary to the federal spirit of the country and, in the absence of a constitutional amendment, had taken away the law making power of the states. The party declared that with the setting up of the NIA, 'the Government of India wants to take responsibility of fighting terror by sidestepping states.' The BJP was also upset that the National Advisory Council (NAC) had drafted a 'perverse' legislation—the Prevention of Communal and Targeted Violence Bill that proceeded 'on the assumption that the majority community is always the perpetrator of communal violence'. This was 'reverse discrimination in its worst form,' the party declared.

The BJP also started slamming the ruling government on matters relating to Jammu and Kashmir, China policy and internal security. The party pitched for full integration of Kashmir with India and said that giving more autonomy (as had been proposed by some circles) was not a solution to the problem. The party passed a resolution at its national council meeting in Indore on 18 February stating: 'The state of Jammu and Kashmir has more powers vested in the state legislature than at the centre. There is no concurrent list; all residuary powers are with the state and not with the centre. Yet the misconceived solution being suggested is to confer more powers. The problem of cross-border terrorism is not linked with inadequacy of political power in the state government and state legislature. The root cause is the inability of Pakistan to accept J&K as an integral part of India. BJP declares an unequivocal commitment to the complete constitutional integration of J&K with the rest of India. Separate and special status to J&K is an instrument of national disintegration,' the party said.

BJP showed concern about China, too. 'There is unquestionably an increased show of assertiveness by China. Its objections to the Indian PM's visit to Arunachal Pradesh and Dalai Lama's visit to Tawang were gratuitous interference in the affairs of India,' BJP said. The party also went hammer and tongs about the issue of internal security in the country. 'The internal security situation in the country remains precarious and fragile. Post 26/11 it was expected that our intelligence networks would be fortified and the infrastructure of our security forces would have been visibly strengthened. None of this appears to have happened.'

With the government's term nearing its last stage, the BJP offensive began to mount and its resolutions began to become shriller. At its national executive meeting at Mumbai on 24 May 2012, the party said that 'there is a fundamental flaw with the political structure which the UPA has followed. The PM must be the natural leader of the country and the government and he should have the last word in matters of policy. Dr Manmohan Singh singularly fails in these tests. There is not only twin leadership but the distance between 7 Race Course Road and 10 Janpath is becoming wider. They are also not on the same page on a whole range of policy initiatives. The PM is in office but not in authority. He gives the impression of being more like a CEO taking directions from the board of a company whose chairman has all authority but practically no accountability'. The consequence of this, the party said, was that there was a policy paralysis and corruption, slowing down of investment and worsening of the industrial climate.

At the same national executive meeting, the party took the opportunity to pat itself on the back by noting that it had recently won the state assembly elections in Punjab along with the Akali Dal and achieved 'the extraordinary feat of being the first incumbent government re-elected in the last forty years'. It also made a mention of 'the outstanding victory in Goa which was unique because the majority of average voters including the Christians saw in BJP the only hope and redemption'. The national executive noted that a large number of minority candidates won on BJP tickets 'demolishing the canard that BJP is anti-minority'.

But the BJP realized that it had done poorly in UP and again missed the bus in the most populous state of India. The national executive noted that 'we could not measure up to the expectation of people there. We need to reclaim UP where, in the past, the party enjoyed enormous goodwill and support of the people'.

At the same time, the party executive was overjoyed at the poor performance of the Congress. 'The Congress has suffered severe reverses in the states and municipal elections in Mumbai, Bengaluru and Delhi. This demonstrates the anger of the people against gross misrule and corruption of the UPA government.'

Meanwhile, Advani, with his considerable experience and vision, began to devise strategies that would bring the party to power after the next elections. At the national executive meeting at Surajkund in September 2012 and again at its national council meeting in New Delhi in March 2013, Advani unveiled the concept of 'NDA plus' to ensure that the party got a chance to rule. NDA plus meant a group that not only included the constituents of the NDA but also others who could come together with the singular object of good governance and as an anti-Congress alternative. Advani said that good governance could be sold by invoking the good work done by the Vajpayee government, the impressive performances by the governments of Punjab and Bihar and with some innovative ideas. Advani also realized that the biggest roadblock in the way of the BJP was the lack of confidence of the minorities in the BJP. Therefore, he proposed that the BJP include a 'charter of commitments to the minorities' in its agenda of governance and development.

While all this was happening, the RSS was trying to tighten its hold on the BJP even further. In the good old days, the RSS had a man deputed to the BJP to keep a watch on the party. The most effective example of such a person in the past had been Govindacharya in the 1990s who later fell foul with Vajpayee. Now the RSS decided that it needed more than one RSS functionary to look into the affairs of the BJP. The three officials who would oversee the work of the party were General Secretary Suresh Joshi (popularly called Bhaiyyaji), Joint General Secretaries Suresh Soni and Dattatreya Hosabale. Their brief was to 'closely observe and guide the BJP so that the party could discover a new leader who could lead it to victory in 2014,' reveals a BJP insider. 'All this was with a purpose. Only if the BJP became victorious could the RSS further its agenda. But let me tell you, the RSS did not start the exercise in 2011 with any pre-decided names. They were open to all options,' the insider says.

The most promising name was that of Narendra Modi whom a lot of people had begun to see as the inheritor of Advani's mantle. Even before the 2009 general elections, leading businessmen like Anil Ambani and Sunil Mittal had started wondering publicly why he could not be the prime ministerial candidate. As a leader of the Opposition and also a woman, Sushma Swaraj was also in the race. Two successful BJP chief ministers, Shivraj Singh Chauhan of Madhya Pradesh and Raman Singh of Chhattisgarh, were also in the running. The leader of the Opposition in the Rajya Sabha, Arun Jaitley, had considerable experience as a strategist and was a leading light of the Delhi establishment. Then there was Lal Krishna Advani who, his age (he was over eighty now) notwithstanding, was the tallest leader in the party. BJP president Nitin Gadkari must also have fancied his chances but he was to get into trouble soon.

It was alleged that Gadkari's Purti group of companies had cornered land meant for farmers in the Vidarbha region. Later, his name came up in the context of an irrigation scandal. A few companies close to him were discovered to have grown very fast at the time when he was the PWD minister of Maharashtra. There were also some doubts raised about some shell companies and their shareholders. 'With interests in sugar, power products, export, solar energy and many other areas, Gadkari was mainly a businessman and less a politician. He was on good terms with businessmen as well as politicians of other parties like the NCP,' says a BJP insider not very happy with him. 'He warmed his way into the hearts of the RSS bosses who, at some level, are very naïve. A person like Gadkari should have never been made the BJP president,' the insider adds.

Just before these controversies broke out, the RSS bosses had got the BJP constitution amended to give a second term to Gadkari. The process had begun in April 2012 when, at a meeting of BJP office bearers, a proposal was finalized to amend Article 21 of the constitution to enable the president of the party—at the national, state and district level—to enjoy two terms of three years each. The earlier provision was only for one term. Significantly, L.K. Advani was not present when the office bearers cleared the proposal. At the party's national executive meeting in May 2012 in Mumbai, the proposal was approved, although again Advani and former deputy chief minister of Maharashtra, Gopinath Munde, skipped the meeting. However, three members of the national executive—Sangh Priya Gautam, L. Ganesan and J.K. Jain—opposed the proposal. In September, the proposal was also cleared by the party's national council.

When the heat turned on the Gadkari matter an internal inquiry was set up and RSS ideologue and chartered accountant, S. Gurumurthy, was given the charge of finding out whether anything was wrong. He gave a clean chit to Gadkari but not to his companies. With pressure mounting, Bhagwat—the main backer of Gadkari—allowed his term to finish in December 2012 and did not push for his re-election. This decision was, however, taken at the very last moment, just a day before Gadkari's term in office ended on 23 December. What prompted the Sangh to drop Gadkari could have been the income tax raids on Purti group, which almost coincided with the end of his tenure. The sage counsel was that allowing Gadkari a second term would have opened the party to attack and cause embarrassment at the hands of the Congress in the run up to the general elections.

When talk of not allowing Gadkari a second term was being debated much before the actual decision was taken, many names came up as his replacement. Primary among them were Sushma Swaraj and Arun Jaitley. At one point, there was also speculation that Yashwant Sinha could be pushed to the post. Also in the contention at one point was Venkaiah Naidu. But due to the opposition of various factions, all the names were shot down.

Finally, it was Rajnath Singh who was called back and brought to head the party once again. Stories suggest that Gadkari himself suggested Rajnath's name, aware that he was acceptable to the bosses in Nagpur. The RSS loved Rajnath because he had allowed Nagpur to micromanage the party in the four years that he was at the helm. Gadkari himself had developed a good rapport with

Rajnath and for this reason cited the old consideration that had made Rajnath acceptable the last time around: his rural background in a predominantly urban party. Moreover, the fact that he belonged to UP, where the biggest electoral battle would be fought for 2014, was quoted in his favour.

▪

Faction fights were rampant in the party—not only at the central level but also in the states—even before Rajnath took over the second time. In Rajasthan, sixty MLAs loyal to Vasundhara Raje Scindia threatened to resign from the house in May 2012 in protest against a planned Lok Jagran Yatra proposed by Gulab Chand Kataria. When Scindia had been chief minister, Kataria had been her home minister but now the yatra plan made her apprehensive. It was the state election year and Scindia saw in the move an attempt by Kataria to upstage her. The BJP central leadership called Scindia for talks to Delhi but she refused to comply. In the end, the party bosses buckled down and reined in Kataria. In Karnataka, the BJP government fell as a result of factionalism. In Maharashtra, former Deputy Chief Minister Gopinath Munde thought nothing of Gadkari who had served along with him in the Shiv Sena–BJP government. Both were reputed to have clashed often even in cabinet meetings during their tenure.

On 31 March 2013, Rajnath Singh decided to reshuffle the office bearers of the party in the run-up to the elections that were a little more than a year away. The top decision-making body of the party, the BJP Parliamentary Board, was reconstituted to include Narendra Modi. Thus, Modi became the only chief minister to be part of the body that included Advani, Sushma Swaraj, Arun Jaitley, Venkaiah Naidu and Rajnath Singh, among others. Incidentally, Modi had been part of the Board till 2007. Rajnath Singh had dropped him then saying that it was not correct to include one chief minister on the Board and ignore other BJP chief ministers. But this time, Rajnath Singh did not find anything amiss in including only Modi in the Board. There was a proposal that Raman Singh of Chattisgarh also be inducted but this was dropped. The party constitution did not allow more than eleven members on the Board. Modi had been taken on board to fill the vacancy created by the death of Bal Apte and there were no other places remaining. Incidentally, Atal Bihari Vajpayee was still on the Board, though he was in unsound health—both physically and mentally.

As part of the appointment of new office bearers, Rajnath Singh appointed Modi's right-hand man, Amit Shah, as general secretary of the party and made him in charge of UP. In doing this, Rajnath had acted brazenly because Amit Shah was being investigated by the CBI for his role in the Sohrabuddin Sheikh case. Amit Shah was the home minister of Gujarat when Sheikh, an underworld criminal and his wife, Kauser Bi, had been kidnapped by personnel of the state police and killed in a fake encounter. In 2010, Amit Shah had to resign after he was arrested for his alleged involvement in the murder. He is presently on bail. Rajnath Singh also inducted many hardcore RSS men into his team under the advice of Nagpur. This included Ram Lal as organization secretary of BJP. He was based in the 11, Ashok Road, New Delhi headquarters of the party and was reputedly the ears and eyes of the RSS.

Three months later on 9 June 2013, Narendra Modi was named the chief of the campaign committee of the party at its national executive meeting at Goa. This was the same venue where Modi's job had been saved at the party's national executive meeting eleven years ago. The anointment did not come without a hitch. Firstly, Advani did not attend the meeting citing health reasons. Then, a day after the appointment, he resigned from the Parliamentary Board, National Executive and Election Committee in protest against Modi's elevation. In a one page resignation letter, Advani said that 'for some time, I have been finding it difficult to reconcile either with the current functioning of the party or the direction in which it is going. Most of the leaders are now just concerned with their personal agendas.' He also lamented in the letter that 'BJP no longer was the idealistic party created by Syama Prasad Mookherjee, Deendayal Upadhyaya, Nanaji Deshmukh and A.B. Vajpayee.' The resignation threw the party into a tizzy. The Parliamentary Board rejected the resignation and said that Advani's 'sage advice' and 'guidance' was required more than ever before. Advani also relented and took back his resignation.

Three months later on 14 September 2013, Narendra Modi was declared the prime ministerial candidate of the BJP by the Parliamentary Board. Consequently, Advani wrote a letter to Rajnath Singh saying: 'It is best that I don't attend the meeting.' He added that he was disappointed in the way Modi was being foisted as the prime ministerial nominee and predicted that this would lead to 'political disaster'. Sushma Swaraj and Murli Manohar Joshi also had objections to choosing the name of Modi but they attended the meeting.

But their protestations were in vain. The RSS bosses had made up their mind about Modi and had come to the conclusion that only he could lead the BJP to victory in the 2014 elections. They also perceived that the opposition to Modi was coming from top leaders of the party who saw the Gujarat chief minister as an obstacle in the way of their ambitions. Nagpur also realized that Modi was immensely popular with the middle-level functionaries of the party and karyakartas who saw him as their only hope. RSS's support for Modi had been expressed publicly even before he was named the PM candidate. For example, Suresh Soni, RSS's joint general secretary, addressing leaders of the BJP in UP on 17 August 2013 told them that the party should act tough with any functionary who criticized Modi. He even suggested that in case someone refused to fall in line, they should be suspended from the party for six years.

Although Bihar Chief Minister Nitish Kumar expressed himself openly against Modi and parted ways with the BJP with whom he had been running the government since 2005, other constituents of the NDA were okay with him. Shiv Sena found nothing amiss with Modi being elevated as the BJP's PM candidate; neither did the Akali Dal of Punjab. The latter, in fact, greatly admired the economic model used by Modi in Gujarat and wanted to emulate it in Punjab. Shiv Sena founder Bal Thackeray had endorsed the case of Sushma Swaraj as the prime ministerial candidate of the BJP, but things changed after his death in 2012 and his son, Uddhav, was on board with Modi being chosen as the prime ministerial candidate.

Epilogue

The pendulum has swung from one end to the other. If the first elections of the Indian Republic in 1951 began with the Congress party straddling like a colossus across the polity, that monopoly has been eroded over the years and has now ended completely. The BJP stormed into power in the 2014 elections with a thumping majority, becoming the only party other than the Congress to achieve this. 'I had never expected to see this happen in my lifetime. This has happened after sixteen general elections,' BJP MP Balbir Punj told television channels in an emotionally-choked voice, moments after the saffron surge became clear on counting day. With this win, Syama Prasad Mookerjee's dream of the Jana Sangh becoming a national democratic alternative got fulfilled. In this election, the Hindu vote substantially deserted the Congress, whose seat tally collapsed to 45: its lowest ever tally. Nationally, the party's vote share declined to about 19 per cent, which is only slightly higher than the population of minorities in the country. Thirty years ago in 1984, the Congress had got 415 Lok Sabha seats, almost ten times the number of seats won in 2014. The BJP had then won only two seats; in sharp contrast, this time the tally has hit 282. The Hindu vote is now commanded almost entirely by the BJP. As Narendra Modi himself pointed out at his victory speech on the banks of the Ganga in Varanasi after winning the polls, all prime ministers of India before him have either been from the Congress or were persons of Congress origin, thereby indicating that a saffron revolution had taken place.

If the BJP rose to power this time, a large part of the credit should go to Narendra Modi. Though the party named him the prime ministerial candidate many months ago and gave him a free hand with the campaign, the Gujarat chief minister worked very hard to successfully complete his mission. Modi criss-crossed the nation and spoke at over four hundred and forty election rallies in an election campaign that seemed almost presidential. Modi and his teams strategized well and positioned the prime ministerial candidate appropriately. There was extensive use of the media in the campaign—not just traditional media like print and television but also social media like Facebook, Twitter and the like. Thus, in a scenario where the Congress displayed weak leadership and organization, Modi came across as the change that the voters wanted. For many voters, the candidate and the party became irrelevant as they voted for the man on top. It was a throwback to the 1970s when voters exercised their franchise in a similar fashion for Indira Gandhi.

In UP, India's most populous state, the BJP won 73 of the 80 seats, exceeding the expectations of even the most optimistic party supporters. In Delhi, the party claimed all 7 Lok Sabha seats, making a clean sweep in what was its first stronghold. In UP, the caste divisions, following the Mandalization of the 1990s, had split the Hindu vote, with a large part of it going to the Samajwadi Party (SP) thereafter. With the rise of the Bahujan Samaj Party (BSP), the vote bank was further divided by the Dalit votes now going to them. This had reduced the percentage vote for the BJP; the party weakened in the state as a result. A similar thing had happened in

Bihar in the early 1990s with the OBC votes going to Lalu Prasad Yadav's Rashtriya Janata Dal (RJD). Now, for the first time in the two decades in UP, the Hindu vote was almost unanimously garnered by the BJP, with both the SP and the BSP collapsing in its wake. The SP got a meagre four seats and the BSP did not get a single seat. For the record, the SP and BSP secured 22 and 19 per cent of the votes respectively. But in the first-past-the-post (FPTP) mode of election in India, this was not enough to counter the winner. It was an almost similar situation in Bihar where the RJD won a mere four seats and Nitish Kumar's Janata Dal (United) won only two. This implies that a huge chunk of OBC and Dalit votes went to the BJP.

But how did this consolidation of Hindu votes happen? If the BJP had managed to mobilize Hindu votes through the Ram Janmabhoomi movement in the 1990s, this time it employed a different strategy. Holding the trump card of economic development in Gujarat, the party's prime ministerial candidate Narendra Modi pressed his advantage in UP and Bihar. 'I was most surprised to find deep in the interiors of villages in backward parts of UP many declaring that they would vote for Modi and BJP,' says Raja Bose, The *Times of India*'s resident editor in Lucknow. 'When I asked them why, they said it was because they wanted a better life. They were sure that Modi's BJP would work for growth because some of their family members worked in Surat and had seen prosperity,' Bose says. 'The youth of UP and Bihar villages who go to big cities like Delhi, Mumbai and Bengaluru for work come back home and tell stories of a better life in metropolitan India. This raises the aspiration levels of those back home. They realize that they should vote for a nationalist party whose appeal is across caste lines and not limited to certain castes,' says Sudhir Kumar, a corporate manager in Delhi. 'The outward migration to metros from UP and Bihar is the highest from anywhere in India. This led to people voting for the BJP on the assumption that their life would improve,' he adds. It is obvious then that the liberalization of 1991 and the reforms thereafter have changed the entire outlook of voters. This is truer of younger voters—almost a whole generation has been born post-liberalization, a generation that is moved less by caste considerations and more by opportunities to pursue their individual dreams.

'The Hindu votes deserted us because the Congress party from 2004 onwards has started being perceived by many as a party of minorities—a party that got into power only with the votes of 15 per cent of Muslims,' says a top Congress leader who does not want to be identified. 'With this perception, a reverse mobilization of Hindu votes happened against the Congress. The BJP was the obvious choice [for the voters],' he adds. Amit Shah, Narendra Modi's right-hand man and the person in charge of BJP's campaign in UP, said the same thing in a different way when he told television channels soon after results started pouring in: 'Our strategy succeeded because of the number of people who are not part of vote banks anymore.'

Vote statistics bear out this analysis. The *Times of India* reported that the saffron party won all the eight constituencies in UP that have a Muslim population of 40 per cent. This includes Saharanpur, Amroha, Shrawasti, Bijnor, Muzaffarnagar, Moradabad and Rampur. However, the saffron mobilization here was probably a fallout of the Muzaffarnagar riots between Muslims and Jats in the winter of 2013 that led to massive polarization. As a result of this, the Jats who were never with the BJP joined their ranks. The Dalits, too, changed sides as they had received the wrong end of the stick during this time. The paper also reported that in UP there are 32 seats where Muslims constitute 15 per cent of the population; of these, the BJP won 30. Under normal circumstances, in constituencies where the voter base of Muslims is as much as 30 per cent, only a Muslim could be expected to be elected. But in the 2014 election, not a single member of the minority community was elected. As per the aggregate, BJP got over 42 per cent of the votes in UP, although the percentage figure differed from seat to seat.

The 2014 election has also resulted in the spread of BJP's influence across the nation. In Assam, a state where the BJP had been only a marginal force till now, the party won 7 out of the 14 seats, making a breakthrough in the hitherto Congress-dominated state. The vote consolidation for the BJP was the result of local angst against the illegal migration of Bangladeshis into the state. Though the issue has influence the electorate since the early 1980s, the early beneficiary of this had been the Asom Gana Parishad which has now almost disappeared. The disgruntled electorate has put their faith in the BJP, whose prime ministerial candidate, Narendra Modi, had strongly taken up the issue of the influx of foreigners in his campaign speeches in Assam.

The most remarkable results for the BJP were seen in Rajasthan and Gujarat, where the party won all the seats (21 and 26 respectively). The BJP polled 55 per cent of the votes in Rajasthan and 59 per cent in Gujarat. The Congress won 33 per cent of the votes in Gujarat and over 30 per cent in Rajasthan. Considering that minorities are less than 10 per cent of the population in Gujarat, this means at least 20 per cent of the Hindu voters also voted for the Congress! Interestingly, 1.8 per cent of the electorate of the state also pressed the NOTA button, implying that they liked neither the BJP nor the Congress. This appears to be a strange verdict for a state that is perceived as the most saffron oriented in the country. In Madhya Pradesh, the BJP secured 54 per cent of all votes cast and won 27 of the 29 seats. In Karnataka, the party polled 43 per cent of all votes cast and won 17 of the 28 berths to the Lok Sabha.

As a result of the great showing by the BJP and the collapse of the Congress, there will not be any officially recognized Opposition in the Lok Sabha. Of course, the UPA as a pre-poll alliance can be recognized as a combined Opposition by the new speaker of the

Lok Sabha. The UPA has got 67 seats—more than 10 per cent of the total tally of 543—and can be recognized as the Opposition. Of course, all members of the UPA have to wish to continue as part of this alliance. As Modi pointed out in his victory speech after the Ganga aarti, in the past, political parties have clamoured to make alliances in order to form the government. But now, he said, the same parties were trying to get together to garner enough numbers to be recognized as the Opposition. This was a wee bit of an exaggeration, but it does make an interesting point. With these results, the BJP has become the supremo of India's polity and other parties are scrambling to forge an alliance to remain relevant in the system. Old-timers pointed out that this was a hark back to the 1960s when various parties, including the Jana Sangh, came together in spite of their ideological differences to form an effective Opposition to the Congress.

The BJP may have become the fulcrum around which the Indian polity will revolve for the next five years, but political life is all about competition. The Congress party will try to get back into the reckoning; many, however, feel that this will be easier said than done because of the virtual collapse of leadership in the party. The BJP slogan of 'Congress-mukt India' (Congress-free India) rings more true today than ever before.

Though the BJP may have aggregated the Hindu votes for the time being, caste-based parties like the SP, RJD and BSP will try to regroup. Nitish Kumar's JD(U) has already made it clear that it will fight back by nominating a 'Mahadalit'—one belonging to the lowest Dalit group—as the new chief minister of Bihar. This indicates its strategy for the Bihar assembly elections to be held in 2015 at present. More such moves to appeal to separate castes are likely to be made by regional parties in the coming months.

In addition to this, parties like the AIADMK of Jayalalitha, the Trinamool Congress led by Mamata Banerjee, and Naveen

Patnaik's Biju Janata Dal (BJD) will work assiduously to consolidate their position. These three parties have effectively countered the BJP's challenge in their states by wielding a two-pronged strategy. First, they have provided effective leadership—something that the Congress failed to offer in the past five years. Second, they are perceived by the electorate as the sole representatives of the ethos of their respective states. For example, the Trinamool Congress is the party that represents the aims and aspirations of the Bengali people. Similarly, Naveen Patnaik's appeal is based on his party being seen as the sole upholder of the interests of the Odia people. Jayalalitha and her party, the AIADMK, have now displaced the DMK and become the sole representative of the Tamil people. 'We do understand that displacing powerful regional parties that reflect regional aspirations is not that easy, especially for a national party like us—even though we try to reflect the ethos of the entire nation,' says a BJP insider. 'In the process of representing the Indian or Bharatiya cause, there is a conflict with the regional cause. We are constantly trying to achieve that "golden mean" that will reflect the cause of the majority of the people of India. This is in addition to Narendra Modi's thrust on economic development, which is born out of the idea that this is something that everybody in the country wants; therefore it acts as a binding force.'

But the party will not just frame overall policies for economic development and hope to consolidate its support base. By the looks of it, the BJP will also design policies relating to specific states where it wants to ramp up support. A good example is the recently divided Andhra Pradesh, where the BJP plan started rolling within days of the party coming to power. The state—which lacked BJP presence for the last fifty years—is now witnessing a polity that is in a flux. There has been angst against the bifurcation of the state and the creation of Telengana, and many top Congress leaders have left the grand old party. Those who stood for the election lost, most of them even their deposits. The party's support base has been unhinged, and both leaders who control the vote banks and their followers are up for grabs. The electorate is seeking a political party that will articulate their concerns and take up rapid economic development in the state. Within days of elections results, and even before the formation of the ministry in New Delhi, Ravi Shankar Prasad has been appointed as the man in charge of pushing the BJP's agenda in Seemandhra. Similarly, in Telangana, where the Congress has lost steam after the bifurcation, the BJP has appointed Prakash Jawadekar to ramp up support for the party.

In the same fashion, the BJP is all poised to make a Herculean effort to establish a base in West Bengal. Though it won only two seats in the state, the party (which fielded candidates in a huge number of seats in the 2014 elections) will make a bid to dislodge the Trinamool Congress in the 2016 assembly elections. Illegal migration from across the border is a huge problem for residents in the border districts and that has changed the composition of the electorate in those areas of the state. The BJP wants to capitalize on the angst of these people and convert it into a support base. West Bengal has a minority electorate of 26 per cent and both the Trinamool Congress now and the CPM earlier were hugely dependent on their support to get into power. Because of factors peculiar to Bengal, like voting on the basis of classes and not castes (promoted by the Leftists who ruled the state for nearly three decades), there has been no attempt to consolidate Hindu votes and this is something that the BJP will seek to do in the coming years.

Though the party has been elected to power based on the same system of elections selected by the Constitutional assembly and the Nehru government, the party has its own set of beliefs about the Indian nation. Though the BJP government in power is not expected to rock the boat and thrust the party's idea of India on to the electorate immediately, there is a way of life the party is expected to work towards in the long run. The essence of BJP's philosophy is contained in a party document published in 2006 titled 'Cultural Nationalism' which states: 'The concept of modern India is philosophically rooted in the Anglo-Saxon model and is institutionally shaped and structured on the experiments and experiences of Christendom, with individualism, secularism and liberalism as symbols of modernity. In short, modern India is an exotic and glamorous laboratory strenuously trying to experiment with the Anglo-Saxon experience on this ancient nation by a cut-paste model without even mixing an iota of nativity or indigenization. To transplant this doctrine of secularism that evolved in a mono —religious set up in the West into India with its multi-religious fabric is contrived. It could not effectively handle a multi-religious terrain like India and dangerously distorted the national mind and confused the national identity of the nation.' In sum, what is 'modern' is actually 'Western'. The party document states that India should be governed on the basis of *dharma*—which means consciousness of duty. This philosophy will hopefully be embraced by not only the individual but also the government.

Whether the efforts of its leaders to further the cause of the party in the various states will bear fruit is not known and how effective the maiden BJP government in New Delhi will be is yet to be seen. But one thing is clear: the BJP has arrived and will remain the primary pole of Indian politics in the foreseeable future.

Acknowledgements

Growing up in Delhi in the mid-1960s and 1970s meant that the Jana Sangh was a visible part of your life, as their supporters were all around. In those heydays of Indira Gandhi, many dismissed the Jana Sangh men as 'khaki shorts' (an allusion to the brown half-pants that were worn at daily shakhas of the RSS) but their influence was inescapable. The young—who are always anti-establishment—hated Indira and raised provocative slogans of '*gali gali mein shor hai*, Indira Gandhi *chor hai*.' One of my most vivid memories is that of the hero's welcome Arun Jaitley and Rajat Sharma received at a public reception at the Maurice Nagar Chowk in the Delhi University campus once they were released from jail after Emergency. The University's union was controlled by the Akhil Bharatiya Vidyarthi Parishad (ABVP) and the duo, the office bearers of the party, had been jailed on the declaration of Emergency. The Student's Federation of India (SFI), the student wing of the CPM, was also active on campus, aggressively seeking adherents. Their apparatchiks came from the rival campus—that of Jawaharlal Nehru University (JNU). The academic courses in our university, much like in JNU, were also influenced by Left-dominated ideology and most of the deans leant left-of-centre.

With this dual influence in my formative years, I have tracked the rise and fall of the BJP over the years with great interest. Therefore, when Prerna Vohra of Rupa Publications called me and asked me whether I would like to do a book on the BJP, I said yes without a moment's hesitation. In that sense, she is responsible for this book and has very efficiently taken me through the project these past few months. A big thank you is due to her, not least for coming up with the proposal at the right time!

Besides witnessing things first-hand, I have also profited from discussions with many people over the years. They are too numerous to be named but I would like to mention my old friend, Dr Jagdish Shettigar, with whom I used to have extended discussions on the party in the 1990s. Shettigar, a former student activist of the ABVP in Mangalore and Bangalore, was in the post-liberalization days the Economic Cell Convener of the BJP and based out of the party's headquarters on 11 Ashoka Road. He gave me deep insight into how the Sangh Parivar worked. This is something that has still remained with me. The BJP is one party that meticulously keeps its records—those of the period after 2005 are online and those of its earlier period (from the Jana Sangh days) are available in published form. Therefore compliments are due to the party organization as well for making the task of research easy.

One last word: India is now going through one of its most eventful periods. The first Republic that was crafted by Jawaharlal Nehru in the 1950s is making way for the second Republic that will be based on a completely different paradigm. This book must be seen in this context.

Kingshuk Nag
May 2014

Index

www.ingramcontent.com/pod-product-compliance
Lightning Source LLC
Chambersburg PA
CBHW021113200326
41577CB00072B/305/J
9788129131270